Phaedra Patrick studied art and marketing and has worked as a stained glass artist, film festival organizer and communications manager. Her books have been translated into twenty-five languages worldwide and her second novel *Rise and Shine, Benedict Stone* was made into a Hallmark film. Phaedra lives with her family in Saddleworth where she writes full-time.

Also by Phaedra Patrick

The Curious Charms of Arthur Pepper
*Rise and Shine, Benedict Stone**
The Library of Lost and Found
The Secrets of Sunshine
The Book Share

* Previously published as *Wishes Under The Willow Tree*

The Little Italian Hotel

Phaedra Patrick

ONE PLACE. MANY STORIES

HQ
An imprint of HarperCollins*Publishers* Ltd
1 London Bridge Street
London SE1 9GF

www.harpercollins.co.uk

HarperCollins*Publishers*
Macken House, 39/40 Mayor Street Upper,
Dublin 1, D01 C9W8, Ireland

This edition 2023

2
First published in Great Britain by
HQ, an imprint of HarperCollins*Publishers* Ltd 2023

Copyright © Phaedra Patrick 2023

ISBN: 978-0-00-841848-9

MIX
Paper | Supporting
responsible forestry
FSC™ C007454

This book is produced from independently certified FSC™ paper
to ensure responsible forest management.

For more information visit: www.harpercollins.co.uk/green

This book is set in 11.5/16 pt. Bembo by Type-it AS, Norway

Printed and Bound in the UK using 100% Renewable Electricity at
CPI Group (UK) Ltd, Croydon, CR0 4YY

For all my readers. Thank you.

CHAPTER I

Mountains

'Hi, it's Ginny Splinter, I'm listening. Tell me your worries . . .'

It was something she said so many times a day on her *Just Ask Ginny* radio show it had become second nature, like sprinkling sunflower seeds on her muesli or kissing her husband, Adrian, on the cheek before he left for work each morning.

Ginny arrived early at the Talk Heart FM studio that day to pass a financial planning article to a security guard who'd confided to her he was struggling to pay his rent. She stopped to chat to the young receptionist whose boyfriend wouldn't commit to anything more serious between them.

'You shouldn't rely on him for your own self-esteem. Never forget you're a prize worth winning,' Ginny told her with a kind smile. 'Come talk to me anytime.'

The receptionist wiped a tear from her eye. 'Do you really mean that?'

'A promise is a promise. Stay strong, sweetheart.'

Ginny walked away with a glow in her chest, touched when others trusted her with their personal issues. She wasn't one to toot her own horn, but when her friends wept into their chardonnay, she was the one they turned to for good advice and packets of tissues. Where others saw paths littered with broken glass, she chose to picture the sun rising over the mountains. It was probably why thousands of folk from Greenham, Ginny's leafy north-west England hometown, tuned in to her daily advice show.

Throughout her fifteen years on the air, there wasn't a problem Ginny hadn't tried to fix, whether it was loneliness, retirement worries, body dysmorphia, noisy neighbours, or bullying at work. She offered solutions for the lost loves, secret loves and the never-been-in-loves. Empathy was her superpower.

Other people's issues made her appreciate her happy marriage all the more. Her twenty-fifth wedding anniversary was just around the corner and she couldn't wait to celebrate it in style. Whenever Ginny thought about the surprise holiday she'd booked for her and Adrian, in Italy, she couldn't help smiling. Next month, in June, they were going to be staying in a gorgeous little village, Vigornuovo in Bologna, for three whole weeks. It would also be the perfect opportunity to renew their wedding vows, to reaffirm their love and commitment to each other and to have some fun, too.

The thought of spending quality time alone with her husband made a rush of warmth flood her skin. Ginny couldn't wait to wander the side streets of Venice at dusk and admire Botticelli's *The Birth of Venus* in the Uffizi Gallery in Florence. More than anything, she wanted to reignite the spark in her marriage. She and Adrian had been so busy recently that they were like cars speeding along a motorway in opposite directions. It made her feel uncharacteristically listless, especially now that their daughter, twenty-four-year-old Phoebe, had left home to move in with her fiancé, Pete, and was busy arranging her own wedding.

Ginny usually advised fellow empty-nesters to keep busy by taking up a new hobby, perhaps home baking or walking a neighbour's dog, but she was struggling to practise what she preached. Her hormones had felt out of balance for some time and sticking HRT patches to her backside, to banish her hot flushes, hadn't proved to be the wonder cure she'd hoped for.

Last week, she'd had a worrying urge to rip open her blouse on the high street and flash her lacy bra to passers-by. 'See, I'm here, still desirable, not invisible!' she'd wanted to shout. But really, she wanted her husband to make her feel that way. The Italian holiday was going to be the perfect solution.

When she stepped into the lift at work, Ginny was faced with a new life-sized poster of herself. She had an auburn high ponytail with a trademark curl at the end, and was wearing a pastel-blue skirt suit with animal-print heels. Her face had been airbrushed, removing every wrinkle, and she'd been given a golden halo and wings.

Ginny Splinter, Advice Angel, said the tagline.

Ginny pursed her lips. She didn't like that her lines had been erased. She'd earned them over forty-nine years of life experience, like gathering stamps in a passport.

In the office, she waved at her latest producer, Tam. There was a conveyor belt of young graduates keen to join Talk Heart FM, using it as a training ground before migrating to bigger and better roles elsewhere. Tam was the latest recruit.

She buzzed with ideas and her oversized black-rimmed glasses screamed ambition.

Tam propelled her chair across the office at great speed while sitting in it. 'Gin, babe,' she said, tapping a pen against her teeth. 'Thought we'd shake things up today and take some live calls, if you're up for it?'

Ginny sat down at her desk and frowned. 'Are you sure that's sensible? We've got time to run through the show and handpick a few problems. It gives me time to digest them and give my best advice.'

Her mind flicked back to a live call during which a woman had set fire to her husband's clothes after discovering his affair. Fortunately, he'd not been wearing them at the time. Afterwards, Ginny had fielded lots of calls from concerned listeners and had to assure them everything was okay. Since then, all her producers preferred to pre-record conversations.

Tam drummed her fingers on the table. 'Come on, Gin. Today's lead news story is about a herd of sheep escaping into Greenham town centre.' She fanned a yawn with her hand. 'You must be bored of the same old format, too. We don't want *Just Ask Ginny* to become the missionary position of advice shows.'

Ginny narrowed her eyes. She knew her audience well. 'Playing some great music, reading out listeners' letters and giving them advice on air, plus a few pre-recorded interviews is a proven formula,' she said. 'And the new poster makes me look like someone off *Love Island*.'

Tam slow-blinked and tapped her teeth again. 'Hmm . . .'

she said, looking Ginny up and down critically. 'Not sure about that.'

Ginny was increasingly aware she was now twice the age of her colleagues. It felt unbelievable, laughable even, that she and Adrian would both turn fifty later that year. She always told callers that age was just a number, but she was finding the milestone confusing. One minute, she treated herself to a new pair of sparkly stilettos, and the next she found herself reading reviews for thermal nightdresses. She bought pretty lingerie and vitamins to improve her energy levels. She was far from being old, but her youth sometimes seemed like a distant memory.

'I've made my decision.' Tam pointed her pen at Ginny's chest like a pistol. 'Let's go for the live calls.'

Ginny tried not to growl.

A few minutes later, she went live on air, playing songs by Ed Sheeran, Adele and Coldplay, slotting in a couple of her own choices by Red Hot Chili Peppers and The Strokes.

Many of the callers seeking advice used a pseudonym and sometimes even affected a fake voice. Ginny nervously gnawed the inside of her cheek as she took a live call from *Confused of Greenham*. The woman didn't know whether to enter a third marriage with a kind, generous man she didn't love, or to pursue a fling with a younger pizza delivery guy.

'Picture yourself five years from now,' Ginny said. 'You're lying on your sofa, wrapped in a blanket with a dose of the flu. A hand gently sweeps the hair off your clammy forehead. You open your eyes and see someone holding out a cup of hot tea and some aspirin for you. Is it your fiancé or the pizza guy?'

'My fiancé, I suppose,' *Confused* said.

'Then there's your answer. You can get pizza anytime from any place. Care and understanding are more difficult to come by.'

Ginny wrapped up the call and Tam's weary voice came through her headphones. 'Try making the next call sexier, Gin,' she said. 'We don't want listeners nodding off.'

'I'm here to help, not titillate,' Ginny said through gritted teeth. She ran a hand down her ponytail and picked up a call from the next person on the line. 'Hello, it's Ginny Splinter, I'm listening. Tell me your worries.'

The woman's voice sounded shaky. 'Oh, hello. It's Miss . . . Peach.'

'Well, hi there, Miss Peach. Thanks for joining me today,' Ginny said. 'Is there anything you'd like to share?'

The caller's words stuttered out. 'I only stayed with my husband for the sake of our child. You make a promise and then you're stuck with it, for life. I wish I'd got out while I had the chance . . . I've wasted so much precious time and now I don't know what to do.'

A familiar ache of compassion rose in Ginny's chest. It was something she welcomed but had also learned to control, so other people's problems didn't affect her too deeply. 'I'm sorry to hear that,' she soothed. 'It sounds like you've been through a tough time. There's nothing you can do to change the past, but you can take control of your future.'

'What if it's too late for *that*?'

'It's never too late to move on. Focus on yourself and consider what you really want from life—'

'And what if I don't know?' Miss Peach snapped. 'What if I've forgotten how to think about *me*?'

Ginny hmm'd and delivered a sympathetic pause while considering what advice to give her caller. People often just needed a gentle push in the right direction. 'Why not make a list of all the things you enjoy, perhaps a walk in the country or a trip to the cinema. Try to get to know yourself again and—'

'As if *that* will work,' Miss Peach interrupted, her tone growing more brittle. 'And what do *you* know anyway? You think you're little Ms Perfect, don't you?'

Ginny's scalp prickled and her mouth dried. Her uneasy sensation made the room tilt a little. She waved a hand, trying to get Tam's attention through the glass partition, but the producer was busy scrolling on her phone. 'This call is about you, not me,' she told Miss Peach. 'Please don't let your regrets eat you up.'

'I've seen photos of you and your husband in a magazine. Adrian, isn't it? You think you have such a *marvellous* life together.'

Ginny's heartbeat began to thump ominously in her ears. A few thousand people would be listening in to this conversation. Oh, god, she hoped Adrian or Phoebe weren't tuning in. Organizing a wedding was stressful enough for her daughter without *this*. Ginny drew a finger across her neck, indicating to Tam she was thinking of cutting the caller off.

Her producer didn't notice.

'Shouldn't you address your own problems before you lecture other people?' Miss Peach continued. 'Do you even know what your husband gets up to at work? How well do you *really* know him?'

Ginny hesitated and rubbed the double lines between her eyebrows. *Of course* she knew Adrian, from the way the moles on his back formed a diamond shape, to how he liked his toast served warm, not hot, and with butter spread right to the edges. He didn't like the bedroom to be stuffy so he slept with the window ajar, even if it meant Ginny had to wear socks in bed during winter. He thought Porsches were works of art but would feel like a cliché owning one. He could be grumpy until his morning coffee kicked in and he enjoyed a nice glass of Rioja most evenings. He loved dogs, hated cats, liked dark chocolate but never white and sang Oasis songs while he shaved.

Nevertheless, something icy seemed to slither down her spine. 'Miss Peach, what do you mean by—?' Ginny started.

'Ask *him*,' Miss Peach said.

'Ask him *what*?'

But there was a click and the line went dead.

CHAPTER 2

Earring

Ginny tugged off her headphones and marched into the office to where Tam sat cross-legged in her chair.

The producer quickly unfurled her limbs. 'Sorry, Gin, I didn't—'

'I told you we shouldn't take live calls.' Ginny rapped the desk. '*This* is what can happen. Now listeners might think there's something wrong with my marriage. My daughter is getting married in five months' time. What will *she* think?'

Tam held up a palm. 'Okay, okay. I get it. This is all my bad. Look, let's line up something calming next, maybe some Fleetwood Mac. I'll make you a black coffee.' She looked around helplessly. 'Or I can buy you one instead.'

'No more live calls,' Ginny said. 'Ever.'

Back in the studio she wriggled her shoulders, struggling to get comfortable in her chair. She read out several emails from listeners and gave them her best advice while her stomach continued to roll. She cautiously eyed the messages dropping into her inbox.

Are you okay?

What on earth has your husband done?

You solve problems but never share your own.

Ginny bristled at the last comment. She needed to project a strong persona to her listeners and not display any weakness, to show she was a warrior, not one of the wounded.

She walked briskly home, staring straight ahead so she wouldn't catch anyone's eye in the street. Did her listeners think Miss Peach was unhinged, or did they believe what she'd said? Adrian could be touchy about any public attention.

A couple of months ago, Ginny had arranged for them both to appear in a feature for a local magazine. Her favourite photo from the 'At Home with the Splinters' shoot was a little cheesy but fun, showing her feeding her husband a spoonful of mushroom risotto in their glossy kitchen. There was another photo of them standing arm in arm with Phoebe in the garden.

Adrian had taken part very reluctantly. He worked as the sales director for an upmarket car dealership, The Vehicle Emporium, and hadn't been happy when the guys in the workshop had blown up photos of his ecstatic expression and plastered them all over the walls. The company owner, Nelson, had given Adrian a dressing-down about projecting the wrong image for the business. Ginny could only pray that Adrian's teammates didn't listen to her show while they worked.

She secretly thought the photos had been worth it. Adrian's eyes were blue like Dutch pottery and his sharp cheekbones still made her belly flutter. The shots proved to Ginny she'd assembled the happy and stable family, marriage and home life she'd always longed for, something her own parents hadn't managed to give her.

When Ginny arrived home, she still felt jittery and couldn't wait for Adrian to return, to reassure her that Miss Peach was deluded. She took a moment to look out of her kitchen window and to take in the glorious view. They lived on a small crescent at the edge of the countryside and were surrounded by rolling hills. The long, landscaped garden had a pagoda at the end they'd built to use for entertaining. She and Adrian loved to invite friends and neighbours over for prosecco and homemade pavlova in the summer.

Her husband had a smooth manner that made others feel relaxed in his company. His throaty laugh sounded like he was about to share a risqué joke. They were useful attributes for charming people and selling luxury cars, but not so much when it came to communication of a more personal nature. Only Ginny and Phoebe could spot the telltale signs of when Adrian was stressed, how his eyelids became pink and how his jaw tensed. If she ever questioned him about any worries he might have, it was like trying to pry open an oyster with a blunt knife.

Ginny made pasta and tiramisu as a cute hint at the surprise holiday location. She put the holiday confirmation printout under her tablemat and rearranged the napkins several times while continually glancing at her watch. Adrian was already forty-five minutes late. Usually it wouldn't bother her, but Miss Peach's words waltzed around in her head.

What am I supposed to ask him? she thought.

While she waited, she browsed shopping sites on her phone.

Her eyes lit up at a pair of peep-toed heels she didn't have in that shade of tomato. An electronic stomach-contracting belt had fifty per cent off, a real bargain.

Although a voice in Ginny's head told her she didn't need any more stuff, she stabbed the buy button anyway. When she heard the front door open, she stuffed the phone into her jacket pocket and rushed towards the hallway. 'Hiya.'

'Hi there,' Adrian said.

'Had a good day?'

'Fantastic.' He kissed her haphazardly on her cheek.

Ginny bit her lip, wondering if his voice sounded a little strained. She hovered around to see if he mentioned her show. As the seconds ticked away, relief trickled over her.

Adrian carried his briefcase into his downstairs home office where he kept a selection of toiletries and casual clothes in a small wardrobe.

She leaned against the door frame while he got changed. 'I've made dinner and then I have something to tell you . . .' she said playfully.

'Yeah? Great, I'm starving. Something smells delicious.'

'I've cooked Italian for us.'

'Wicked,' Adrian said.

Ginny's eyebrow twitched upwards. Since when did he use *that* word? When he emerged from his office, she tried not to stare at the indigo jeans that were so tight they made his legs look like chicken drumsticks. Surely, they were too young for a man of his age? When he walked into the dining room, she glanced at the logo on the back pocket and almost coughed at the expensive brand.

Last week she'd found a tube of fake tan in the bathroom and felt like giving him a hug. Just like her, Adrian must be trying to keep up appearances with his younger teammates at work.

Some of Ginny's friends' husbands had commissioned sleeve tattoos or bought motorbikes when they hit middle age, so she was getting away pretty lightly. She didn't want to embarrass Adrian by mentioning anything.

'It's not fair that Nelson keeps you at work late,' she said as they sat down at the dining table. She poured them each a glass of Chianti.

'It's fine, the nature of the job.' Adrian checked out the label on the bottle and nodded approvingly. 'There's several new car models on the market at the moment and customers are taking more time making decisions in the current financial climate. Electric cars throw a whole new range of technologies into the mix.'

Ginny stifled a yawn. She sometimes found their dinner table conversation to be a little dull but, from her problem-solving, she knew lots of long-married couples felt that way. 'I do think you've been working too hard recently, and you're looking a little tired. Perhaps we should increase your B12 vitamins. . .'

Adrian spun his wedding ring around on his finger, something he did when under pressure. 'I'm *fine*,' he said. 'Let's eat.'

He made appreciative noises about the pasta but Ginny found it difficult to swallow. She had a strong urge to tell him about the holiday and hoped it would expel the Miss Peach incident from her brain. 'Our wedding anniversary is coming up fast,' she said.

'Thirty-one years together and twenty-five of them married,' Adrian said, gulping his wine. 'I mean . . . wow.'

Ginny liked his sentiment, though his voice sounded strangely flat. When she touched the booking confirmation, her heart began to race. 'I know you're busy at work, so I've planned a celebration for us. I've found an amazing hotel in Italy called Grand Hotel Castello Bella Vista. It's got a fabulous spa and gorgeous bedrooms and I think—' She halted when Adrian held up a finger. He made a counterclockwise motion.

'Hold on a minute,' he said. 'We *can't* go on holiday this year.'

Ginny tightened her grip on her fork. She felt a vein pulsing in her neck. 'We always go away in June,' she said.

'I should have said something sooner. I'm too busy at work to take a break.'

The air between them turned chilly.

Ginny cleared her throat. 'Our silver anniversary calls for a special celebration, and our fiftieth birthdays are coming up, too. Three weeks together in sunny Italy will be perfect. It's a chance for us to chill and' – she lowered her voice to a whisper – '*reconnect*. I thought we could renew our wedding vows while we're there . . .'

'*Three* weeks?' Adrian stared at her. 'No can do. I can't take that long off.'

Overcome by panic, Ginny started to babble. 'Surely Nelson will understand if you ask him. You're his right-hand man and usually take two weeks' holiday in June anyway.'

Adrian slowly massaged his chin while he thought. 'We can

mark it in some other way, perhaps a nice meal with Phoebe and Pete or something . . .'

Ginny pursed her lips. She'd never admitted her feelings of listlessness to him, not wanting to bother him. She liked to appear cheerful and poised for her husband, but a solitary meal wasn't going to give her the passion she was yearning for. She glimpsed the cost of the holiday on the booking confirmation and it suddenly seemed extortionate. 'I've already booked our trip,' she said quietly.

Adrian clattered his knife and fork onto his plate. '*What?*'

'We're going to Bologna.'

He groaned and pressed his palms to his eyes. 'You *can't* do things like this without consulting me first, Ginny. The guys at work still call me *Dreamy Adrian* from that magazine shoot you agreed to. Stop trying to organize my life.'

Ginny stared at him in shock, cut to the core by his words. 'I'm only trying to help, and those photos are something Phoebe can treasure forever.' She laid her hand on his arm. 'A summer holiday might relieve some of your stress.'

Adrian glowered for a while. 'You're turning into Ginny the Patron Saint of Problems.'

Ginny thought about this and decided it was a compliment.

The rest of their main course was conducted in a prickly silence. When Adrian eventually said, 'This is great tiramisu,' Ginny took it as an apology.

'Thank you,' she said.

Adrian slumped back in his chair and eyed her. 'I didn't want to worry you, but there are going to be several job losses at work and I need to prove I'm indispensable. I'm nearly fifty and the employment market is ferocious out there. There are younger, more dynamic guys snapping at my heels. And I'm sure we'll want to contribute to Phoebe's wedding and honeymoon, rather than pay for a fancy Italian break.'

Ginny's cheeks grew hot. She wondered how much was left in their bank account now that she'd paid for the holiday.

Adrian stood up and made coffee for them both, setting the cups down on the table. The air settled a little as they sipped them together. 'Anyway, how was your day?' he asked.

Ginny recalled slicing her finger across her neck in the Talk Heart FM studio. 'Um . . .' she said lightly, focusing on her cup. 'Did anyone mention my show to you today?'

'And why would they do that?' Adrian's shoulders crept upwards, as if preparing for a slap in the face.

'I took a crank call. The woman sounded really regretful about her life. I tried to be sympathetic, but she turned on me, accusing me of trying to be Ms Perfect.' She flicked her eyes to his. 'She asked me how well I know you.'

Adrian's left cheek started to spasm. 'Did this go out live on air?'

'Yes,' Ginny said quickly. 'But don't worry, it will be okay—'

Adrian screeched back his chair. 'It's *not* okay. What if Nelson hears about this?' He jumped up and started to pace the room. 'It's humiliating.'

Ginny felt her lungs deflating. Oxygen was vacating her body at an alarming rate. 'It's not my fault,' she said quietly. 'It was Miss Peach.'

'*Who?*' Adrian threw up his hands. 'This is great, just *great*.'

She stood up and faced him, rubbing her hand down his

arm. 'Please come with me on holiday. This will all blow over quickly and . . .' She stopped speaking when she spotted something she hadn't seen before, a tiny hole in his left earlobe, and her forehead furrowed. 'When did you get your ear pierced?'

With his skinny jeans and fake tan, Ginny felt like she was looking at an actor on stage, or an ageing boy band member, not her husband.

'I had it done a while ago,' he muttered, turning his head so she couldn't see his ear.

She squinted at him, suspecting this wasn't true.

'I decided I didn't like it,' he said. 'It sounds like you don't trust me or something.'

Ginny shook her head. 'Of course I trust you.'

'It doesn't sound like it.' Adrian squeezed past her and marched towards his office.

He sounded angry and she didn't know where it was coming from. It felt like he was trying to twist things back around on her and her ankles wobbled as she followed him.

How well do you really know him? Miss Peach sang in her head.

'I understand the potential job losses must be worrying,' Ginny started. 'I have some leaflets on . . .'

Adrian ignored her and shoved things around on his shelves, as if looking for something. 'We've been drifting apart for some time,' he said, bending down to pull out a suitcase from under his desk that she hadn't seen before. 'We don't have anything left in common, especially now Phoebe's moved out.'

Ginny's jaw dropped open. 'That's *not* true. We enjoy inviting friends over for dinner, and watching movies together . . .'

She trailed off her words, recalling their usual Saturday evening debate about which film to watch. The gritty crime films Adrian liked were too violent for her taste, and he didn't share her love for rom-coms and period dramas. They usually had to compromise with a blockbuster action movie or thriller.

Adrian scratched the back of his neck. 'Our relationship has changed over the years and we're not the same people any longer. There are cracks in our marriage and they're getting wider.'

'*No*,' Ginny protested wildly. 'We're happy . . .'

'You're so hooked on solving other people's problems that you don't even recognize ours. I need to get away from here, from you. I feel like I'm suffocating, being analysed and told what to do all the time. It's bad enough at work without facing it at home, too.'

'You're not thinking straight, Adrian. We just need some time out together. You can't leave, like my dad used to—'

'*Ginny*, stop.' He spun around and took hold of her arms, looking directly into her eyes.

For a moment she thought he was going to kiss her. Every molecule of her body hoped that he would.

'We need a break *apart*,' he said. 'I've been thinking about divorce for some time and should have raised it sooner. I didn't mean to tell you in this way.'

'*Divorce*?' Ginny's voice quavered. How had their lovely dinner come to this? Was this really happening? She looked on in horror as Adrian grabbed hold of his suitcase and wheeled it into the hallway.

'I really think it's the way forward,' he said.

'No—'

Adrian paused with his head bowed for a moment, thinking before he opened the front door.

Ginny placed her hand on her husband's back, but he stepped out into the street and slammed the door shut behind him. She wrenched it open again and watched helplessly as he sped away. 'Adrian—' she called after him, to no avail.

Back inside the hallway, Ginny's arms hung numbly by her side. *Divorce.* The word reverberated in her head, turning her body to jelly.

She furiously tried to think what guidance she'd offer to someone else in her situation — *stay calm, don't panic and think positively.*

For once, her own advice felt totally useless.

CHAPTER 3

Rope Ladder

Ginny's heart beat so fast she thought it might burst out of her chest. Her mind spun as she strode from room to room, worrying about Adrian. Was he going through some kind of midlife crisis or breakdown? How could she help him? Claiming he wanted a divorce was ridiculous. They'd spent their entire adult lives together and were a family. They hardly ever argued. Sure, they'd both been busy with other things, but it was good not to live in each other's pockets all the time. It gave them things to talk about.

This was so unlike her husband. He usually hid his troubles away, or let them run off him like water from a waxed raincoat. When his dad died, a couple of years ago, Adrian didn't show any outward signs of grief. He went on a walking holiday with his school friend Dave, trekking up the highest mountains in England, Scotland and Wales. He threw himself into his job and never said a word to Ginny about how he was feeling. Could his outburst be the aftermath of his grief finally showing through?

Adrian was her rock. He'd been by her side, helping with her breathing exercises when she gave birth to Phoebe. He'd joined her for the endless night feeds where they both yawned and marvelled at their daughter's tiny hands clenching as she suckled. He'd held Ginny's hair back on holiday when she was sick after drinking too many strawberry daiquiris during the cocktail happy hour. She'd never been able to judge how many drinks were too many, especially when they tasted of fruit.

Ginny sat stiffly on the sofa, listening for the sound of Adrian's key in the door. She didn't text or phone him, wanting to give him some time to come to his senses. Hopefully a walk around the town with his suitcase would help him to calm down.

The clock ticked, the air cooled and Ginny rubbed her arms. It started to rain outside and her stomach felt as small and hard as a hazelnut.

At two in the morning, she eventually forced herself to go to bed. She tossed and turned, tangled up in the bedsheets. Her chest was hot and clammy, then she was shivery and cold. Her hormones often ran riot at night and Adrian was contributing to their chaos.

She finally drifted off into a fractured sleep by telling herself he'd be back home when she woke up. He'd mutter, 'Sorry,' and they'd hold each other tightly and talk things over.

However, when Ginny woke at 4.30 a.m., she was still alone. Her self-control cracked and she clutched her phone.

Where are you? she texted. **Let's talk. I'm sure we can work things out.**

Adrian didn't have a big social circle compared to the wide

array of people Ginny had amassed from school, her various counselling and advice jobs over the years and from being a mum. His main friends were Dave and his wife, Linda.

Ginny waited but Adrian didn't reply.

As the sun rose, the sight of his pillow all plumped up without a dent made her queasy with worry.

She lay in bed and waited until 8.00 a.m. to ring him. When he didn't pick up his phone, she called Dave at home instead.

Linda answered. She was a playgroup assistant who spoke to Ginny like a naughty three-year-old and the two women had never bonded.

'Hi, is Adrian there?' Ginny asked, adopting the casual manner she used to make hair appointments.

'Yes, he's here,' Linda said curtly.

Ginny screwed her eyes shut with relief. 'Great, that's good.' She took a moment. 'Can you put him on the line, or ask him to call me?'

Footsteps sounded as if Linda was moving to a different room. A door closed. 'It's not a good time. He doesn't want to talk to you right now.'

Ginny's irritation rose. Linda sounded like she was enjoying her self-appointed role of Adrian's protector. 'I'm his wife, not a patient asking for a doctor's appointment,' she said. 'Please tell him that.'

'He wants some time alone.'

'I *need* to speak to him . . .'

'You're not listening to me, Ginny,' Linda said. 'He'll call you when he's ready.'

'But—'

'Sorry, I have to go to work.' Linda hung up.

Ginny scowled at the phone and threw it across the bed. What had Adrian told his friends about her? She stared up at the ceiling for a couple of hours in a daze. When the doorbell rang, breaking the silence, she pulled on her dressing gown and ran downstairs, hoping to find Adrian waiting on the other side of the door.

Instead, a postman handed a pile of packages to her. Ginny sighed as she clutched them to her chest and carried them upstairs.

Somehow, watching TV shopping channels and browsing online sales had become addictive to her. She found classy Italian leather handbags, new face serums, and cordless vacuum cleaners with fantastic suction power impossible to resist.

Many of the things she bought disappointed her and it was a hassle to return them, so Ginny hid them on the top shelf in her wardrobe behind a pillow, out of Adrian's sight.

Back in her room, Ginny opened the parcels and couldn't remember ordering Luscious Locks hair thickening lotion, or vitamins especially tailored to her age and lifestyle. A pair of leopard-print heels looked exactly like ones she already owned. There was a contraption that used sonic waves to firm jowls and a 'miracle' under-eye cream. It was the kind of stuff she needed to look and feel better for Adrian's return.

Ginny set to work. The machine buzzed as she pushed it up and down her face. She took a bath, washed her hair and curled her ponytail. She applied coatings of peachy gel under her eyes, and she still felt dreadful. She ordered herself not to chase Adrian again; he would have to call her.

When her phone eventually rang at lunchtime, Ginny snatched it up, only to see Phoebe's name flash on the screen.

'Hey, Mum,' her daughter said. 'How's things? Got any anniversary plans yet?'

Ginny sat on her bed and hung her head. Phoebe sounded cheerful, so she probably didn't know about the Miss Peach incident, or that her father had left last night. Ginny usually advocated honesty, but didn't want to worry her daughter, especially during her wedding plans.

'Oh, hi, darling. All's great, thanks. We're thinking about escaping to Italy for a nice break, if your dad can get the time off work. The hotel is like a white castle,' she said. Before her daughter could ask anything, Ginny quickly swerved the conversation. 'How are all your wedding plans going?'

Phoebe exaggerated a sigh. 'Okay, I *suppose*. Pete's mum only wants to invite his *entire* family to the wedding. It'll be like Glastonbury! We need new carpets for our home, not buckets of champagne for his long-lost relatives. They're also pushing us to honeymoon in Barbados, like they did. It all feels too much.'

Ginny could empathize. There was pressure these days for weddings to be nothing less than epic. Fortunately, Phoebe had inherited Adrian's sensible, level-headed genes alongside Ginny's caring DNA. Phoebe's job as an accountant for an animal rescue charity suited her.

Recalling Adrian's mention of divorce, she swallowed away a lump in her throat. They were both supposed to be role models for their daughter. 'Is it somewhere you'd like to go?' she asked.

'Yeah, who wouldn't? We don't have the cash though.'

Ginny chewed her lip when she thought about the holiday she'd booked. She supposed she had acted impulsively. The money could have helped Phoebe out instead.

'Anyway, Pete wants Dad's advice on a car or something,' Phoebe said. 'Is he there?'

'Oh, um, not at the moment.' Ginny's voice cracked a little. 'He's gone out for a while . . .'

'What time will he be back? We'll pop over.'

'I'm not exactly sure. He's really busy at the moment.'

'Oh . . . right.'

Ginny heard the house phone ringing downstairs. Could Adrian be calling her? Perhaps they could sort things out before they saw their daughter. She ran downstairs with her mobile clamped to her ear. When she saw her husband's number on the screen, her breath quickened.

'Are you out jogging or something?' Phoebe laughed.

Ginny hated to cut her off, but she *had* to pick up Adrian's call in case he vanished again. 'I'm sorry darling, I have to go. Love you lots, bye.' She hung up and snatched up the house phone. 'Adrian. Where are you? I've been worried sick.'

'I'm fine, at Dave's house,' he said glumly.

Ginny paced around, needing to keep moving. She circled the living room and then the kitchen. 'I understand if you need some time out. It's good you recognize that. Why not come home and let's talk things through?' She didn't want to use their daughter as a trump card, but it slipped out. 'We don't want to worry Phoebe.'

She added silently, in her head, *Don't you remember, how we both cried when we saw the two blue lines on the pregnancy strip and how you came with me for all the hospital scans?*

'Ginny.' The tone of his voice said *stop*. 'I've been unhappy for some time and I think you have, too. We both need time to think about what we really want in life.'

She continued patrolling the house and found herself in his home office. Adrian had left his MacBook behind, a good sign. 'I know what I want and it's you,' she said. 'Are you coming home?'

'Not yet.'

Yet. She clung onto the word like it was a rope ladder dangling from an air ambulance while she was drowning at sea. She hated feeling so helpless.

'I'm *not* going on holiday with you,' he said firmly. 'You have to cancel it. It must have cost a fortune. What's the cancellation policy?'

She sank into his office chair. How could he sound so glacial? 'I don't know. There was no need to check at the time.'

'We need that money for other things. I can stay with Dave and Linda for a short time, then I'll need to find somewhere to rent.'

Ginny felt like an earthquake was shaking her home and she screwed her eyes shut. With the threat of Adrian losing his job, cancelling was the best option. She didn't even want to think about him living elsewhere. 'I'll check it now. There might be a cancellation fee.'

She wondered if she could access the travel website on her phone without cutting him off the call.

Not wanting to risk it, she switched on his MacBook, knowing he used the same password across all his devices.

'Ginny, I have to go . . . ring me back.' Adrian's voice sounded small and tinny from her mobile.

'*You* asked me to do this,' she called out while logging into the travel website.

'Okay, *okay*.'

Adrian's MacBook pinged as email notifications started to appear in the top right-hand corner, virus protection software and something from Vodafone.

Ginny ignored them and clicked on the holiday cancellation policy. It was several pages long and her eyes flitted as she tried to find the relevant information.

A direct Facebook message briefly flashed on the screen, from Dave. **Sorry things are tough right now, mate** . . .

Ginny narrowed her eyes. So, Adrian could talk to his friend about their problems but not to her? *Great*.

Another ping sounded and a pink face icon grinned at her. **You have a wink**, it read.

Ginny frowned. A wink? What did that mean? It didn't look like any app she knew. She clicked on it, to get rid of it.

Instead, the face grew larger on screen. Pink hearts burst forth and twinkled.

She found herself staring at a photograph of Adrian she hadn't seen before. He grinned and wore mirrored sunglasses, resting his head on his hand. From the angle of his shoulder, she could tell it was a selfie and her blood cooled in her veins.

'Are you still there?' Adrian asked.

Ginny read the website name, *ChainReaxions – Confidential Connections*.

Oh, god. She bit her lip so hard she almost drew blood. Swaying with nausea, she had a masochistic urge to read more.

Adrian, age 45, looking for interesting women, for fun and companionship . . .

Her vision fuzzed and Ginny gripped the desk to stop herself from keeling over. Even though she felt sick, she couldn't tear her eyes away from the screen.

'Ginny?'

Her hand shook as she clamped the phone to her ear. 'I'm trying to cancel the holiday on your laptop and your dating profile has popped up,' she said numbly.

'Why are you using my stuff?'

'You're cheating on me . . .'

'No, I'm not.' He went silent for a while. 'I was just curious and wasn't actually going to—'

'It's still cheating . . .' Ginny squeaked. She felt like she was falling off a skyscraper, tumbling through the air and ready to hit the pavement. 'Miss Peach was right.'

Adrian's breath grew hoarser. 'No, it's not like that. I swear I don't know *her* . . .'

Not able to bear listening to his excuses, Ginny ended the call.

Adrian made several attempts to ring her back and each time she cut him off. Eventually, he stopped trying and his office fell silent.

Ginny pressed her hands against her chest and felt the heavy thrum of her heartbeat. She stared at the total cost of the holiday on the laptop screen and felt like curling into a tight ball. She fumbled with the mouse and located the holiday booking policy again.

Cancellation within 28 days – 100 per cent of the cost.

She did a quick calculation of the dates and swallowed hard. There were only twenty-six days to the holiday, but surely there must be some way to get the money back, a cooling-off period or a get-out clause.

Scanning through all the details again, she prayed she'd read them wrong. However, they were there in black and white. Ginny slumped down in her chair and cried.

Her husband was gone, she wasn't going on holiday, and now she was going to lose all their money, too.

CHAPTER 4

Roar

Keep calm and be kind to yourself. Get dressed, clean your teeth and style your hair. Confide in close friends or a therapist if you need to. Indulge in self-pity in private, but keep your dignity in public and show your heartache who's boss. Relationships can be like roller coasters with as many downs as ups. Things aren't over until they're over.

No matter what Ginny told herself, it wouldn't sink in. Adrian's dating site image was seared in her mind. As the weekend progressed, questions raged in her brain. How long had he been active on the site? Why had he lied about his age? Had he met up with anyone? Were his late nights at The Vehicle Emporium really just work, and what did Miss Peach know? She felt terribly naive for missing any warning signs.

It felt like aliens had kidnapped her husband for a scientific experiment and removed the part of his brain that governed tact and decency.

She took a shower and let hot water bounce off her face. Afterwards, she put on her dressing gown and rang the local independent travel company she'd booked the holiday with.

She briefly explained her situation to a woman with a robotic nasal voice who took great pleasure confirming that if Ginny cancelled, she would lose all her money.

'You could go on your own,' the woman suggested.

'*Really*?' Ginny threw a hand in the air. 'It's a *romantic* resort for couples.' She pictured waiters in the dining room exchanging pitying looks as they allocated her a tiny table next to the toilets. Other diners would whisper about her over their steaks.

'Please speak to your supervisor, to see if there's any other options.'

The travel assistant sighed. When she returned to the call she sounded a little more amiable. 'Apparently you can change the name of your guest, or guests, for a small fee. You can switch your hotel to a different one, up to the same value. That's all.'

An optical migraine brought dancing spots before Ginny's eyes. She conducted a quick search and found there was only one other hotel in Vigornuovo available for three weeks in June. Hotel Splendido was much cheaper and nowhere near as posh as the Grand Hotel Castello Bella Vista, meaning she could afford five people to go on holiday rather than two. She felt too overwhelmed to look at other locations.

Ginny tried to think who she'd take with her instead of Adrian. Her married friends would probably spend the holiday secretively phoning their children and partners. The single ones would want to go out dancing and drinking. Ginny would most likely end up crying on a sun lounger after too many martinis and Adrian wouldn't be there to hold back her hair. Phoebe was about to become knee-deep in confetti and Ginny didn't want to tell her about Adrian's misdemeanours. Her head was too achy to think about all this right now.

'You have forty-eight hours to amend your booking,' the travel assistant said. 'Have a great holiday.'

Ginny trudged into the kitchen and automatically took two plates out of the cupboard. She looked in the fridge and asked herself why packets of pasta came in two-person-size portions. When she picked up a cup, it proclaimed, *The World's Best Husband*.

She stared at it before lobbing it across the kitchen. It bounced off a wall and thudded down onto the linoleum where it lay intact. 'I can't even break a bloody cup properly,' she yelled, balling her hands into fists.

Ginny flurried around the house looking for evidence that Adrian might be having an affair. She didn't discover anything, other than a silver stud earring and instructions for how to look after a new piercing in his bedside drawer. Seeing it felt like a kick to her bare shin, but she was relieved not to find anything more incriminating.

Adrian didn't answer her calls and texts for the rest of the weekend.

On Monday morning, Ginny curled her ponytail and applied lipstick, telling herself the people of Greenham needed her, even if her husband didn't.

Inside the Talk Heart FM building, the confident version of her in the poster looked like an imposter. The real Ginny felt bruised black and blue inside.

Tam had left a message to say she was going to be late into work, and Ginny was glad she didn't have to face her. She would sort out her own show for the day. She sat down at her desk and texted Adrian.

Hi. Sorry but I can't cancel the holiday, she messaged.

This time, he replied within seconds. **Are you sure? Let me try.**

Ginny ground her teeth. What could he possibly do that she couldn't?

Send me the link, he added.

Ginny messaged him the holiday details. Let him try if he wanted to. She drank two cups of black coffee to give her an energy boost and scanned her emails to find some problems to address. The message she'd received last week nagged in her head.

You solve problems but never share your own.

Now that Adrian had christened her the Patron Saint of Problems, being authentic was more important to her than ever. Ginny had always prided herself on her empathetic abilities, but when she read through listeners' issues that morning, she truly *felt* their pain as if it was her own.

She cried for a man whose wife had left him for their next-door neighbour, and a woman who'd been unemployed for three years and was about to lose her home. Big, fat tears streamed down her face, joined by a river of snot, making jotting down any advice difficult. How could she help others when she felt so useless and hollow inside? She gulped another coffee and it made her feel a little high. She hadn't been eating properly and her head was light when she took to the airwaves.

'Hi, and a very good Monday morning to you all. I hope you had a fabulous weekend,' she said, thinking how fake her cheeriness sounded. 'I'm Ginny Splinter and you're listening to *Just Ask Ginny* on Talk Heart FM. Let's all enjoy "Adore You" by the adorable Harry Styles, then I'll give you a helping hand with your issues.'

Ginny set the track playing, wiped her cheeks and drank more coffee. Her phone vibrated and her stomach skittered when she saw Adrian's name. She quickly lined up 'Roar' by Katy Perry and answered his call off-air.

'You're right,' Adrian said. 'I spoke to someone at the travel agency. There's no way to get the money back.'

'I know I'm right,' she said, dismayed he hadn't bothered to say good morning to her.

'Are you still going to go?'

Ginny shook her head, overwhelmed by the rush of sadness she felt. 'I don't want to go alone,' she said stiffly. 'I can't think of anyone else to invite . . .'

'We can't let the holiday go to waste. There're only a few hours left to amend the booking. Can't Phoebe and Pete use the tickets for their honeymoon?'

'A honeymoon *before* a wedding? What a great idea,' she said, more sarcastically than she intended. Her brain felt floaty and sporadic tears kept escaping.

'I'm only trying to solve the problem, just like you always do,' he snapped.

Ginny couldn't remember ever feeling this low before. Perhaps she could forgive Adrian's dating site presence if it was a one-off, something he'd done out of confusion or experimentation. They had a great marriage and he'd never given her any cause for concern before. He knew about all the trials and tribulations her parents had put her through, and he'd

34

promised never to do the same thing. Ginny still saw her and Adrian's troubles like a loose thread on a sweater. If you left it alone it might be fine. If you kept on pulling, everything would unravel. 'It'd be silly to lose all the money,' she said. '*Please* can we go to Italy together, to work on things—?'

Adrian cleared his throat. 'I can use the tickets,' he said.

'*What?* Who would you take with you?'

'I'll find someone . . .'

When she realized her husband was willing to go on holiday with someone else but didn't have the time to go with *her*, Ginny reeled. 'Have you met someone else? On the dating site?' she demanded.

Adrian didn't speak for a while. 'Forget it. It was just an idea.'

Ginny shook her head, wondering how her marriage had come to *this*. They were acting like boxers in a ring, ducking, diving and jabbing. There was *no way* her husband was taking someone else on their anniversary holiday, to the castle hotel she'd booked, with the posh spa treatments and tennis courts. The thought made her shoulders shake. As Katy Perry sang about roaring, Ginny felt like doing the same thing. 'Hold the line,' she commanded, placing the phone down so Adrian could still hear her. 'I need to go back on air.'

As she looked at the listeners' problems she'd jotted down, Ginny recognized she wasn't a superhuman with all the answers. She was a real woman with real problems. Problems that were too big to deal with alone. Problems that were swelling inside her, fighting to get out. Her cheeks felt fiery and she was overcome by a rage that made her feel like she was going to explode.

The record stopped. Ginny opened her mouth and scrambled for something to say.

Seconds ticked away and frost seemed to crackle over her skin. The airwaves were silent.

Get a grip, Ginny. Inhale and exhale. Thousands of people are listening to you.

But her tongue was bone-dry. She couldn't find any words.

Tam arrived and stood in front of the glass partition, gaping as Ginny sat there motionless and speechless. 'What's up?' she mouthed.

Ginny saw the disdain in her producer's eyes. She heard Adrian shouting her name from her phone and felt like she was about to crack in two.

She wrenched the scrunchie out of her ponytail and shook out her hair. She unfastened the buttons on her jacket and then the one on the back of her skirt. She kicked off her shoes and pressed her bare feet against the carpet, needing to feel something solid.

Emails pinged into her inbox.

What's happened to the music?

Do you know Talk Heart FM has gone off-air?

Are you okay, Ginny?

The last question made her cry. No listener had ever asked her that before.

No, she shook her head. *I'm not okay.* She felt she had more in common with the strangers who contacted her radio show than she did with her own husband.

Ginny remembered what she always told her callers, 'It's okay to *not* be okay,' and she took a deep breath. For once, she was going to lead by example.

She lined up the next song on her playlist, a golden oldie, 'Strangers in Paradise' by The Supremes, and it felt like some kind of message to her.

'Sorry for the slight delay there, folks, just a small technical hitch.' Ginny swallowed painfully. She turned her head so she couldn't see Tam and ignored Adrian's voice.

'There's something I want, something I *need*, to share with you . . .' Ginny inhaled, to summon more strength. 'I sit here each day considering your problems and giving you answers, trying to do my best to advise you. I thought I was in a good position to do so. After all, I have the perfect life and perfect husband. Or, so I thought . . .' she laughed wryly.

'Ginny, *Ginny*. Don't do this,' Adrian shouted.

She ignored him and carried on. In her current headspace, she wasn't thinking about his reputation at work, or about Phoebe. She couldn't stop her words from tumbling out.

'I feel so foolish because I've been living a lie and didn't realize it. My marriage has been crumbling and I've been in denial. I thought a holiday might paper over the cracks, but our issues are more like the Grand Canyon.

'You may have heard a caller last week asking me how well I know my husband. Obviously, it's not very well at all. He's walked out on me after twenty-five years of marriage and refuses to join me on the special holiday I've planned for our anniversary. He'd actually prefer to go away with a stranger. And, considering the way he's treating me, so would I.'

Out of the corner of her eye Ginny could see Tam gesturing wildly. She took a few seconds to gather her thoughts. 'So, if you're listening to this, and you're heartbroken, too, why not join me on holiday, for three weeks in Italy next month?

'I'll pick up the hotel bill for four lucky listeners if you can cover your flight costs. We can all be heartbroken together.

'Pick up the phone during the next song and leave your name and a few details with my producer, Tam. She thinks my show is boring, so it will give her the shot of excitement she's craving.'

Ginny set 'Strangers in Paradise' playing and sat back in her chair. She cut Adrian off the call and turned off her phone. After removing her headphones, she picked up her shoes and walked barefoot out of the studio and into the office, feeling strangely serene.

'What the f—?' Tam asked, her glasses sliding down her nose.

'The phones are ringing and I need some fresh air,' Ginny said calmly. 'Please field the calls from listeners and select four winners. You can WhatsApp me their details later.'

Tam opened and shut her mouth like a fish lying on dry land.

Ginny put her shoes back on and left the building.

By the time she'd walked home (taking back streets to avoid seeing anyone), Tam had sent her three messages, starting with the list of strangers who'd be accompanying Ginny on holiday.

I hope you know what you're doing. Your holiday mates are . . .

Heather Hall, 43. Schoolteacher. Likes yoga and talks too much. Her mum is ill.

Eric Sanderson, 28. Carpenter. Quiet. Had some kind of bereavement.

Edna Edgerton-Woods, 80. Ex-seamstress. A bit grouchy. Missing her family.

Curtis Dunne, 38. Property developer. (Sounds fine, if you ask me).

Curtis will replace Adrian on your flight and the others will make their own way there.

BTW. Take all the time off you need. Talk Heart FM takes mental health very seriously.

The last message sounded like Tam had been instructed to send it by the radio bosses and Ginny was relieved to read it. There was no way she could face going back on air before her holiday.

Needing to change the booking before time ran out, she quickly logged into the travel website and deleted Adrian's name, humming The Supremes track as she added the strangers' names instead.

As she reread their brief descriptions, Ginny gave herself a firm nod. She would prove to Adrian, to Tam and also to herself that other people needed her.

And she needed them, too.

CHAPTER 5

Splendido

Nico

The holiday booking had come as a welcome surprise for Nico, almost a miracle. His little Italian hotel had been struggling since the pandemic, but now his five guest rooms were going to be fully occupied for three weeks in June. He couldn't wait for Hotel Splendido to be filled with chatter and laughter again.

The booking was made under the name of Ginny Splinter for five people in total, arriving on four different flights. It would take several trips to the airport to pick everyone up. Not that he minded too much. If the guests liked his hotel, they'd hopefully spread the word so he could start to earn a living again.

Nico couldn't help flourishing his right arm when he practised greeting them. 'Welcome to my hotel,' he said, under his breath. 'Greetings, my home is your home.'

He was very proud of his bedrooms. They were all comfortable with lemon-painted walls, and trendy coral duvet covers and curtains. The compact ensuite bathrooms each had blue and white ceramic wall tiles, a toilet and small shower enclosure. Along the upstairs corridor and his downstairs hallway, framed photos on the walls showed a younger Nico with his mamma, papà, nonna and nonno.

He personally cleaned each of his rooms daily and picked fresh flowers to place in small glass bottles on the bedside tables. He made fresh bread and hoped the delicious aroma would reach the Vigornuovo village where tourists might lift their noses, sniff and head to his hotel in a trance.

Unfortunately, his seventeen-year-old daughter, Loretta, didn't share the same fondness for Nico's decor. 'Nothing says *Benvenuti* like our dead relatives,' she often said with a roll of her eyes. 'They might give our guests nightmares. Why can't we update our hotel, to make it more modern?'

Nico could admit some of their relatives looked rather stern, even angry. To him, they showed Splendido was a place where he treated everyone like family.

That morning, he had washed all his bedsheets and duvet covers and hung them on the washing line in the courtyard, to dry in the early morning heat. He sat down at one of the white outdoor tables to eat breakfast with Gianfranco, a fellow hotel owner and his best friend since childhood. They often spoke to each other in English to practise the language.

Breakfast was treated lightly in Northern Italy. The two men drank cappuccinos and ate cornetti, a croissant with a light sugar glaze. Nico could never understand why anyone would want to cram their stomachs full of eggs, cheese, ham, yogurt and bacon as soon as they woke up.

He liked to feel streamlined and his waist had remained the

same size since he was Loretta's age. There were only a few strands of silver in his flock of dark curls.

'Why are you still using the old bed linen?' Gianfranco asked, eyeing the washing line. 'It isn't nice.'

'It is good quality.'

'It is orange.'

'Coral,' Nico corrected. 'A pretty colour.'

Gianfranco shook his head. He was squat with bulging eyes and a wispy goatee beard. Despite his stalwart appearance, he could be moved to tears easily, making his big eyes glisten like wet marbles. 'In my humble expert opinion, guests like everything to be white. We only have white pillow cases and white sheets at the Grand Hotel Castello Bella Vista.'

'I am running a hotel, not a dental surgery. My guests like colour.'

'I *know* what they want,' Gianfranco nodded sagely. 'And it's not tangerine sheets. They want fine bedding and sophisticated activities to stimulate their minds and bodies. A coffee, brioche and a nice view are no longer enough. I have asked you several times to come and see my new spa, to give you inspiration.'

If anyone had overheard the two men, they might think they were shouting at each other, rather than having a normal, friendly conversation. Their discussion was accompanied by much gesturing of their hands.

Gianfranco had added a huge extension and turrets to the roof of his once-modest *pensione* and now claimed it was a castle. He served a sumptuous buffet breakfast that included twenty types of cereal and even champagne and caviar.

Nico preferred his own modest offering of *caffè latte*, bread served with butter and jam, *fette biscottate* and fruit. Even though Gianfranco's hotel was usually fully occupied, he wanted his own guests to sit down at the oak kitchen table that had been in his family for centuries, to enjoy traditional food.

Nico also didn't want to risk the feelings of awe, envy and inadequacy that Gianfranco's new facilities might conjure up. He knew Splendido needed an update, though not in such a drastic way.

The two men took a moment to sip their cappuccinos and admire their surroundings. Hotel Splendido nestled in a valley between two lush hills, one mile along the slender road leading into the pretty medieval village of Vigornuovo. Gianfranco's castle hotel sat on top of one of the hills, gleaming white in the sunshine.

Vigornuovo had a pretty square with a few cafés that weren't bothered too much by tourists who preferred the art and beauty of Florence, the romance of Venice, or the golden coastline of Lido di Jesolo. The village had enjoyed a swell in popularity a few years ago when scenes from a Hollywood movie, *A Glorious Escape*, were filmed in the streets, featuring the weathered stone fountain and the river that twinkled like a length of glittery blue ribbon.

The lead actor, Tim Vincenzo, was supposedly a heartthrob, but Nico and Loretta saw him sitting outside a café one day and he looked surprisingly haggard. He had been smoking a cigarette and lowered his sunglasses, as if to look at Loretta's legs. Nico had thrown the actor a disapproving stare, especially because his daughter had just turned fifteen at the time, but Vincenzo just smirked and flicked ash onto the tablecloth.

Gianfranco studied Nico and raised a bushy eyebrow. 'My offer is still on the table, *amico mio*,' he said pointedly.

Nico wiped away a milky moustache. Each time he saw Gianfranco, his friend offered to buy Splendido. Each time, the price dropped by a few thousand euros. 'My hotel is not for sale. You know I made the promise,' he said.

Nico let his thoughts slip back in time, to four years ago. His eyes stung as he recalled sitting at his beloved mother's side as she lay dying in bed. In the midst of her last breaths, she had squeezed his hand. 'Splendido is yours now, Nico. Never sell it.'

'I promise, Mamma,' he whispered, just before she slipped away.

His wife, Maria, had been incensed when he'd told her of his mamma's last wish. '*Nico*,' she scolded. 'I am sorry your mother has gone, but we've talked about moving to the coast. A seaside hotel will attract more tourists and Loretta can play on the beach.'

'I didn't promise this,' Nico said. 'There is much we can do with Splendido.'

He'd taken Maria's hand, leading her from room to room. He tugged down dusty curtains and rolled up the threadbare rugs. He told her stories from his childhood, of playing hide and seek with Gianfranco in the wardrobes of the unoccupied rooms, and showed her the kitchen stool he used to stand on to make bread with his mamma.

Maria gradually came around to his way of thinking. She stood in the courtyard with Nico and surveyed the peeling pistachio-coloured window shutters and the juicy figs that hung in the trees surrounding the hotel. 'If we stay here, we could install an outdoor swimming pool,' she mused. 'We could open a trattoria and make improvements to the road. We need to do *something* to make Splendido stand out.'

'Yes, I want this, too,' Nico said, aware they only had enough money to repaint the bedrooms and to update a couple of bathrooms.

Maria's big plans remained as pictures in his head. Nico didn't fit a pool or introduce fancy food. He watched as other families in the area transformed their *pensiones* into posh hotels, just as Gianfranco was doing. He stalled and got left further and further behind, especially when the pandemic took hold.

And, sadly, Maria had moved on, too.

'Your promise to your mother was made under pressure. You should plan for your future, and Loretta's, too.' Gianfranco said, side-eyeing Nico's minibus parked a few metres away. It had once belonged to a hospital and the word *ambulanza* showed through the white paint. 'Your hotel would make the perfect sister hotel for Castello Bella Vista, or perhaps a set of apartments. You could still live here and be the manager. Maybe Romeo could help you when he finishes college.'

Nico tried not to wrinkle his nose at the mention of Gianfranco's son. Romeo was studying media at college and had promised to design a website for Splendido. It remained half-finished and featured stock images in place of real photos. The copy (also written by Romeo) claimed that Nico's hotel was only fifteen kilometres away from Venice, when it was actually one hundred and fifty kilometres away.

Nico had told Romeo numerous times that the distance was a mistake, but the lazy boy had not made the change. Nico's written English wasn't the best, but he was sure Romeo's description of his hotel wasn't that great either.

> Only fifteen kilometres from Venice, Hotel Splendido presents a rather drab inauspicious exterior to the outside world. Do not be dismayed! As you cross the threshold, you enter a different world. The aim is to create an elegant, friendly atmosphere. A nice breakfast from the territory is served with love in a light dining room and the landlord is always available for conversation. The spotless bedrooms are of modest size, not cramped. Some have little terraces looking over the courtyard where guests can view the white-painted tables, chairs and chickens. Bathrooms are functional and graced with adequate towels. Splendido is the art of creating good memories!

'At my castle, I host well-being workshops and guests can have ten different massages. They lie down and someone hits gongs around them,' Gianfranco said. 'The vibrations are supposed to cleanse the soul. What can you offer your guests?'

Nico ignored the question and frowned. 'Do the gongs work?'

'It does not matter,' Gianfranco replied with a shrug. 'I charge fifty euros per person.'

'This is robbery.'

'This is business. You should follow your head, not the heart.' Gianfranco tapped his temple and then his chest.

Nico bristled. 'I think you will find it is the other way around. My guests want simple living, not strange therapies.

I can drive them to Florence, and Loretta can show them the best shops. There is also Venice.'

At the mention of her name, his daughter appeared outside with a swish of her white cotton dress and glossy long brown hair. She planned to attend a local college to study fashion, when she left school in one year's time, and Nico was forever finding her draped around the hotel and courtyard, taking selfies for social media. She was growing more reluctant to help him out around the hotel, even though it was now the school summer holidays.

'Venice. Ha,' Loretta said, biting into an apple. 'It is a theme park for tourists.'

Nico shook his head at how his daughter mocked the romance of the city. He loved its canals, meandering streets and multitude of bridges. If you went there early in the morning, or stayed late at night, there was a magic that didn't occur anywhere else. He and Maria had spent many happy moments slipping along the back streets, and kissing in doorways at dusk. He loved how the canals rippled golden at daybreak and pink at sunset, and how the shops sold handmade marbled paper and carnival masks. He even enjoyed the overpriced *gelato*.

'Venice is beautiful,' he said. 'It is *not* fifteen kilometres away.'

Gianfranco raised a hand and sighed. 'I will speak to Romeo again. He will change the website.'

'*Grazie.*'

Gianfranco finished his coffee and waited until Loretta had gone back indoors. 'Seriously, you need to get with the times, Nico. Your hotel needs *something* new, or it might shut down. What Hollywood actor would ever want to stay here?'

'Maybe one I have heard of, who does not stare at my daughter,' Nico said. 'Do not worry about me. I have five guests arriving soon and my hotel will be full for three weeks. It will be the beginning of good times again.'

'I really hope so, my friend.'

After Gianfranco left, Nico washed their cups and plates in his kitchen. Everything was just as his mamma had left it. Her cooking pots sat on the shelves, and a chipped floor tile reminded him of where she'd once dropped a ladle. He recalled his family's laughter as they sat around the kitchen table together and, one day, he hoped to hear it again.

He picked up a pink Murano glass vase he'd bought Maria for their first wedding anniversary and held it up to his eyes. They used to look through it together, to see the world tinted rose. It hurt him deeply that she'd not taken it with her when she'd left.

Nico ordered himself to look forwards and not back. Soon his hotel would be full of life again, giving him lots to be proud of. Hopefully, one day, his wife would also realize this, too, and come back to him.

CHAPTER 6

Suitcase

Since Ginny's live announcement on air (or *rambling meltdown* as her local newspaper called it) the time leading up to her holiday passed by in a blur. The worst experience of her life, even worse than Adrian asking for a divorce, was when Phoebe called her in floods of tears. Ginny couldn't stop replaying the moment in her mind.

'Mum, what's going on with Dad?' her daughter had sobbed. 'You went on the radio and told *everyone* you're splitting up, without telling me first. I heard it from a friend.'

Ginny had sat down heavily on her bed. Her recollection of what she'd done in the studio was hazy, as if it was a strange dream. 'We are *not* splitting up, darling,' she'd said firmly, also trying to convince herself. She had to keep thinking positively. 'We're just having a little break from each other, that's all.'

'I listened to a recording of your show. You said Dad walked out on you, that your marriage is falling apart . . . Is it true?'

Ginny's gut had twisted with regret. 'I'm truly sorry,' she'd said. 'It was a culmination of lots of things, the menopause, stress at work . . .' *And I miss you*, she'd wanted to add but didn't. 'I got carried away.'

'Where's Dad gone? Why are you going on holiday with strangers? It's weird.'

Ginny had chewed the inside of her cheek. She hadn't wanted to tell Phoebe about Adrian using a dating site in case it destroyed her faith in marrying Pete. She usually advocated complete openness to her listeners, but in this case, the less her daughter knew, the better. 'Your dad's staying with Dave and Linda for a while, having a little rest. I didn't want to vacation alone, so I invited four lucky listeners to join me, instead. I'm sure they'll be perfectly pleasant people.' She'd crossed her fingers.

'So, Dad'll be back soon?'

'Of course he will. Try not to worry and focus on your wedding. Everything will be just fine.'

Ginny had used more reassuring words and distraction techniques until Phoebe eventually calmed down. When she'd wrapped up the call, her daughter still wasn't totally happy, but Ginny promised to keep in touch while she was in Italy.

On the lead-up to her holiday, she focused on the trip rather than on Adrian. Ginny selected her outfits and bought toiletries in the supermarket at night, when she was less likely to be accosted by concerned listeners. She ordered too many sarongs and sunglasses on the internet and greeting the postman each day made her feel a little less alone. She emailed property developer Curtis Dunne details about their flight and received a brief *cheers* back.

One day, she went out for a walk and detected the smell

of Adrian's aftershave in the hallway when she returned to the house. He must have let himself in while she was out. He'd taken some of his clothes and his MacBook, making his request for a divorce seem even more real. She tried phoning and texting him for an explanation, but he didn't reply.

A statement appeared on the Talk Heart FM website.

Ginny Splinter is currently taking a well-earned break from her show. She'll be back with more tunes and advice soon! Keep on listening.

Ginny felt lost when she arrived at the airport. Adrian had been at her side for the last three decades and she'd never been overseas without him before. She wandered around the shops buying things she didn't need; nail varnish, perfume and a new relationship book titled *The Power of Two*. She boarded the plane and lifted her chin each time other passengers walked past her down the aisle. Her eyes were drawn to the couples, especially the younger, gorgeous ones who chatted excitedly while trailing their fingers up and down each other's backs.

As the takeoff time grew closer, she questioned if Curtis was actually going to show up.

Just as Ginny had convinced herself he wasn't coming, a man dressed all in white strode down the aisle as if he owned the airline. He grinned at the seated people who tutted at his tardiness. He examined his boarding card for his seat number and stopped to stuff his travel bag into an overhead compartment.

'Ginny, right?' he asked, sticking out a hand so large it looked like a bear's paw. 'How's it going?'

'Great,' she said, trying not to wince as his handshake made her knuckles crack. She didn't detect a hint of heartache in his smile.

Curtis's box-fresh white Nike running shoes, cargo shorts cut off at the knee and baseball cap made him look younger than thirty-eight until Ginny saw the crow's feet spanning from his eyes.

'Awesome to meet you. The traffic sucked.' Curtis thumped down in his seat, taking up much more room than Adrian did. He rustled around in the bag fastened around his waist and produced a big bag of Skittles. 'Want some of these? They'll stop your ears from popping at takeoff. The red ones are the best.'

'I'm fine, thanks,' she said.

'No worries.' He fastened his seat belt. 'Can't beat flying, can you? I don't usually listen to the radio, but I heard you offering the free trip and I thought, Curtis, you should go for it. Have some fun, meet some new people. There's five of us, right?'

Ginny nodded. Curtis made it sound like he was purely here for a freebie rather than trying to solve any of his problems. She was about to ask him more about himself, but he'd already put on a pair of headphones and was busy messing around with an iPod. Ginny hadn't seen one of those things in years.

She'd never been keen on flying and opened the book she'd bought. Authors Ben and Ally Prince were a married couple who'd once been on the verge of divorce when they wrote *The Power of Two*. They gazed adoringly at each other in their author photo and Ginny read the blurb.

On the brink of despair, our love reignited. We battled adversity together and so can you. Whether you're a couple in danger, or alone and trying to stop your world from crumbling around you, *The Power of Two* will illuminate the way through the rubble to a fresh landscape ahead.

Ginny nodded and pushed her shoulders back. She and Adrian had made a promise to love each other forever and the book confirmed all was not lost. Helping the four strangers on holiday would prove she was a good person and show Adrian what he was missing.

As the plane careened along the runway, she focused on her book again and read about the seven stages of heartbreak.

Stage One. Shock and denial.

The end of a relationship is akin to bereavement. You may feel numb and be in a state of disbelief. How can someone you love cause you so much pain?

'Yes, how can he?' Ginny muttered, devouring the chapter without looking up. Adrian didn't like self-help books, but she wished she could show this one to him, so he could understand his confused feelings better.

The plane cruised at thirty-five thousand feet in the air and Curtis snored for the entire flight.

By the time they touched down in Italy, Ginny felt like Ben and Ally Prince were her new best friends. If they could get through their issues, so could she and Adrian.

Through the plane window she could see the sky was cloudless and powder blue. The light was golden and excited chatter started up from the seats around her.

Ginny placed her hand on Curtis's hairy arm and gave it a gentle shake. 'Wake up, we're here,' she said.

'Cool,' Curtis said with a yawn. 'Can't wait to jump in the pool.'

Ginny thought about the website photos she'd seen for Splendido and frowned. 'Um, I don't think it has one.'

'*For real?* What kind of hotel doesn't have a pool?'

She wondered why he talked like someone a decade younger. In fact, all his clothes looked more suited for someone in their twenties. Curtis and Adrian might get along.

Curtis wore his travel bag over his shoulder and they waited by the luggage carousel to collect Ginny's suitcase. They both stared at the juddering rubber belt for ages until the only luggage left was a broken buggy and a child's pink rucksack circling repeatedly.

The Manchester flight details disappeared from the information screen, replaced by one from Amsterdam. Ginny glanced around her uneasily. What was going on? Where was her case?

She overheard someone muttering that a container of luggage had been left behind in the UK and she told Curtis.

'Bummer,' he said. 'Lucky I've got all *my* stuff.'

They headed towards a long queue stretching from a small desk. At the front, an airline representative gripped a clipboard, his face shiny and red. There was lots of jostling and raised voices. Curtis busied himself by talking into his phone like it was a walkie-talkie. Ginny couldn't hear what he was saying and saw him gesturing with his other hand as if performing a rap.

'What happens now?' she asked the crimson-faced airline representative, after she'd finally completed a form at the desk.

'When the luggage arrives, we will contact you,' he said wearily.

Ginny ran her tongue over her fuzzy teeth. 'When will that be? I only have the clothes I'm wearing. All my toiletries are in my case, and my phone charger. . .' The more she spoke, the more she wished she'd packed these things in her handbag rather than her suitcase.

The man exaggerated a shrug. '*Mi scusi*,' he said, looking harassed rather than sorry. He beckoned the next person in the line towards him.

'Don't worry.' Curtis nudged her. 'I have spare socks and an iPhone charger. Sorry, no make-up or dresses though.'

Ginny couldn't decide if his joke made things worse or not. She longed to get changed out of her jeans and blouse. 'My phone is a Samsung,' she said.

They exited Arrivals almost two hours late. Someone called Nico was supposed to be meeting them and Ginny hoped he'd stayed around.

There was a handful of people waiting. One was a slim man, sinewy like a greyhound. He had black curly hair and his tanned skin was lined like tree bark, contrasting against his pale blue shirt. His eyes looked sad, or perhaps he was just tired from standing there so long. His handwritten sign said SPLINTER.

Curtis pointed at it. 'That's us, right?'

Ginny nodded and approached the man with her head cocked. 'Nico?'

'*Sì. Ben arrivata, Signora Splinter.*' He looked down at her feet. 'The luggage is still in England, yes?'

She forced a smile and shrugged. 'It's just me and my handbag.'

'And she's got me, too.' Curtis grinned. He shook Nico's hand.

'*Prego.* Please follow me.'

Ginny already loved Nico's lilting accent and how he seemed to add 'ah' to the end of his words. He wore his clothes well and she admired how his leather shoes looked handmade.

Outside, Ginny shielded her eyes against the sun with her hand. She reached into her handbag for her sunglasses and remembered they were in her suitcase. Oh, god, all her clean underwear was in there, too. She glanced at Curtis and the thought of potentially having to borrow a spare pair of his boxer shorts made her wince.

As Nico led them towards a shiny grey BMW, Ginny felt a little better, thinking that Adrian would *love* this car. Her lips straightened when Nico walked past it and opened the passenger door of a scratched white minibus. He gestured for them both to get inside.

Ginny froze on the spot. She was used to a sleek coach delivering her and Adrian to their hotel in style. She liked the chirpy holiday representatives who used a microphone to tell them about the weather and local waterpark. This vehicle looked like an old ambulance.

'Nice wheels,' Curtis said, winking at her.

'My minibus is good on the roads,' Nico said stiffly.

Ginny climbed inside. She shuffled to get comfortable on the rock-hard seat and fastened her seat belt. Nico handed her a cold bottle of water and she gulped it readily. As they drove away and pulled onto the road, a solitary tear wound down her face. She turned her head and took a tissue from her handbag.

Nico noticed. 'I'm sorry,' he said. 'They will find your suitcase.'

'Yeah, don't worry. It'll turn up,' Curtis said, avoiding looking at her. He started to chat to Nico.

Ginny gripped her seat and rested her forehead against the side window, watching as road signs and grey tarmac sped by for miles, until they filtered out to rows of trees and little trattorias. She spotted the white castle hotel on top of a hill and swallowed a sigh.

'That is my friend Gianfranco's hotel,' Nico said, as he pulled off the road. 'He will collect the other three guests in his minibus. The vehicle has air-conditioning and he will enjoy telling them about it.'

He drove through open black iron gates and crunched to a halt. A battered sign read *Hotel Splendido. Benvenuti!* Nico got out and opened the minibus door for Ginny. He performed a small bow and swept his hand towards the building. 'I am pleased you are here,' he said. 'My home is your home.'

Ginny stepped out and breathed in the warm tranquil air. The hotel's white walls peeled prettily, and pale green window shutters added a splash of colour. She could smell pink bougainvillea and lemons, and evening sunlight glistened through the trees making everything seem more enchanting.

The sound of distant church bells chiming and the trickle of water made her heart swell.

'You like the hotel?' Nico asked.

'Oh, yes,' Ginny nodded. 'Very much.'

'This way.' He beamed.

Inside the hotel, the terracotta floor tiles felt cool through the soles of Ginny's sandals. The hallway was long and its uneven white walls displayed black and white photos of people she assumed were Nico's family. They looked like a serious bunch. Glancing through a door, she saw a wooden farmhouse table and copper saucepans on shelves. She could smell cooked tomatoes, oregano and fresh bread.

Everything looked homey, yet the hotel had a strange air, as if it had been closed for the winter and the sheets covering everything had only just been whisked off.

Nico selected a key from a hook on the wall, number five. 'My very best room,' he announced. 'The bridal suite.'

Ginny gripped the strap of her handbag. She followed Nico up the creaky wooden stairs, leaving Curtis in the hallway.

When Nico opened the bedroom door, Ginny wasn't expecting the sea of coral and lemon. The bed, desk and small chair looked as tired as she felt and the colour of the painted woodwork could best be described as autopsy red. Not a great way for couples to start married life. The room didn't look like the ones she'd seen on the website, or perhaps she was mistaken. She took a moment, trying to find something positive to say. 'What a colourful room.' She walked towards the window and looked outside. 'The view is beautiful.'

'*Grazie*.' Nico presented the ensuite bathroom to her and

the pile of towels topped with a tiny guest soap. 'Perhaps you would like juice, coffee, or a bowl of soup? I made it fresh today, my mamma's recipe.'

Kindness was just what Ginny needed, and it also made her wilt. 'Soup and a glass of juice would be lovely. And do you have a charger?' She waved her phone.

'Only for iPhone.'

'Oh, okay. My battery is very low.'

They both paused, not sure who should speak next. Nico went first. 'The others will arrive later tonight. Would you like your soup served in the dining area, or——?'

'My room, please,' Ginny said. She was drained from travelling and wanted to relax. She didn't really want to spend the evening talking to Curtis on her own.

Nico nodded. '*Prego*, I understand. I'll leave you to unpack your, um . . . handbag.' He left and closed the bedroom door.

Ginny sat down on the bed and ran her fingers over the faded orange cover. At least the room looked spotless. She texted Phoebe to tell her she'd arrived safely, though her luggage was delayed. She unpacked her handbag, setting out her tissues, purse and mints in a line, trying to restore some order. Tomorrow she would meet the three other heartbroken strangers she'd invited on holiday.

At least they were all in this together.

CHAPTER 7

Breakfast

Ginny woke to the sound of a cockerel crowing outside and light shining through her curtains. Instead of taking time to come around from her sleep, she grabbed her phone to see if the airport had been in touch. She had no missed calls and her battery level was three per cent. It was still only 5.25 a.m. and she let out a small groan.

Glancing back over her shoulder, she half expected to see Adrian with pillow lines marking his cheeks. In her imagination, he grinned and huskily said, 'Morning', as if everything was still okay between them and he was here on holiday with her. If Ginny closed her eyes, she swore she could feel his breath on her arm as he pulled her towards him.

A sense of longing for him tickled her belly and made her grip the sheets. She couldn't help wondering whose bed he was waking up in while she was in Italy. Was he still staying with Dave and Linda, or had he already found somewhere else to live? Perhaps Adrian was lying in bed thinking about her, too, or was that something he'd stopped doing years ago?

Ginny was naked under the bedsheets and she felt suddenly vulnerable. She'd washed her underwear with soap last night and placed it on her bedside table to dry. It was still damp and she squirmed when she put it on.

Knowing she wouldn't get back to sleep, Ginny wrapped the sheet around her like a toga. She stuck her head around the curtain, watching the sun sparkling behind the turrets of the castle on the hill. Birds were singing and, in the lilac light, she could see church spires and vineyards more beautiful than any photograph. The air was warming up and she could tell it was going to be a beautiful day.

Ginny heard the front door open and watched as a man wearing a backpack strode across the courtyard. He sported sturdy boots and a vest top that displayed his muscular arms. She wondered where he was going so early in the morning and if this was Eric the carpenter.

Her stomach rumbled and Ginny found that she was ravenously hungry. Nico's soup had been delicious but had left her wanting more. There was no sound from the rest of the hotel and it felt too early to go downstairs for breakfast.

She picked up the guest book from her bedside table and leafed through the leaflets for walking trails and places to eat in the village. At the back of the book was an evaluation form for guests to score the accommodation, facilities, meals and atmosphere out of ten. Ginny decided to hold back judgment until she was properly settled in.

She washed her hair in the shower, using soap that made it tangle and squeak. There wasn't a hairdryer in the room and, without make-up, her face looked pale and featureless.

She sniffed her worn blouse and was sure it smelled like the monkey enclosure at a zoo. She was glad Adrian couldn't see her like this.

Ginny finger-combed her hair and spoke to her reflection in the bathroom mirror. 'We've got so many reasons to work things out, so many things we still have in common,' she said, practising for when she next spoke to her husband.

She browsed through *The Power of Two* again and pondered her and Adrian's relationship. Sometimes the sound of him crunching toast made her want to strangle him and his snoring was no longer cute. Perhaps his dating profile *was* an experiment and they *had* become stuck in a rut, like he claimed. Thank goodness Ben and Ally Prince could help her to find a way out of it. A dog barked in the distance and Ginny wondered why people never grew bored of their pets in the same way they did with other humans.

She read her book until she heard movement in the hotel. Putting on yesterday's clothes made her wince and she went downstairs to breakfast.

There was one large table in the dining room, the size of a single bed. Two long benches ran down either side and there was a throne-like chair at one end. A large bowl of fruit fit for Roman gods sat in the centre. She could smell freshly baked bread and heard Nico singing in the kitchen. His voice was a rich baritone that she could listen to all day. She welcomed the light breeze that wound around her ankles and lifted the corners of the tablecloth.

'*Buongiorno*,' Nico said, entering the room holding a basket of brioche and croissants. 'Did you sleep well?'

'Yes,' Ginny nodded. 'Like a baby.'

'That is good.' He gestured with his hand towards the spread of food. '*Prima colazione*. The breakfast is served.'

There was a smell of almonds and a flash of white cotton as a teenage girl appeared and helped herself to an apple from the fruit bowl.

Nico shooed her away. 'For the guests only. Please bring the milk.' He turned to Ginny. 'This is my daughter, Loretta.'

Loretta smiled, exaggerated biting into her apple and vanished into the kitchen. Seconds later, she plonked a jug down on the table before exiting the room again.

Ginny sat down and waited, wondering what time her four companions would wake up and join her.

Heavy footsteps sounded along the hallway and the man she'd seen earlier sat down on the bench opposite. His long strawberry blond hair was roughly tied back and he had a full beard. With his muscular physique, it was easy to imagine him wielding an axe to chop down trees. He placed a round yellow tin on the table, the type that might be used for storing tobacco.

'You must be Eric,' Ginny said brightly. 'I'm Ginny Splinter, the lady off the radio.'

'Hi,' the man mumbled, reaching out for an apple. He took out his penknife to peel it.

'I think I saw you going for a walk this morning. The light was so beautiful.'

Eric munched an apple slice and kept his eyes fixed on his tin. 'Yeah, it was.'

'It's nice to clear your head before the day starts, with only the birds for company, isn't it? Though maybe not *that* early.' She laughed gaily.

He reciprocated with a short nod.

'So, do you have any plans for today?'

Eric whistled to himself and picked an orange from the bowl. He peeled it with his fingernails. 'Nope, not yet.'

Ginny's smile faded. Tam had noted Eric was quiet, perhaps due to his bereavement. If she could offer him some good advice, it might make them both feel better. 'Do you usually listen to my show?' she asked.

'Sorry, no.' He shook his head. 'I'm sure it's great,' he added.

Nico brought out a pot of coffee. As he poured cups for Ginny and Eric, a small woman with blonde corkscrew curls bounded into the room. She wore striped leggings and a pink T-shirt with a mandala on the front. She set a bottle of vitamins down on the table and pressed a hand to her chest. 'Oh. My. Word,' she said, her lips parting when she fixed her eyes on Ginny. 'I can't believe I'm standing here in front of *the* Ginny Splinter. I love listening to your show with my mum. You're *so* caring and wise.'

Ginny felt her cheeks flushing. It was nice to hear kind words after the turmoil of the last few weeks, but also rather embarrassing. 'Heather?' she presumed.

'I most certainly am.' Heather edged so close Ginny could see the rusty brown patches in her green eyes. 'I'm looking forward to getting to know you better.'

Ginny wanted to inch back, but didn't want to appear rude. Heather had the energy of an overwound clockwork toy, which felt too overpowering at breakfast time. 'Yes, me too. Let me introduce you to Eric, he's a carpenter.'

'Hello there, I'm a primary school teacher,' Heather enunciated as if addressing her class. 'I'm used to planning and organizing everyone. I've been teaching my kids mindfulness and teamwork, so I'm here whenever anyone needs me.' She unscrewed her bottle and popped a tablet in her mouth, washing it down with a glass of water. 'Who else is joining us?' she asked.

'Curtis arrived with me yesterday and then there's Edna,' Ginny said. She paused when she heard tapping, like a metronome ticking out a slow beat. The tip of a walking stick appeared around the corner of the dining room.

'Loretta,' Nico called out. 'Please help our guest to sit down.'

The person that followed the stick had steel-grey eyes that gave her slim face a disapproving quality. Her white hair formed a neat bun secured by a tortoiseshell comb. She wore a black skirt that reached her shins and swamped her petite frame, reminding Ginny of a Victorian statue that had come to life in a graveyard.

'Good morning, everyone.' She pronounced all her words crisply as if she'd had elocution lessons. 'It's a pleasure to meet you all. My name is Mrs Edna Edgerton-Woods.'

Loretta held out a hand to help her.

Edna batted it away. 'Please don't fuss. I'm perfectly capable of sitting down on my own. I have the agility of a ballerina.'

'You're using a walking stick,' Loretta muttered.

'I only use it occasionally, when I'm tired. I spent yesterday travelling.'

'Please make yourself at home, Mrs Edgerton, um . . .' Ginny said, momentarily forgetting the rest of her name.

'You must call me Edna, my dear. You all must.' She addressed the table. 'Well, I must say this is all very pleasant. I appreciate you bringing us all together like this, Ginny. It's extremely kind of you.'

'You're very welcome.'

They all made polite conversation until Nico finished laying the table. 'I have made fresh butter,' he said proudly.

Ten minutes passed and Ginny peered at her watch. 'We're just waiting for one more person, Curtis,' she told her guests.

Heather sat rolling her thumbs and Edna's rumbling stomach sounded like thunder.

Nico glanced at Ginny. 'I will see if Signor Dunne is awake,' he said before disappearing.

A few minutes later, Curtis appeared. 'Morning,' he said cheerily, though his eyes looked red and bleary. He was dressed from head to toe in white sports brands again, including a baseball cap.

Edna smiled tightly, fixing her eyes on it. Her stare sent a silent message to Curtis who sheepishly removed his hat and stuffed it into his pocket. As he sat down, he displayed a bald patch the diameter of a tennis ball in his thatch of black hair.

After Ginny had made all the introductions, the five of them tucked into breakfast. While eating her brioche, she couldn't help glancing around the table at each of her guests. She knew heartbreak could be like a fractured bone, not always visible until X-rayed. It took time to heal and if you acted too fast, it could shatter. Even so, she longed to know why each of them was here.

Curtis tore off pieces of bread and stuffed them into his mouth as if he hadn't eaten for days.

Edna gave him a gimlet-eye again and finished her bowl of cornflakes. She spoke loudly to Nico. 'I'm looking forward to my cooked breakfast. I'd like scrambled eggs, not fried, please. Crispy bacon, not burnt. Please don't grill my tomatoes and I'll have mushrooms if they're not served in butter. I have to watch my cholesterol levels.'

Nico's smile flattened. '*Scusa, non capisco.*'

Loretta breezed in and deposited a jug full of freshly squeezed orange juice.

Edna turned to her instead. 'Did you hear my requirements, dear? I'd like scrambled eggs, bacon—'

Nico swept his hand around the table. 'This is the breakfast.'

Edna struggled to conceal her disappointment. 'Oh, yes, a continental breakfast. Of course.'

Ginny hoped she wasn't going to be fussy about her meals for the entire three weeks. 'Everything here is fresh, Edna. There's bread, butter and fruit.' She briskly loaded a small plate and set it down in front of her guest. 'It's all delicious.'

'Yes, lovely.' Edna nibbled on a piece of bread for a while. After placing her large leather handbag onto her lap, she took out several scraps of grey fabric and deftly threaded a needle.

Ginny admired her eyesight. She doubted her fingers were ever as nimble. 'What are you making?' she asked.

'It's going to be a quilt.'

Ginny thought the gloomy fabric would make a bed look like a slab of concrete. 'Oh, how clever,' she said.

'Do we have an itinerary for the day?' Edna asked, flicking her eyes between Ginny and her sewing. 'Perhaps an interesting excursion? That nice man Gianfranco offers lots of activities at his hotel. He told me all about them, when he collected me from the airport.'

Ginny saw Nico stiffen. Eric, Curtis and Heather looked at her expectantly, awaiting her plan of action. She plucked at the underarm of her blouse, not wanting to do anything or go anywhere until her clean clothes showed up. 'I can't arrange anything for today,' she said. 'My luggage has gone missing and I need to wait here for an update. I don't have any clothes, or make-up, or a phone charger and . . .' Embarrassingly, she found a lump swelling in her throat so she couldn't speak. The emotions she'd tried to suppress over the last few weeks were creeping back again.

Pull yourself together, Ginny. These people need you.

Edna lifted her chin. 'Perhaps we can all play bingo. Surely, that's available here?'

Loretta wrinkled her nose and shook her head.

'We can't swim because there's no pool,' Curtis said.

'My class recently enjoyed reflexology,' Heather offered, hopefully and unhelpfully.

Ginny felt pressure rising in her chest. For a few moments, she felt like she'd made a terrible mistake by coming here, especially with a bunch of strangers. Perhaps Adrian was right and she was a problem junkie, after all. Maybe it was better to give up on the idea of healing everyone's heartache, and her own, right here and now. It was a monumental task she had no chance of achieving.

She rubbed the top of her own arm. 'I'm sorry I haven't planned anything for us yet,' she said scratchily. 'I just want to wait until I feel clean and human again. Is that too much to ask? Let's all take some time to acclimatize and reconvene here at lunchtime.'

An awkward silence descended around the table. Loretta surveyed everyone with a slight smile on her lips.

Nico picked up an empty bread basket and tucked it under his arm. 'Loretta has too many clothes,' he said. 'She can help you.'

His daughter shot him a stare. '*Papà!*'

Eric toyed with his penknife. He handed it to Ginny on the flat of his palm.

Ginny slow-blinked at it. She didn't need a knife to feel better, she needed a miracle. Though somehow the offer sparked warmth in her chest. 'I believe we're all here because we're heartbroken,' she said, looking at each of them in turn for confirmation.

Edna, Eric and Heather reluctantly nodded while Curtis pursed his lips and looked up at the ceiling.

'Then let's all support each other and plan things together,' Ginny said.

'A democracy,' Eric said quietly.

She stared at him, surprised he'd spoken.

'The main issue with democracy is that people collectively make the wrong decisions,' Edna chipped in.

Ginny ignored her, wanting to explore an idea that was forming in her head. 'We all need to try out new things that will keep us busy, that might make us feel better. We can see

69

what works and what doesn't and can all take turns coming up with ideas.'

'Like a committee,' Nico said.

'Yes,' Ginny said. 'That's it!' She thought for a while before she raised her glass of orange juice. 'We can all be a team, together. Welcome to Team Heartache.'

CHAPTER 8

Fabric

Edna

Everyone returned to their bedrooms after breakfast and Edna opened her wardrobe to survey the T-shirts, long skirts and cardigans she'd packed for her holiday. She thought how woeful they looked all bunched together.

She hadn't bothered to buy anything new; she was only here for three weeks and her primary clothing needs these days were comfort and warmth. She had some pride and refused to wear shoes with Velcro fasteners or tights the shade of gravy, but colour had exited her life three years ago and she missed it dreadfully.

She was eighty years old and there wasn't much joy in that. People tutted at her in shop queues when she was a little slow unfastening her purse. They spoke to her too loudly even though she had better hearing than a barn owl. If she ever used her walking stick, people sometimes exaggerated stumbling over it, even if it merely brushed their shoe. Wherever Edna went, she felt like a shrivelled lemon in a bag full of rosy apples.

The few friends she had left only phoned her to grumble about the weather, their children never visiting, bowel movements, or to report that someone had died. They rarely had any good news and contributed to giving older people a bad reputation for complaining. Edna supposed she should welcome anyone bothering to call her at all, but the continuous moaning made her feel worse than she already did. She longed for more scintillating conversation, such as the best conditions in which to grow orchids, or which sewing machine needle to use when tackling organza, to stimulate her mind.

Her solitude was a waste because her brain was as tack sharp as always. She listened to current affair shows on the radio and reeled off answers to questions on *Mastermind*, saying 'Ha' when she got one right and the contestant didn't. She only wished her daughter, Daisy, was still around to clap her hands and shout, 'Yes, go Mum!'

Without Daisy in her life, Edna's loneliness felt like an unwelcome house guest that wouldn't leave. It shadowed her and convinced her she didn't deserve any better. She kept the radio playing all day for a bit of company and even called in to a couple of shows, just to speak to someone more positive than her friends.

The producer lady on the *Just Ask Ginny* show (Tim? Tom? Tam?) had sounded uninterested when Edna told her a little about Daisy, so it had been a pleasant surprise to receive the invitation to Italy. The most she'd ever won were vouchers for a DIY store that were languishing in a drawer somewhere, and she hadn't been abroad since before Daisy was born.

Edna pulled a shapeless black dress out of the wardrobe and

held it up to her neck. It was hard to believe that, as the mistress of monochrome, she'd once been fascinated by fashion. Edna used to wear the brightest colours that didn't belong together, a red dress with purple tights, or a yellow hat with a striped ribbon. She used to turn up the music on the radio and put on pretend fashion shows for Daisy who clapped her hands together with glee.

Going to fabric shops together had been their favourite pastime. Daisy picked patterned cotton that Edna made into dresses for her. It was cheaper than buying them and her daughter's arms and legs were too short for anything in the shops anyway.

When she and her husband, Desmond, first held their baby daughter in their arms, the midwife warned them that Daisy was 'different' and would be reliant on them all her life.

Edna held her limp pink baby and felt her tiny heart thumping against her own. 'She'll just have a different life than the one we imagined,' she said defiantly. 'There's nothing wrong with that and we'll have to adjust.'

Desmond had remained very quiet. He was a proud, stoic man who made Edna feel protected while not having much to say. It took him much longer to accept that their only child was never going to graduate college, get married, or give them grandchildren. It was unlikely she'd ever leave home.

Edna had two jobs, one as a fashion designer and the other as a seamstress, and she gave up both to become a full-time mother. She didn't resent it one bit, though she did miss being surrounded by creative people and the occasional sojourn to France for fashion launches. Desmond was a kind man and a good provider, but his idea of adventure was to have both cheese *and* ham in a sandwich.

Looking after their daughter was hard work for Edna, even if there was a loving innocence about a child who would never grow up.

Though, inevitably, Daisy did. The smiling, funny little girl became a confused teen, and then a challenging young adult. She was loving yet also angry at times and Edna had to develop the patience of a saint. In addition to being a wife and mum, she was a nurse, personal aide and cleaner. Desmond remained working as a police officer, so Edna inherited the majority of Daisy's day care. It was just how it was.

She supposed that couples nowadays relied on each other for everything – friendship, excitement, support, equal childcare responsibilities, talking about feelings and entertaining each other, while also having red-hot sex. Something had to give, probably hence the divorce rate.

Women of Edna's generation mostly kept their mouths shut and got on with things. In her younger days, you went on a date if someone asked you, and carried on until you were going steady. Engagement was expected after a few years and marriage followed soon after. A few of her friends had put more care and attention into looking for a party dress than into finding a man they'd love for a lifetime and who would love them back.

Daisy had grown older and frailer before her time, so in her later years it had felt like there were three elderly people living together.

She had died aged fifty, followed a couple of months

afterwards by Desmond. Losing them both, especially so close together, made Edna's life instantly grey, like an old silent movie stuck on repeat. And now there was just Edna left, with her heart worn and cracked.

She'd never expected to feel *this* alone without them. She even missed the monotonous tasks, such as helping Daisy get dressed in the morning and cutting the crusts of her toast. Edna felt like she was no use to anyone any longer.

Her home was an empty shell and was too large for her to keep clean. A bigger family would benefit from it more, so next month she was moving into a one-bedroom apartment in the Shady Pines retirement village. Even though it had a common room for residents, bingo on Thursdays and buttons to call for help in each room, she did not want to go. It was a necessary move rather than one she embraced.

Whittling down decades of belongings into a handful of boxes was proving painful and making her act all pernickety. Being pedantic was a symptom of her sense of loss.

'You'll feel much better when you're free of all this stuff,' a tattooed young woman from Caring Companions social care said, as she'd helped to pack Edna's king-size duvet covers and sheets into a bin bag. 'It'll only bung up your new place. You won't have enough room to take all your old clothes.'

Edna no longer wore her favourite red velvet Laura Ashley jacket because the poshest place she went to these days was Tesco. Bagging up Desmond's yellowing shirts had been easy. Getting rid of Daisy's clothes proved to be more of a wrench.

Each outfit Edna had made for her daughter had a memory or milestone attached to it, a trip to the seaside or a prize won at dance class. Each button Daisy helped to choose for a dress reminded Edna that her daughter had achieved far more than anyone expected, including herself.

Some of Daisy's clothes were faded with age, not even good enough to give to a charity shop, yet Edna couldn't let them go. As a halfway measure she cut some of them into squares, bringing the pieces to Italy to make into a quilt.

Edna reached down to take them out of her handbag and pressed her cheek to the grey cotton printed with tiny white flowers. She imagined she could still smell her daughter's scent, talcum powder and fabric conditioner, and a tear spilled down her cheek.

So, Ginny Splinter thought that a holiday with strangers could magically snuff out Edna's loneliness and make her feel better? She doubted that very much. Edna wasn't sure she even had the strength to try herself.

She took an assortment of her clothes out of her wardrobe and glumly hung them over her arm, to pass to Ginny.

CHAPTER 9

Milkshake

Ginny sat on her bed and groaned at the sliver of battery on her phone screen. Just making one call would deplete its one per cent of power. She felt torn between phoning the airport for an update on her missing suitcase or trying to call Adrian. Either call might bring a soar of delight or crash of disappointment.

She sent Phoebe a text instead. Hi darling. My phone battery is about to die. I hope all's okay with you and Dad. Speak soon x

She heard a scuffling noise outside her door and went to see what it was. The other bedroom doors were closed and a pile of clothes lay on the floor outside her room. She carried them inside and sat back down on her bed to browse through them.

They included a very small striped beach dress and an even tinier yellow bikini that obviously belonged to Loretta. A pink T-shirt with People Power written in the middle of a large flower must have come from Heather. On top of the pile were several of Edna's black skirts and T-shirts.

Ginny didn't know whether to laugh or cry at the assortment.

She tried on a baggy black skirt and the daisy T-shirt, then looked in the mirror. The outfit looked confused, like she was destined for both a music festival *and* a funeral. Her once-smooth ponytail resembled the end of a broomstick. How on earth could she go out like this in public? She missed how her usual, smart clothes gave her confidence, as if she was wearing a suit of armour.

She sighed and stretched out her forehead using her fingers. It was difficult to remember how unlined it had once been. Ginny was too scared to indulge in Botox or fillers, in case her face resembled an overinflated beach ball. She tried to respond to ageing with humour, cosmetics and electronic contraptions.

On a good day, she might pass for her mid-forties, possibly late thirties if she was in a dimly lit pub. At other times, she caught sight of her skin in broad daylight and noticed every line and wrinkle. Inadequate lighting in shops made her face look like a craggy cliff face, and no amount of miracle cream would fix that.

Ginny searched through the clothes pile again and caught sight of a lipstick nestled in the bikini top. It was sealed with cellophane and when she twisted it up, its frosted pink colour reminded her of something her mum used to say, to try to lift her own mood whenever Ginny's dad let her down.

'How can the world seem dark when you're wearing pink lipstick?'

Ginny applied the lipstick and gradually felt a bit brighter. Something scratched her neck and she noticed the People Power T-shirt still had its tag attached. She was the first to wear Heather's new garment and it made her feel honoured.

Ginny rolled over the waistband on the black skirt to shorten it, tucked in the T-shirt and added the belt from her jeans. She tied her hair into a low bun and her reflection in the mirror reminded her of the teenage version of herself who'd fallen in love with Adrian Splinter all those years ago.

She often missed the people they once were.

She'd first seen him in a café when they were both eighteen. Ginny had been with her friend Sufrana who never shut up about the long list of boys she fancied.

'Don't bloody look now,' Sufrana had hissed and prodded Ginny. 'Adrian Splinter is at the table in the corner. He's really fit.'

Up until then, Ginny had found reading books more interesting than dating boys. But when she'd flicked her ponytail to surreptitiously glance at Adrian, she'd changed her mind.

He had the brightest blue eyes she'd ever seen and she loved how he offered his Victoria sponge cake to his friends first before taking a forkful for himself. Manners and kindness were important to her, so she appreciated how he swept his own crumbs away using a napkin.

Ginny had tried to look cool while sipping her milkshake, whereas Adrian's two friends (one of them was Dave) flicked tinfoil balls at each other.

Adrian had caught Ginny's eye with an apologetic shrug that made her laugh. Sufrana kneed Ginny's leg and they exchanged excited glances.

Ginny went to the bathroom to apply more lip gloss, but when she'd returned, Adrian had left.

'Don't worry, he left you a bloody note,' Sufrana had said

rather jealously, passing her a napkin on which Adrian had written a message, *Party at 8, next Friday?* followed by his home phone number.

He'd arrived spot on time to pick Ginny up at home in an ancient BMW, bringing her a huge bunch of flowers. She didn't have any friends who could drive and had felt all swanky and precious sitting next to him in the front seat.

Adrian worked for his dad's car business, so he dressed in sharp suits when the other lads she knew wore baggy jeans and T-shirts. His influence rubbed off on her and Ginny started to buy smart clothes for herself, too.

Upon leaving sixth form, Ginny had taken up an admin job in an accountancy firm, as recommended by her dad.

'You don't seem like a numbers kind of person,' Adrian had mused on one of their dates. 'It's better to do something you enjoy. What are you *really* good at?'

Ginny told him how she *felt* things on behalf of other people. Her emotion-packed creative writing had scored her a top grade in her English A-level.

TV advertisements, especially ones for donkey charities, could reduce her to an emotional wreck. Spotting a dead rabbit on a country road, charity phone-ins and other people's bereavements made her tears flow, and she always avoided weepy movies and arguments.

Teachers and early employers labelled her as *sensitive*, and not necessarily in a good way. Over time she'd learned to harness and channel her feelings, and to use them for good, such as being there for her friends after their breakups.

'People interest me,' she'd told Adrian. 'I like helping them.'

'Then why don't you do that instead?'

With his encouragement, Ginny left her job and went to college, to study counselling. Finally, she felt like she'd found her forte in life. And a lot of it was thanks to Adrian. He was solid, caring and kind, offering her the stability that had been missing throughout her childhood.

Ginny *had* to find a way to draw them both back together again. Surely, that was the only genuine way to harness her heartache.

She took *The Power of Two* off her bedside table and reread a passage.

Stage Two. Sadness and remorse.

You probably feel like withdrawing from the world, it's an important part of the healing process. Lick your wounds and prepare yourself for the next stage, even if you feel like there'll never be one. Your sadness might be all-consuming and that's okay – for a while. Try to make friends with it rather than treating it like an enemy.

It sounded easier said than done, but Ben and Ally's smiling faces gave her hope.

At lunchtime, Ginny re-entered the dining room and heard Nico singing and clattering around the kitchen. Although his cooking smelled delicious, Ginny sensed unease among all her guests sitting around the dining table. Eric sat rigidly, toying with his tin, and Edna's eyes were glued to her sewing.

She gave a small cough to get their attention. 'Thanks so

much for the clothes. I'm sorry if I was tetchy before, I've been under a lot of stress.'

Heather looked directly at her. 'You've got this,' she said. 'We're all friends here.'

Ginny nodded thanks. 'Let's push ahead with the plan to select activities that will make us feel better. What works for you might work for others, too.'

'Hmm,' Edna said doubtfully, staring at Curtis.

'How can we measure heartache?' Heather asked, taking a pencil and paper from her pocket and jotting down a formula.

Ginny glanced at Eric. He hadn't said more than a few words since they'd all met, so it was unlikely he was going to suddenly express his feelings. He might even feel awkward putting forward a suggestion. 'We could write our ideas down,' Ginny offered. 'It gives us more time and freedom to think of something.'

Eric nodded gratefully.

Ginny remembered the evaluation scale she'd seen in Nico's information pack. Scoring their heartache before and after each activity could track its effect on their emotions. It would help to remind her she hadn't made a big mistake by bringing everyone here.

She told the others about her idea.

'Sounds cool,' Curtis said. 'I usually write reviews for books, hotels and stuff.' He squirmed when Nico flashed him a disparaging look.

'Measuring heartache isn't an exact science.' Edna tutted. 'Everyone thinks they're an expert these days.'

Curtis folded his arms. 'I'm entitled to my opinions.'

'I'll design a form,' Heather said. 'Teachers have to assess and grade everything we do in school.'

'Gianfranco has a . . .' Nico mimed paper sliding out of a printer. 'He can make copies.' He headed back into his kitchen.

Ginny thought about what activity to put forward first. Venice seemed too romantic and a spa treatment together seemed too intimate when they'd only just met. They all needed something to lift their spirits and she thought of something that fitted the bill. 'I've always wanted to visit the Uffizi in Florence, to see *The Birth of Venus*,' she said. 'The gallery is supposed to be wonderful.'

Nico reappeared carrying huge bowls of ravioli, served with butter and cheese. 'I am happy to drive you all there.'

'*Grazie*,' Ginny said.

'The journey takes around ninety minutes and we should set off early to avoid traffic and queues.'

Appreciative murmurs soon sounded around the table as everyone tucked into their lunch. The pasta was the best Ginny had ever tasted. She closed her eyes as the delicious flavour lit up her taste buds. The dining room brightened as shafts of sunlight cut through the windows, warming her face. She was proud that she wasn't sitting at home, moping around about Adrian. Listening to her guests chatting together gave her a renewed sense of purpose and Nico's photos on the walls added to a sentiment of family.

Perhaps things were going to be okay in Italy after all.

CHAPTER 10

Venus

The next morning, Ginny stifled a yawn as the others filtered into the courtyard to join her. An air of sleepiness and irritation clung to everyone like a damp duvet. Looking around her, she wondered if there was ever a greater mishmash of people holidaying together.

The yellow light from the downstairs windows of the hotel made the flagstones shine like gold nuggets and a crescent moon lingered, silvery and low in the sky. Birds sang a morning chorus accompanied by the *coo-coo-coo* of a wood pigeon.

Eric sat down on a garden chair to dig stones out of his boots with his penknife and Ginny wondered if he'd already been out for a walk. The hills on either side of Splendido looked too dark and imposing to explore this early.

She was surprised that Edna hadn't brought her walking stick. The older lady was dressed in dark shapeless clothes again, even wearing grey socks with her sandals. The only bit of colour about her person was a patchwork fabric bag slung over her shoulder.

At least she won't need sunblock, Ginny thought to herself.

She pursed her lips when she surveyed her own outfit of Heather's People Power T-shirt and Edna's skirt, missing the professional feeling her suits gave her, like she was ready to take on the world. Hopefully her missing suitcase would turn up soon.

Ginny pushed back her shoulders regardless. 'Morning everyone,' she called out. 'We want to get to the museum nice and early, before it gets busy. The weather's supposed to be gorgeous again, so let's embrace the day and have fun.'

Nico appeared in the courtyard with his arms wrapped around a multitude of brown paper bags. 'I have made breakfast and also sandwiches for lunch,' he said. 'Food can be expensive in the city.'

'Great. Thanks,' Ginny said, relieved they didn't have to find a restaurant for the group. Edna seemed like a fussy eater and she suspected from his fruit intake that Eric might be vegetarian.

As the others boarded Nico's minibus, she helped him to hand out the bags, heartache forms and tourist maps. She was impressed to see Nico had circled the gallery and noted down the ticket costs. 'It's so quiet I can hear a pin drop in here,' Heather said, sitting down. 'Shall we all sing a song?'

Everyone ignored her.

Ginny selected a seat next to the window and was a little relieved when no one sat down beside her. Adrian liked to sit next to the aisle so he could stretch out his long legs or get out quickly if there was a crash. Laying her palm flat against the black vinyl of his vacant space, she let out a sigh. Being without him felt disorientating.

Nico drummed an impatient tune on the steering wheel before clamping his mobile phone to his ear. 'Loretta,' he hissed, followed by words in Italian.

His daughter appeared several minutes later. 'Why *this* early?' she asked with a yawn. Her crumpled dress looked like she'd scooped it off the floor. 'I do not need to come with you.'

'We want to get to Florence before the tourists,' Nico said aloud so everyone could hear.

'We *are* the tourists.' Loretta climbed in and slammed the door shut.

Nico drove onto the narrow road and Loretta switched on the radio. Pop music blared out and Nico turned it down. Father and daughter argued with each other. Loretta pointed to a sign for Grand Hotel Castello Bella Vista, as if to say they should go there instead.

Ginny gazed up at the white castle on top of the hill. The sun was rising, making its turrets glow orange. In an alternate reality, she and Adrian would be staying there, curled up under crisp white sheets in a king-size bed. She felt a surge of disappointment and clasped her breakfast bag on her lap.

The further they drove, the more the sun poured through the streaky windows, making shadows dance on her face. Ginny squinted and wished she'd put her sunglasses in her handbag.

The events of the last few weeks had left her feeling drained and she dropped her head forwards to take a little nap.

When she next opened her eyes, she felt groggy and realized the minibus had come to a standstill. The countryside had vanished, replaced by hordes of people swarming around the pavement outside. Ginny looked at her watch and found that she'd slept for the entire journey. Heather and Curtis were busy gathering their things together and the minibus door was open. Eric took hold of Edna's arm, trying to help her disembark.

'Thank you, but I don't need any assistance. I have the balance of a tightrope walker.' Edna waved a hand as if swatting a fly.

'Everyone, try to keep close together so you don't get lost,' Heather called out.

Ginny stepped off the minibus and rotated her arms to stretch them. The bustle of people around her sounded extra loud after the peacefulness of the countryside. Cars and mopeds beeped their horns and tourists chattered while examining maps and their phones. She heard Nico and Loretta exchanging words again as they stood in front of the minibus.

'I've been to the gallery before,' Loretta said. 'I will meet you here later.'

'Where will you go?' Nico asked.

She pointed over her shoulder. 'Somewhere.'

He called out to the back of her head as she walked away. 'Where? What time will you be back?'

'The middle of the afternoon.' Loretta didn't turn back around.

Nico watched her with his shoulders rounded. He sighed deeply as he returned to his flock. 'Follow me, friends.'

He led them further into the city where ochre stone build-ings contrasted against the periwinkle sky. Offices, shops and hotels had arches of every description and were topped with statues of cherubs and saints. Flags fluttered and pigeons strutted. A man on a bicycle rang his bell as he rode along a narrow street followed by his two young sons, wobbling on their own bikes. Ginny heard the peal of church bells and glanced around her in wonder, admiring the gelaterias, tiny coffee shops and designer boutiques. She saw Nico's eyes were pained after his discussion with Loretta and she caught up with him to talk.

'My daughter, Phoebe, went through an argumentative phase in her teens, too,' Ginny said gently. 'Young girls can be challenging when they're finding their independence. Patience is key. My advice is to keep a good sense of humour and grit your teeth.'

Nico bared his molars to her. 'Soon, I will have none left,' he said. 'How old is your daughter?'

'Twenty-four. She's getting married soon.'

'Ah, congratulations.' Nico placed a hand on his chest. 'I will have to wait a long time for Loretta to marry, maybe forever. She is . . .' He struggled to find a word.

'Determined? Spirited? Feisty?'

'All of these things.' He laughed. 'She reminds me of her mother, Maria.'

Ginny hadn't seen any photos of Maria around Splendido and wondered where she was.

Nico, Ginny, Eric, Curtis and Heather walked together at Edna's pace until they reached the Uffizi Gallery.

Portrait artists sat outside the building, using pencils and burnt-umber pastels to sketch tourists in the Renaissance style. Living statues posed on top of plinths with their faces and clothes painted chalk white. They moved and waved whenever passers-by dropped coins into their hats on the pavement. Tour guides raised their voices to inform visitors about Florence and the gallery.

Fortunately, the queue outside wasn't too long. People talked as they filed alongside the curved grey walls of the U-shaped building. Majestic Doric columns were punctuated by ancient statues set in arched hollows and a replica statue of Michelangelo's *David* flanked the entrance, standing almost three times Ginny's height.

Nico ushered Ginny and the others around him. 'The building was constructed in the sixteenth century, originally to house the Florentine magistrates,' he said.

Ginny looked up and around her with her mouth agape, admiring the three storeys of windows and sculpted balconies. She felt honoured to be in the presence of such history and beauty. As she inched along in the queue, she didn't look down at her feet once.

When they reached the entrance doors, Edna already looked withered from the morning heat. She slumped and a damp strand of hair stuck to her forehead. 'I don't need a wheelchair,' she announced to no one in particular. 'My legs work perfectly well without assistance.'

Nico sidled up beside her. 'There are forty-five halls over three floors in the building, with many corridors,' he said. 'I wish *I* could use a chair with wheels. You will be like Boudicca riding her chariot into battle against the Romans.'

Edna lifted her chin and considered this. She rearranged her bag on her shoulders. 'I suppose you can all be my generals . . .' she said.

Nico winked at Ginny. She grinned back and noted it was

the first time she'd smiled properly in weeks. It felt strange and most welcome.

She paid for everyone's tickets and guides to the gallery and handed them out, trying not to think about her bank account balance. It was unlikely that she, Nico and the strangers would stay together in one group. 'Let's meet outside the gift shop in two and a half hours' time,' she said.

Curtis immediately headed off on his own. 'Catch you guys later,' he said, twisting his baseball cap back to front. He pressed his mobile phone to his lips and talked as he walked.

Ginny helped Eric settle Edna into a wheelchair. When a security guard stopped Eric to search through his rucksack, she felt quite territorial.

The guard took Eric's tin out of his bag and held it on the flat of his palm. The two men had an animated conversation until Eric took the tin back and twisted off the lid. They both peered inside it and the security guard raised an eyebrow. He took a pink collar out of the tin.

Eric's bottom lip wobbled a little and the guard patted his arm sympathetically.

Is Eric's bereavement a dog? Ginny thought as she watched. Surely there must be more to his heartache than that? She still missed her childhood Jack Russell, even though it bit her many times, so she could understand his sense of loss. Was it really enough to take up a free place on holiday with her?

Eric checked his rucksack into the cloakroom and paid for a pair of headphones. He hurriedly placed them on his ears before anyone had the chance to talk to him. Taking hold of Edna's wheelchair, he whisked her away.

'I'm going to take photos and make notes for my class,' Heather said. 'They'll be useful for one of our art history projects.'

Ginny frowned, trying to remember when the UK school holidays fell. She was sure it wasn't in June. 'It's term time now, isn't it? Are you taking some time off?'

Heather's movements became twitchy and she scratched her neck. 'Yes, yes, I've been granted special leave from my job until the autumn term begins.' She opened her mouth to say something else, then changed her mind. She skirted off into the first gallery, homing in on a painting of cherubs.

Ginny was left standing with Nico, feeling thankful she didn't have to solve anyone's heartache that morning. Her guests seemed like a random bunch with random issues and, hopefully, the art would make them all feel better.

The art gallery brought on a touch of nostalgia and Ginny thought back to when Phoebe was young. It had been awkward going to galleries and museums as a family of three. She needed eyes like a hammerhead shark to keep track of both Adrian and Phoebe. Her daughter grew bored easily and preferred to draw rather than look at paintings. She dragged her feet so Ginny had to constantly look back over her shoulder, to tell her to keep up. Adrian strode ahead, so if Ginny wanted to discuss any of the artwork, she had to rush to catch up with him.

They'd only been able to have one child and Ginny thought she, Adrian and Phoebe would be like an equilateral triangle, with all sides and angles the same. However, their family was often scalene-shaped, a little spiky and askew. Sometimes they were all best friends, and sometimes they weren't. It was easy for one person to feel left out of their trio, and she supposed it was most often Adrian.

Ginny and Nico silently admired works by Raphael, Caravaggio, Leonardo da Vinci, and ancient statues from Rome. The artists had left great masterpieces behind that would be cherished for centuries to come and Ginny considered what her own legacy might be. Helping others was noble, if not as visible as the art.

There was a buzz of excitement emanating from the small crowd gathered around *The Birth of Venus*. Ginny caught her breath when she finally stood in front of the painting she'd always wanted to see. The canvas was much larger than she'd expected, almost two by three metres. Painted in the fifteenth century, it depicted the goddess of love and beauty standing on top of a giant scallop shell in the sea and arriving on land. She was naked and her hands and long hair covered her modesty.

Ginny was struck by how serene and nonplussed Venus was by her own nudity, ignoring a woman on her right who held out a red shawl. Ginny wanted to grab it and wrap it around the goddess. ('Come on. Let's get you nice and warm and you can tell me why you're standing in a shell with no clothes on.') She loved how Venus was calm and beautiful in the face of adversity.

Look and learn, Ginny told herself.

'The painting is superb,' she whispered to Nico.

'*Sì*,' he said. 'I have seen it on several occasions and each time feels like the first.'

'It makes me feel quite emotional.'

'Me, also.'

Ginny suspected Adrian would have glanced at the painting, nodded and moved on to the next one, treating the gallery like a checkbox exercise. It made her appreciate Nico's patience.

'What would you like to see next?' he asked, after a while.

Ginny looked around her. 'There are so many rooms, it feels overwhelming.'

'Perhaps I can show you my favourite painting?'

'Yes, please. Surprise me,' she said, thinking it was something she'd never usually say. She let Nico lead the way, trying to guess which piece of art he'd choose, perhaps a small vase of flowers or a cockerel, to match his hotel decor.

She was surprised when he stopped in front of a Piero della Francesca. It was a double portrait diptych of the Duke and Duchess of Urbino, facing each other across a strip of ornate gold frame. Their expressions were stagnant and Ginny thought they looked rather passionless. They were together while also separate, a little like her and Adrian, she supposed.

A wave of sorrow washed over her and she accepted they might have drifted apart, just like her husband claimed. 'I can't tell what they're thinking,' she told Nico.

'The duke lost his right eye during a tournament, so the painting only shows his left side,' he explained.

Ginny thought the duke had a strong noble nose, not dissimilar to Nico's. She envied people whose prominent features made their faces more interesting to look at, especially because she considered her own profile to be unremarkable. 'Why do you like this one best?' she asked.

Nico opened his gallery guide and pointed to a picture. 'The two paintings have another side, different scenes on the back. It is like a secret.'

The images on the reverse showed the duke wearing armour and the duchess sitting on a chariot. These pictures were more dynamic and Ginny would have displayed these sides instead.

'Maria does not like the painting of the duke,' Nico said. 'She says it is miserable.'

Ginny admired the portrait. 'The duke has a lot of character so it's shame he hides half of his face. He should be proud of his appearance . . .' She let her words fall away, realizing how much time and effort she spent trying to enhance her own.

Nico nodded. 'It is always better to show your real self,' he said.

Ginny stared at the painting again and nodded, thinking it was something she really had to try for herself.

CHAPTER 11

Rickshaw

Everyone met up as planned outside the gift shop. When they filtered outside, the sun was high and the day had grown hotter.

Heather pulled a giant tube of lotion out of her bag. 'Don't forget to top up your sun cream, everyone. We don't want any burnt shoulders.'

Edna folded her gallery guide, concertina-style, to make a fan. Her white hair fluttered as she waved it in front of her face. She took Eric's arm again as they strolled back towards the minibus.

Nico drove them a short distance to Boboli Gardens and retrieved their lunch bags. 'I already have tickets and we can sit in the shade to eat,' he said.

Built in a series of terraces, the gardens boasted symmetrically cut hedges that formed hexagons and squares. Tall cypress trees stood to attention, surrounding them like bodyguards, and bees buzzed between the rose bushes. A turquoise dragonfly shimmered past Ginny, settling on the edge of a fountain of Neptune brandishing his trident. Edna's eyes lit up when she saw wild orchids. 'They're breathtaking,' she whispered.

The sandwiches Nico had made were delicious, filled with provolone cheese, shredded lettuce and onion, with oil and vinegar. Ginny didn't care when it trickled down her chin.

She pictured Adrian sitting in The Vehicle Emporium, nursing a boring cheese sandwich at his desk, and it brought a slight smile to her lips.

When lunch was over, four sets of eyes fixed on her, especially Heather's. 'What's next on the curriculum?' the teacher asked.

Ginny hadn't thought of anything beyond the gallery and she racked her brain, trying to think of something to do that might suit everyone.

Perhaps the heat was making her feel uncharacteristically selfish, but she wanted to think about herself for once. It was *her* holiday after all. Convinced her suitcase had vanished forever, she wanted to buy new clothes, make-up, toiletries and underwear. She wasn't sure where to source a phone charger in the city.

'Why don't we all go shopping?' she suggested, choosing to ignore the look of terror that flashed across Eric's face. 'Retail therapy usually works for me.'

'I'll join you,' Heather offered. 'Two heads are better than one if you're buying things.'

Eric and Edna opted to stay in the gardens and Curtis strode off on his own again, talking into his phone. Nico texted Loretta to tell her he was parked at the Boboli Gardens and he gave everyone a time to meet. He warned them that, just like in any city, they should look after their belongings.

It soon became apparent that Ginny and Heather had different tastes in everything. Heather was interested in organic cotton, vegan shoes and candles. She liked bracelets made out of tiny beads and handbags that looked like cloth sacks. Ginny's eyes shone at all the labels and shops she'd seen in glossy magazines: Jimmy Choo, Prada, Longchamp and Gucci. She drooled at the clothes and winced at the price tags.

Heather peered over Ginny's shoulder a lot, saying, 'My goodness, it's fabulous but pricy. Are you sure?' Ginny felt pressured into buying a cream linen dress she didn't love because Heather extolled the sustainability factor of the fabric. They spent fifteen minutes in a shop while Heather decided whether to buy an amber scented candle or one that smelled of patchouli.

'I've become interested in aromatherapy recently,' she said. 'Smells can help to evoke memories and I think it's helping Mum.'

'Is that why you're here?' Ginny asked. 'Because of her?'

Heather gave a slight nod that made her blonde curls bounce. 'Sorry I was evasive in the gallery earlier. Mum's poorly and I've been looking after her for quite some time. It's been taking its toll on me and that's why the headmistress insisted I take some time off school.' She ran a hand down her yoga trousers several times. 'I'm sure Mum and I will be back on our feet in no time.'

'Is there anything I can help you with?' Ginny asked gently.

Heather smiled but her eyes were sad. 'Remember when you were little, when you thought that all teachers were invincible, and that they knew everything? That's the person you *try* to become in my profession. And when you don't feel that way, can't act that way, it's difficult to pretend.'

'You don't have to pretend here.'

Heather took a moment to gather her thoughts. She turned away from Ginny and fixed her sights on a musical instrument shop. 'I'm sure Mum and I will be fine, nothing that a little rest, recuperation and vitamins won't sort out,' she said. Her tone indicated this part of their conversation was now over. 'Oh, would you look at that shop over there. My class is learning to play the recorder. Do you mind if we take a look?'

Ginny desperately wanted to find a lingerie store. Her underwear was crispy from the soap. 'Perhaps we should go our separate ways for a while,' she said. 'I need to buy some *personal* items.'

'Oh, okay, I don't mind,' Heather said, sounding like she did. 'Don't forget that heartache feeds on solitude.'

Too hot to think what that meant, Ginny tried not to feel guilty when Heather bounded off to look at a display of violins.

Ginny experienced a new sense of freedom going into whichever shops she wanted without Adrian standing outside looking at his watch or Heather assessing what she was buying. There was no one to question if she really needed another pair of shoes or not.

Ginny bought a floaty zebra-print dress, underwear and a smart linen jacket, getting changed into them in the shop's fitting room.

Each time she took out her purse, a floating sensation lifted her up for a few minutes before she came back down to earth. It was like being dunked in and out of a river for witchcraft, the euphoria of being alive soon cancelled out by water flooding the lungs. She really shouldn't be spending money like this.

Ginny applied make-up in a cosmetic store and almost cheered when she saw herself in a mirror looking poised and sleek again.

Her celebration was short-lived when a nagging voice appeared in her head. *Isn't this the version of you that Adrian has rejected?* it asked. *The problem-solver, the helper who looks composed on the outside, but who is struggling underneath? Which person is the real you?*

Ginny wasn't sure. Was *Ginny Splinter, Advice Angel* a role she'd grown used to playing? Who was the real person underneath the pastel suits?

As she strolled around the city, Ginny realized she'd been so fixated on the shops that she hadn't noticed the architecture surrounding her. She found herself in a vast square where the smooth surface of the grand white buildings looked like icing on a wedding cake. Grey piping scored the arches, windows and doorways.

She spotted a rickshaw and waved to grab the driver's attention, wanting to see more of the city. She climbed on board and gasped at the view when he turned the corner. The River Arno rippled petrol blue and the Ponte Vecchio bridge looked to be constructed of lemon, tangerine and peach blocks stacked on top of medieval stone arches. They drove along and, in the distance, she saw the terracotta dome of the Cathedral of Santa Maria del Fiore and the slender white, pink and grey of Giotto's Campanile. They looked pretty enough to eat.

The driver stopped the rickshaw and gestured for her to

get out and take photographs. With her phone battery now totally flat, Ginny meandered around instead, happening upon an ornate carousel in the middle of a piazza. It was easy to imagine Phoebe as a little girl, riding up and down on a red and gold horse.

One day, Ginny would love to feel tiny fingers grasping her own again. Her heart melted whenever she heard laughter in school playgrounds and she wondered if Phoebe would ever have children of her own. She hoped so.

A tap on her shoulder brought her out of her daydream.

Ginny turned to see a bride and groom holding out a phone, for her to take their photo. When she looked through the screen at the happy couple, they looked too young to be making a lifetime commitment to each other. She supposed no one ever went into marriage expecting it to blow wide apart, like her own parents' relationship had.

Coming from a broken family, she hated the idea of history repeating itself for her and Adrian. A sense of melancholy made her shiver as she took several shots. Feeling the need to impart some advice to the newlyweds, she handed back the phone.

'Treat your life together like a piggy bank that you both want to keep full of pennies,' she said. 'Do things for each other and treat your needs as equal. When you talk to each other, really listen. I'm not sure I've managed to do it fully in my own marriage. That's why I'm in trouble.'

The bride arched an eyebrow and the groom laughed. '*Scusa, non parlo inglese,*' he said with a shrug as he pocketed his phone. '*Grazie.*' The couple kissed and walked away, entwined in each other's arms.

Ginny smiled and waved them on their way. 'Naive,' she muttered to herself.

The rickshaw rumbled along cobbled streets where the strum of guitars mingled with conversation and laughter. Window boxes burst with geraniums and petunias, and an illuminated green cross outside a pharmacy displayed the temperature, twenty-nine degrees.

Ginny's eyes were drawn to the handsome man standing beneath it crooning an Italian love song. His words and face were full of passion and the rickshaw stopped again. The singer stepped off the pavement and walked towards her, taking hold of her hand. '*Ciao, bella signora,*' he said.

The rickshaw driver rolled his eyes.

Ginny felt colour rising up her neck as the singer fixed his hazelnut eyes on hers. When he rubbed his thumb across her fingers, her chest fluttered and she wished Adrian was here to witness her receiving this attention.

After finishing the song, the man lowered his head and brushed the back of her hand with his lips. Even if he made a living by flattering tourists, he'd made Ginny feel more desirable than she'd felt in years. The experience was worth every penny of the twenty euro note she gave him.

'*Grazie, ciao.*' The singer grinned, blowing her a kiss as he disappeared back into a crowd of people.

Unable to stop grinning, Ginny settled back in the rickshaw feeling all balmy inside.

The driver set off again and she brushed her hair from her eyes. Then she stopped with her hand mid-air. Something felt very different about it. When she lowered and rotated her fingers, her heart almost juddered to a halt. She was no longer wearing her wedding ring.

Ginny's throat constricted and she looked around her frantically. Could the singer have slipped it off her finger and taken it? She hadn't felt it vanish but knew pickpockets could be adept and quick. 'Stop,' she cried out to the driver. 'My ring has gone.'

He did as she asked and halted the rickshaw. They both stepped off and looked around helplessly. 'Thieves can take things without you knowing,' he said.

Ginny felt faint in the heat. Deep down, she knew they had no chance of finding the singer again. They'd already travelled a fair distance and there were too many people around. She felt foolish at being flattered by a professional thief.

'*Mi dispiace.*' The driver shrugged dolefully and Ginny slumped back into her seat. The beauty of Florence dimmed around her and her ring finger felt naked and too light.

A flash of memory came to her, of spotting the ring in a shop window. She'd fallen in love with it right away and just knew it would be a perfect fit. It came housed in a green leather box and she kept peeking at it in Adrian's drawer. She'd rarely taken it off since he slid it onto her finger on their wedding day. And now it was gone.

Adrian was always the first person she turned to in times of trouble. She desperately wanted the old version of him, here with her, so he could hold her and tell her that everything was okay. The ring was only a band of gold and he'd buy her another one. But her phone battery was dead and her husband was hundreds of miles away, living his life without her. Ginny had never felt more alone.

She asked the driver to drop her off at Boboli Gardens and her knees almost buckled when she saw the others. Nico strolled towards her.

'What is wrong?' he asked, noticing Ginny's hunched frame.

'My ring is gone . . . stolen.' Her words came out in gulps.

'I am sorry,' the rickshaw driver said from behind her. 'This has never happened before.'

Nico spoke to the driver in Italian, asking him to relay what had happened.

Edna bustled towards Ginny. 'This is absolutely dreadful,' she said. 'We need to contact the police and report this, pronto. They must try to catch the rapscallion who did this.'

Heather wrapped an arm around Ginny's shoulder and spoke softly into her ear. 'There, there. No point crying over spilled milk.'

For the first time, they didn't all feel like strangers thrown together in an odd situation.

'You do not need to pay me,' the driver insisted.

'No, I must.' Ginny's hand trembled as she took out her purse.

Nico shook the driver's hand then paused with his fingers outstretched. He cocked his head, squinted and bent down. He picked something up from the floor of the rickshaw and held it up. Ginny's ring winked in the sunshine. 'It was here, in a crack,' he said. 'Perhaps you dropped it.'

Ginny blinked at it, as if it was a mirage. Her stomach swooned with relief as Nico placed the wedding ring on her palm. She regretted suspecting the singer and apologized profusely to the driver.

'This could be an omen,' Heather said, looking over her shoulder. 'Perhaps your marriage isn't over after all.'

Ginny pushed the ring back on her finger and hoped this was true.

'I have more good news,' Nico said. 'Your suitcase arrived at the airport and Gianfranco has brought it to my hotel.'

Ginny felt light-headed with gratitude. She spontaneously threw her arms around Nico and hugged him close. 'Thank you,' she said.

His body was initially tense until he relaxed into her embrace. 'No problem. I am pleased you are happy.'

Ginny thought how nice it was to have some human contact again.

When they arrived back at Splendido, one of the wheels of Ginny's suitcase was missing. Strips of brown tape held the ripped fabric together and the clothes she'd packed so neatly were a jumble inside. Even so, she felt overjoyed to see it.

Nico carried the suitcase up to her room, returning to deliver a few items that had become separated, her jowl exerciser and some teeth-whitening strips. Ginny's cheeks burned as she thanked him. After the emotion and beauty of the art in Florence, she no longer felt the need to use either of the items.

As she completed a heartache form that evening, she noted that her mood was lifting and changing. And Ginny felt that she might be changing, too.

CHAPTER 12

Sunrise

Eric

At six o'clock the next morning, the Italian sky was pale yellow, the colour of stripped timber. Dew shone on the grass as Eric strode up the hill. This was his favourite time of day, before the relentless chatter of the world took hold, adding to the noise already in his head. He wanted to keep it at bay for as long as possible.

A song on the radio, an argument in a café or a raised voice in the street could sometimes feel like a flare going off in his brain, an unwanted personal soundtrack to everything he did. He wanted to clamp his hands to his ears to muffle it out.

The trip to Florence and mingling with the others had left him feeling weary. Focusing on the strain in his calf muscles, birdsong and his own breathing helped to quiet his mind.

Eric was still getting used to walking alone, without Bess. It had been three months since he'd lost his faithful companion.

His dog used to go everywhere with him, rarely grumbling about his habit of waking early in the morning because it meant more time to play for her. If Bess was here now, she'd probably fix him with a stare and urge him to cheer up. She used to spring around in the long grass like a lamb, which always made him smile.

He'd found her as a puppy, unwanted and left to fend for herself under a bush in the park. She was so tiny that he could cradle her in both hands. When Eric had gently held the whimpering tan and black dog to his chest, they'd formed an unbreakable bond. He'd carried her home and named her Bess. His friends teased him about preferring a walk in the countryside with his new pet rather than a night in the pub, and Eric couldn't disagree. She went into work with him each day to the Sanderson Fine Furniture showroom.

Eric lovingly crafted chairs, tables and bookshelves using traditional tools and techniques passed down through generations of the Sanderson family. His father and grandfather had shown him how to use a chisel before he could write his own name. Eric's dad had the hands of a craftsperson, scored and ragged from years of working with wood, and Eric's own hands were similar, looking much older than his twenty-eight years.

His parents had retired from the business a few years ago, but still helped him out occasionally. Eric's mother looked after all the invoicing and proved a dab hand at setting up a website with the help of a local marketing company. Whenever she tried to show spreadsheets to Eric and teach him how to update the company website, it was like she was speaking a foreign language to him.

Eric wasn't a talkative sort and he often felt awkward in company, so Bess wagging her tail to greet customers helped him to start conversations about his work. Sanderson Fine Furniture cost almost double the amount of the mass-produced wares sold on the high street or online, so it was useful to be able to share its story. Eric even made a mini four-poster bed for Bess and added a red velvet blanket. When customers saw her reclining and modelling it in the showroom, they said, 'Aww,' and bought one for their own pet.

At first, Eric hadn't been too worried about the virus that was being talked about everywhere. Customers started to wear masks to visit his showroom but they could still see and feel the superiority of his craftsmanship compared to other furniture. They could picture it in their houses.

Things got worse when greater restrictions came in. Sales died down as people cut back on their nonessentials, but Eric kept on making his furniture even though fewer customers were buying it. In the evenings and on weekends, he sat in his small one-bedroom flat sketching out new ideas and was glad he had Bess for company. They went out for walks together before anyone got up in the morning and when everyone was in bed at night.

Talking to his parents and friends on the phone didn't help Eric's plummeting mood. As he watched his meagre savings dwindling in his bank account, he hugged Bess close and told himself he was lucky to have her. She didn't need much money to be happy and he tried to follow her lead.

But soon things went from bad to worse with the business. Eric had to sell some of his machinery and furniture to an auction house dirt cheap so he could pay his household and business bills. Watching the equipment his father and grandfather had used for generations get loaded into the back of a van was the worst day of his life.

Or so he'd thought at the time.

When Eric stumbled home, Bess had been waiting for him and seemed to detect something was wrong. She wagged her tail warily and Eric reached out to envelop her in his arms. He cried into her fur, feeling like she was all he had left in the world. She helped to chase away the blues that were closing in and tightening a grip on him.

Over the months that followed, he reopened his workshop and showroom, but customers didn't flock back. Eric no longer had adequate machinery to make his furniture and his feelings of melancholy dragged on. He also noticed that Bess was slowing down. She was reluctant to get out of her bed in the morning and her chest rose and fell quickly when they walked. He wondered if she was picking up on his low mood.

Eric took her to the vet who said she had a bacterial infection and prescribed anti-inflammatories and antibiotics. Bess improved a little, but still walked more slowly than usual.

Then, one day, Eric found her curled up in her bed and couldn't wake her up. He dropped to his knees and stroked her fur. She looked so peaceful, just like she was asleep. 'I'm so sorry I wasn't with you,' he whispered, bowing his head. He wished he could have saved her, but didn't even know if that was possible.

Losing her was the last straw in his run of bad luck.

Eric knew there were no set rules for bereavement, but he was surprised by the magnitude of his feelings of guilt and pain. He'd battled his way through tough times and Bess's death was the thing that finally floored him. Everything felt dark and pointless from then on, as if he was surrounded by thick fog. He couldn't be bothered to eat properly, nibbling on grapes and biscuits. He let his hair grow out and stopped shaving.

One day, when he couldn't even rouse himself to get out of bed, Eric switched on his radio and lay there, feeling as low as possible while listening to an advice show. A lady named Ginny Splinter sounded anguished about her husband leaving and Eric could relate to her outpouring of grief. Calling the show was an act of desperation for him, an uncharacteristic cry for help, and he was astonished to secure a place on the holiday to Italy. His parents were worried about his state of mind so they paid for his plane ticket, knowing he might otherwise stay moping around at home.

And now he was here in Bologna.

Eric carried on climbing until he reached the top of the hill and the ache in his calves overtook the emptiness in his heart. He looked down at the pretty buildings and winding streets of Vigornuovo and knew Bess would have loved it up here, too. He took her collar out of the tin and slipped it onto his wrist like a bracelet. Slinging off his backpack, he sat down on the grass and reached out for a broken branch.

He used to be able to look at wood and picture it as a box, chair or even a bed, depending on its size. Now, he saw only a piece of a tree. Without Bess at his side, he felt as fragile as a curled shaving of wood.

Eric had hoped being around others might help him to fight his sense of hopelessness. Curtis was a fellow business owner, but Eric found him to be rather brazen, and Heather was annoyingly upbeat. Surprisingly, he felt the closest affinity to Edna, who appeared to be struggling with loss, too.

Pushing her wheelchair around the art gallery in Florence hadn't been as dull as he'd thought it might be. When he'd removed his audio tour headphones, Edna had proved to be funny with her observations about the paintings and her assessments of other people's clothes. He'd coughed a laugh when she'd said a woman's black and white hat looked like she had a skunk sleeping on her head. And then Edna had laughed, too.

In the animal portrait gallery, Eric had found he enjoyed looking at the paintings of horses, dogs and birds. He'd admired the finer details; a cocked ear, how the artist painted fur, or a dot of light bringing eyes to life. His pleasure from the art was like a tiny crack of light breaking through a storm cloud and he hoped there'd be more to come.

But for now, Eric looked up at the Italian sky, gold turning to blue. He whittled the broken branch until only a stick remained in his hands. Then he batted wood shavings off his shorts and stood up, welcoming the strain in his muscles as he carried on hiking.

CHAPTER 13

Selfie

The sound of Eric shutting the front door to go out for his early morning walk woke Ginny up. She initially felt weary after the day out in Florence before remembering she had all her belongings back. She sat up and pulled her cosmetic bag towards her, embarrassed at how excited she felt by the sight of her eyebrow tweezers and concealer.

She'd left her phone charging overnight and Phoebe had sent her a message.

Hi Mum. Glad you've arrived safely. Have fun! X

To her dismay, Adrian hadn't called her and she felt like her emotional piggy bank was running dangerously low on currency for him. The distance between them seemed to be increasing with each day that passed.

It was too early to ring either of them, so Ginny sat up in bed and reread another page from *The Power of Two*.

Stage Three. Resentment and bargaining.

Hold back your negative thoughts. They'll make you feel bad when you need to be strong. This isn't a time for begging and bargaining. Assessing your own needs and desires, and putting them first, will prove to be a powerful tool. Good luck.

Ginny straightened her back, telling herself she was doing well, considering the circumstances. She was actually starting to have a good time and it was Adrian's loss that he wasn't here in Italy with her. They'd had some great times together on previous holidays.

In one hotel, the maids had folded their towels, like origami, to resemble swans. They'd looked more like dodos and Ginny and Adrian had laughed so hard they cried. In Tenerife, the sea stole Adrian's swimming trunks, so he'd had to perform a naked dash along the beach to reach his towel. Ginny had kept inching it away from him, giggling as he tried to grab it. A woman covered her toddler's eyes, protecting him from the sight of Adrian's bare bottom, which had made Ginny laugh even more. She loved their candlelit dinners sampling local delicacies and stumbling back to their hotel room together after drinking too much wine. They lazily made love, knowing they could stay in bed each morning without being awoken by an alarm clock.

Now that they were apart, was Adrian remembering all their good times, too? Or was he still intent on pursuing a divorce? She hoped his actions had been a heat of the moment thing and that he was taking time to collect his thoughts.

Thinking about him made her neck feel hot and Ginny pulled her nightie away from her skin. She lowered her chin to blow onto her chest.

Her mum used to lower her voice whenever she talked about menopause, calling it 'the change'. It had arrived early for her, in her early forties, and Ginny had thought it sounded mysterious, like a magic trick performed on stage behind a satin cape. Perhaps a shiny top hat would disappear to be replaced by a cute bunny.

'The change' seemed to spark a fresh resolve within her mum, prompting her to issue an ultimatum to Ginny's dad about their marriage.

While Ginny waited for her hot flush to subside, she heard a thudding noise outside her room, followed by a female voice muttering. Ginny listened more intently – could Edna be sleepwalking? She peered at her watch and saw it wasn't yet 6.00 a.m. When another bang sounded, she slipped on her dressing gown and crept across her room.

Ginny inched her door open to find Loretta crouching down on the landing. Her white cotton dress hung off one shoulder and her smudged eye make-up looked raccoon-like. She picked up one high-heeled shoe then the other. 'Shhh,' she said, pressing her finger to her lips. She tiptoed barefoot towards her room and smiled secretively before slipping inside.

Somewhere in the distance, Ginny heard a moped chugging away and couldn't help wondering what adventure Loretta might have been on. It made her feel rather envious. About to close her bedroom door again, she heard creaking along the hallway downstairs. Someone else was up and about, too.

Thinking Nico might have woken up early to prepare breakfast, Ginny padded down to offer to help. She assumed he didn't know Loretta was creeping around at dawn. Father and daughter must have just missed each other.

She almost collided with Curtis who jumped back with widened eyes. He was fully dressed in his customary white sports gear and instantly moved his phone away from his mouth. 'Oh, hey, Ginny,' he said.

'What are you doing?' she whispered.

'Recording a few thoughts,' he replied, as if it was obvious.

Ginny noticed a notepad tucked into his pocket. In the dimly lit hallway, she could see the paper was topped with the Splendido logo.

'Also, writing a letter or two . . .' Curtis added. He deftly swerved around her and headed towards his bedroom. 'Catch you later.'

Ginny's eyes narrowed as he closed his door. There was no sign of Nico around, so she retreated to her own room. She showered, washed her hair and let it dry loose. It was a relief to shave under her arms, and to wear deodorant, mascara and lipstick again. She placed *The Power of Two* back on her bedside table and thought about Adrian. Was his profile still on the ChainReaxions website?

She checked it out on her phone, hoping that he'd deleted his photos, but he was still there grinning out at her from behind his mirrored sunglasses. She needed to be a member of the site to view his full profile information and additional photos.

Although she knew it would be torturous, Ginny had an

insatiable desire to take a look. What was her husband seeking out that she wasn't currently offering him?

She quickly entered her email address, adding a fake name and location. She became 'Jenny' from Leeds rather than Ginny from Greenham. Following Adrian's lead, she shaved four years off her age.

Her new account allowed her to view several more images of her husband. He wore a wolfish grin in each, mainly posing alongside flashy cars at work.

How well do you know your husband? Miss Peach's words nagged in her head.

Ginny's ribcage tightened as she read on.

Adrian, 45. Caring, loving and honest. *(Ha! Ginny thought.)* Loves cars and the simple things in life. I'm a down-to-earth family man with a lovely grown-up daughter. I'm at the end of a long-term relationship and feeling bruised, so I'm primarily looking for friendship. If you're chilled out and like coffee and good conversation, you might be my kindred spirit.

Ginny almost choked. Her husband describing himself as *caring*? She hadn't seen much evidence of that recently. She was the one who cooked their meals, who bought family birthday cards and always cleaned the bathroom. And *kindred spirit*? The words made him sound like Heather.

Ginny dissected Adrian's sentences and supposed no one would ever describe her as *chilled out*. Her anger slowly subsided, replaced by a gloom that made her bones feel leaden.

Was she looking at the *real* Adrian on the site, or a persona he'd invented? He wasn't the only one feeling confused.

At least it sounded like he was looking for a brew and a chat rather than a torrid affair. If he'd been conversing with any women online, Ginny could only hope they'd quizzed him about his situation and given him good counsel.

She had to accept that Adrian no longer felt the same way about her, and she wasn't sure how she felt about him. Would telling him about her worries have made a difference in their relationship? Had she also been projecting a persona to her husband, and to the world, that wasn't truly *her*?

She felt devastated that Adrian was willing to liaise with strangers online while avoiding any contact she tried to make with him.

Ginny spun her wedding ring around on her finger and couldn't help questioning if she was still attractive to other men. She was sure admiring glances in the street had died out a decade ago and she'd never thought she'd miss the occasional toot of a car horn. She used to hate it when it happened.

She brushed a hand through her hair and pondered what would happen if she uploaded photos of herself to the site. Would anyone want to send her a wink?

After reading Adrian's profile again, she *needed* to feel desirable again.

Ginny changed into her new zebra-print dress and used a scarf as a headband around her hair. It had already lightened a little in the sun and her sunglasses covered a lot of her face. Instead of smiling, she pouted and took a couple of selfies on her phone, making sure her face was half-hidden in the shadows. She felt ridiculous but her shots looked rather sultry, like she was a different person completely.

She uploaded the images and took a long time to perfect her profile.

Jenny, 45. Friendly and caring. Living in Leeds. I'm a real people person who loves cooking, shopping, reading and helping others. I'm looking for someone I can be myself with. People think I have all the answers when really, I don't. I've been badly hurt recently and am trying to rediscover the real me again.

When Ginny read her words back, she bit her nails, recognizing she'd managed to express her own vulnerability for once. Pretending to be someone else had allowed her to open up. She'd never revealed this side of herself to Adrian or her friends before and it brought a tear to her eye. On ChainReaxions, she and Adrian were two people on display while hiding a different side to their lives, like the Duke and Duchess of Urbino.

She checked her watch and saw that time had flown. It was now past 9.00 a.m. and she'd probably missed breakfast. She hoped the others wouldn't mind.

Gazing at Adrian's profile again, her finger hovered above the pink winking face icon. He was avoiding all her attempts to contact him, so what other option did she have?

Before she could talk herself out of it, Ginny sent a wink to her husband.

CHAPTER 14

Chapel

Ginny found a completed batch of heartache forms waiting for her on the breakfast table. Edna had particularly enjoyed the paintings by Titian and Raphael, and the lovely gardens. Her heartache rating had dropped from a nine to an eight.

Heather claimed the paintings of cherubs in the Uffizi had 'spoken to her soul', and she'd adored all the artsy shops in the city. Her heartache score had made promising progress, too.

Ginny sighed when she saw Curtis had written *Not Applicable* across each section of his form in thick black letters. He'd left his suggestion box and heartache score uncompleted.

Only Eric had suggested something to do next.

Hiking. Meet on Thursday in the courtyard at 6.00 a.m. Wear strong footwear.

Ginny blew out her cheeks. She didn't relish the start time or the activity, but at least he'd put forward an idea.

The table was full of used breakfast plates and bowls and she carried a pile of them towards the kitchen to help out.

Nico and Loretta stood side by side, washing sheets in the sink. They didn't notice Ginny standing behind them, in the doorway. They were talking in Italian and their voices rose in volume, culminating in Loretta throwing up her hands in frustration. Soap suds flew off her fingertips.

The teenager picked up a towel, dried her hands and stormed off, squeezing past Ginny without acknowledging her.

Nico spun around and his face crumpled. 'Lolo . . .' he called after his daughter.

Ginny tightened her grip on the crockery, feeling like she'd been caught eavesdropping.

'Ginny,' Nico said, his voice all flustered. 'Sorry, I didn't hear you . . .' He took the plates from her.

'I just arrived,' she said quickly. 'Sorry I missed breakfast. I didn't notice the time.'

'I can get you something, coffee or a croissant . . .' He looked around him without focus.

'Don't worry, there's still a few things left on the table. I can help myself.' She paused for a moment. 'Is everything okay with Loretta?'

Nico's Adam's apple bobbed. 'We had an argument about the bedsheets. She reminded me that Grand Hotel Castello Bella Vista has a laundry room with washing machines we could use. I told her there is nothing wrong with soap and sunshine.'

'I bet the sheets dry more quickly on your washing line,' Ginny said.

He cast her a grateful smile. 'She wants me to visit

Gianfranco's new spa. Apparently, his guests wear fine clothes and have good taste. She said I am stuck in my ways and this is why her mother left. I called her Lolo, Maria's name for her, and . . .' He looked down. 'She didn't like it and has told me never to use it again.'

Again, Ginny wanted to know where Nico's wife was, yet the sadness in his eyes prevented her from asking him. 'Eric wants us all to go walking tomorrow. Perhaps you'd like to join us for some fresh air?'

Nico thought for a moment. 'Yes, I would like this, though I doubt Loretta will want to come, too.'

'Eric wants to set off at six a.m. Can we take something with us for breakfast?'

'Of course. I will arrange it.'

A stilted pause followed and Ginny's gaze fell upon a pink glass vase. 'That's very beautiful,' she said.

Nico picked it up. 'It belongs to Maria. She forgot to take it with her. It will be here for her when she returns to Splendido.' His words were doleful with only a hint of hope.

Ginny rocked on her heels a little, wanting to say something that would make him feel better. 'I think your hotel is charming. If it was big and luxurious like the white castle, it wouldn't have the same friendliness and character.'

Nico set the vase back on a shelf with a thud. 'Thank you, that is kind of you, though I think Loretta is right. Splendido is not a good place for excitement or romance and I need to change it. I just do not know how.'

★

When Ginny, Eric, Heather, Curtis and Nico met the next morning, the moon was still visible, a crescent of platinum in the sky. Ginny had convinced herself that a hike meant a leisurely stroll, until she spotted Eric's boots caked in mud. Her Converse lace-ups were the most sensible shoes she'd brought on holiday and she wore them with thin white socks, her jeans and a cashmere sweater.

'What's the plan for the day?' she asked Eric.

He shrugged a shoulder. 'Walking.'

Curtis interjected. 'I think Ginny is asking *where* we're walking *to*? What's the strategy? How far are we going and how long will it take?' He tapped his G-Shock watch. 'I have a Zoom at noon.'

Eric didn't reply, acting as if he hadn't heard.

'It takes twenty-five minutes to walk into Vigornuovo village,' Nico told Eric. 'The countryside looks pretty as the sun rises.'

Eric nodded and pointed in the opposite direction to the castle. 'Then we'll climb that hill.'

Ginny shuddered at the word *hill*. It looked steep and possibly too challenging for Edna to tackle. 'Has anyone seen Edna this morning?' she asked, looking around her. 'A hike might prove difficult for her to . . .'

There was a cough and the elderly lady appeared in the doorway of the hotel. 'I am actually here, not a figment of your imagination,' she said snippily. 'I can walk and talk for myself.'

Nico stepped forwards. 'We are only thinking of your comfort, Edna. Did you know that Vigornuovo is so beautiful a film called *A Glorious Escape* was made here? There is a display of costumes in the town hall. Actor Tim Vincenzo's trousers are so small they could fit a doll.'

Edna lifted her chin. 'I've seen the film several times and he looked much taller than Sharon Sterling.'

Nico whispered in her ear. 'Camera tricks.'

Edna stared dreamily across the village square. 'Sharon Sterling wears a vintage red Chanel dress when she dances around the fountain with Vincenzo,' she said. 'It's exquisite, made from the finest silk.'

'You can see that dress and others, too,' Nico said. 'If you do not want to climb a hill, you can stay in the village. There are several cafés and shops to visit.'

Edna hitched an inquisitive eyebrow.

Ginny thought Edna looked like she'd be more interested in clothes on a supermarket clearance rack rather than couture. Perhaps there was more to her than met the eye.

As they all set off walking along the bumpy road, Nico's minibus had never looked more inviting. Eric led the way like a shepherd taking his sheep to new pastures. They were all accompanied by the tinny sound of hip-hop coming from Curtis's headphones. It prevented Ginny from asking how he was feeling.

After half a mile she spotted a roadside sign for Gianfranco's hotel.

Grand Hotel Castello Bella Vista
Spa. Pool. Luxury Rooms. Six Stars.

Nico stared resolutely ahead, refusing to acknowledge the white turreted building on top of the hill.

Ginny dropped back to walk with Edna.

'I'm fine, sturdy as an ox,' Edna rasped. She flexed her arm to display a slender forearm with pronounced blue veins and a half plum-sized bicep.

They all walked over a medieval stone bridge that curved above a rushing river. An archway led them into the heart of Vigornuovo village where narrow cobbled streets meandered and washing lines laced the old buildings together like a corset. Stone walls were the colour of vanilla ice cream and roof tiles were burnt orange. Terracotta plant pots sat on every corner, springing with multicoloured pansies, and a black cat slinked lazily across their path.

The main village square was waking up and coming to life. Edna's eyes lit up when she saw the famous fountain from *A Glorious Escape*. Water cascaded onto the heads of four stone dolphins. 'It's magnificent,' she exclaimed, after catching her breath.

Coffee bars had huge striped umbrellas and tiny iron tables outside. Cups and saucers clattered, and two men stood talking and smoking on a corner. Nico chatted to them for a while before gesturing for everyone to follow him towards a building with a tall carved oak door. He produced a large key and opened it, inviting Edna to follow him inside.

He reappeared a few minutes later, alone. 'Edna is staying here to look at the costumes. I knew she would like them,' he said. 'The building does not usually open until later, so she is receiving a special viewing.'

Eric nodded towards a long passageway with a glimpse of emerald countryside beyond it. 'Let's climb,' he said.

For the first half hour of their trek, Ginny didn't really look around at the vineyards that made stripes on the hill and the clusters of white villas with autumnal-coloured roofs. Instead, she ruminated on future conversations she might have with Adrian, trying to solve all their problems in her head. Perhaps they could see a marriage guidance counsellor when she got home, so they could find a positive way forward.

Ginny might use an abdomen cruncher and walk to work, but she couldn't call herself fit. Pain soon shot up her shins and she pressed her fingers into a stitch in her side. Heather slowed down to join her.

'You're fitter than I am,' Ginny panted.

'Staying healthy is essential, especially keeping the brain active. I always do sudoku before I go to sleep. Mum used to love it, too. She was a school teacher, the same as me, until . . .' She let her words filter away and her eyes dimmed. Stopping to take in the view, Heather tried to brighten her conversation. 'Anyway, that's enough about me. Tell me all about Ginny Splinter.'

Although Ginny didn't mind doing photo spreads for magazines, she'd always found talking about herself cringe-inducing. Thinking of what to say made her toes curl.

'When did you discover your gift of empathy?' Heather prompted.

Ginny explained how she'd originally found her ability to tune into other people's emotions to be a painful affliction, and that it'd taken her a long time to embrace it as something

Ginny shot him a warning glance. She wasn't sure how stitching pieces of fabric together could cure heartache, but she was willing to give it a try. 'It sounds less strenuous than hiking,' she said.

'Creativity is intelligence having fun,' Heather added.

'Yeah?' Curtis raised an eyebrow. 'I can think of better ways.'

'Well, maybe you should put something forward, too,' Ginny said firmly.

'Toosh,' Curtis replied, which she assumed was short for 'touché.'

Later that afternoon, when Ginny returned to her hotel room, heartache forms completed by Eric and Heather appeared under her door. Edna had also filled out details for her quilting activity, to take place the following afternoon. Ginny was pleased to see her three guests' scores had dropped after the country walk. Again, she had no idea about how Curtis was feeling.

She showered and rubbed body lotion into her tight calf muscles. She'd left her phone behind during the walk and checked it to see if she'd received any new messages.

Her heart almost stopped when she saw Adrian had sent a winking face back to her.

Ginny gave a blast of surprised laughter and performed a twirl. Her husband had shown interest in her again and, even if he didn't know her true identity, the sensation was truly delicious.

CHAPTER 15

Feather

Heather

In the bedroom opposite Ginny's, Heather eased her way out of her downward dog yoga pose. It helped to stretch out her legs and back after the hike. She hoped that it was good at easing guilt, too. The emotion felt like thick soup slopping around in her stomach.

She was trying to relax in Italy, attempting to be positive and cheerful, for others as well as herself. She'd once read that you could trick your brain into feeling happy by smiling, even if you didn't feel that way. She kept trying to give it a go, without much success.

It was difficult to be upbeat when her mum, Renee, was back home in England, in a place she didn't want to be or even recognize. Heather felt like she was letting her down by being here. She was also missing the school bell ringing throughout the day, giving her proper structure, and even the children calling out, 'Miss, can I please use the toilet?' and 'I've broken my ruler, Miss Hall.'

Heather had known she wanted to teach primary school children from an early age. It was an honour to be part of young people's lives, to help them learn, grow and nurture their minds. No one ever forgot a good teacher.

She loved how kids thought Plasticine was the most exciting substance on earth, and how lemon sponge served at lunchtime brought on squeals of delight. School Christmas fairs, with a visit from one of the dads dressed as Santa, were beyond magical.

Her mum had retired from teaching several years ago, though the profession remained in her blood. Heather couldn't keep Renee away from her school's sports days, summer fairs and pantomimes.

The two women had always been close, so when Heather's long-term relationship ended a few years ago, she was happy to move back home with her mum. They both enjoyed watching old movies on Sunday afternoon together, making chocolate brownies and sewing costumes for shepherds and wise men. Heather got to enjoy lots of home comforts again and Renee loved having some company.

Things had been great, until Heather noticed her mum beginning to act oddly. Renee started to ask her what year it was and for reminders of her friends' names. She put a plastic kettle on the gas hob so it melted, and Heather found her standing in the middle of the kitchen a couple of times, unsure where she was.

At first, Heather tried to laugh it off. 'You'd forget your head if it was loose,' she'd said. Her mum had laughed, too, failing to conceal the confused look in her eyes.

One day, Renee knocked over a candle in her bedroom and set her duvet on fire. She'd sat on her bed regardless and Heather had to pull her out of the room and throw water on the flames. She'd bundled the burnt bed linen together and threw it into the garden. Renee had stared at it and then at her daughter. 'What are you doing? Where's Heather?' she'd asked. 'She won't be happy with your behaviour.'

The blood had chilled in Heather's veins. 'Mum. It's *me*. There's been a fire . . .'

Renee tutted and her eyes hardened. 'Don't be silly. Heather's a little girl and I'm going to tell her about you.'

Heather had stood frozen to the spot, unsure what to say or do. The sharp-minded, vivacious woman who'd raised her single-handedly, who'd taught hundreds of children, was turning into a different person. Glimpses of Renee were still there, like when you spy someone's head bobbing up and down in a crowd but can't manage to push through, to reach them.

She took her mum to see a doctor who arranged for a series of tests. When the results came through, he explained to Heather that the brain is made up of nerve cells that communicate with each other to send messages.

'Dementia damages the nerve cells so that messages can't be sent to and from the brain properly. It means the body doesn't function as usual,' he said. 'There are over two hundred types of dementia and some can be combined. In your mum's case the disease may progress quite rapidly, so I'll prescribe medication to help slow down some of the symptoms. I'll also give you information about supporting someone with the disease.'

Heather had listened in a daze, wincing each time he said the words *dementia* and *disease*. Surely, he wasn't talking about her mum. Renee was fine, perhaps a little confused, and couldn't that be due to dehydration, low blood sugar or a nutrient deficiency? She was only seventy-two and there must be *some* cure to bring her back to normal.

Heather had always tried to live a healthy lifestyle, even turning down freshly made cakes at school lunchtime. She did twice-weekly yoga sessions and took vitamins, things that might benefit her mum, too. After Renee's diagnosis, Heather visited her local health food store to buy organic fruit and vegetables, and she read online about homeopathic remedies. She implemented a new healthy lifestyle regimen for them both.

One day, Heather was helping out at a school Christmas fair when one of the parents insisted on reading her tarot cards.

'You're currently looking after someone close to you who's very poorly,' the woman said. 'Your love is helping them to recover. Keep doing what you're doing and things will get better.'

Heather had never really believed in such stuff, but the words gave her hope and she clung onto them as things got tougher.

Her mum slept sporadically, no longer sure if it was day or night, meaning that Heather couldn't sleep either. She found herself yawning in lessons and got migraines for the first time in her life. She tried to organize her mum in the same way she did her classes, explaining things clearly and firmly, only for the information to fade from Renee's grasp within seconds. Heather went into school with a sense of dread, hating to leave her mum home alone and relying on neighbours to check in on her throughout the day.

One of the things the two women still enjoyed together was listening to the radio. Renee's short-term memory might be faulty, but she could still remember songs and lyrics from the past. She and Heather sang Beatles songs together and listened to *Just Ask Ginny*, discussing other people's problems while unable to resolve their own.

As doctors delivered yet more unsettling news about Renee's health, Heather turned to alternative therapies even more. She paid for Reiki treatments for her mum and also tried aromatherapy. She downloaded brain-training apps on her phone and tried to get Renee to give them a go. Something *had* to help.

Soon, Heather was running on empty and struggling to function. The kids pointed out her wrong answers to sums in maths class and Heather fumbled to correct her workings out.

While attending yet another hospital appointment, a doctor had told her, 'Your mother needs specialist round-the-clock care and you can't offer her that. You also need a break.'

'I'm absolutely fine,' Heather said, even though her body felt like it was encased in concrete.

'You're heading for a breakdown,' the doctor said firmly. 'Then you'll need specialist care, too.'

Heather broke down in front of him and couldn't stop crying. As tears dribbled down her cheeks, she knew deep down that he was right.

'Take a holiday,' he said. 'You need to look after your own health as well as your mum's.'

'Mum's is more important.'

'Everyone's needs are the same. Don't neglect yours.'

Heather knew she couldn't afford a holiday and felt like she didn't deserve one.

On the day Renee moved into residential care, Heather felt like she'd failed as a daughter and a human being. She'd curled up on the sofa and cried, needing to hear some positive news for once.

A message from the radio came through instead. Advice expert Ginny Splinter was inviting four heartbroken strangers to join her in Italy, and Heather felt like the invitation was meant for *her*. It had to be a sign.

Here in Italy, Heather knew her mum was safe and being well-looked-after, and that friends and family were also helping out, but there had to be something *more* she could do. Some hope, some answer, some new way forward that would help Renee become the woman she once was.

Shopping, hiking and art had offered Heather a distraction for a while and now she needed assistance of a more spiritual kind.

When she spotted a tiny white feather on the floor of her room, she picked it up and cupped it in her hands. She desperately wanted to believe it was a sign from the universe, telling her that things were going to get better. All she could do was keep hoping and trying.

CHAPTER 16

Quilt

Edna placed her handbag on a table in the courtyard and set out a line of needles and reels of cotton. She took out several paperback-sized pieces of fabric and weighed them down with small stones. 'I'm sure a day spent sewing will do us all the world of good,' she said.

Heather stared at her display. 'Did you bring all those things with you?'

'They don't weigh a lot and I like to sew.'

Ginny, Eric, Heather and Curtis sat down on chairs surrounding Edna and awaited her instructions.

Heather stroked a piece of material. 'I could make a kimono if the pieces were prettier,' she mused.

'We're making a quilt,' Edna said firmly. She passed pieces of fabric to them all.

Curtis's face was blank. 'I don't understand crafts,' he said. 'Why would anyone try to make something you can buy from a shop? I like stuff with labels.'

Edna cast him a withering look.

Ginny was finding it difficult to feel inspired, too. All she could think about was Adrian's wink and what it meant. Did he like her photograph, want to chat with her, or something more? His attention made her feel excited and nauseated at the same time.

Edna held up a series of rectangles she'd already stitched together. 'Today we're going to create blocks to add to my quilt, or you can start your own project.'

'Blocks?' Curtis asked.

Edna nodded. 'You create an image or scene on your fabric, using embroidery, applique or fabric paint. It's a bit like collage and should represent something important to you.' She tapped her forefinger on the table as if readying herself to share something more personal with them. 'I call this piece my memory quilt.'

'I'd prefer a fluffy feather duvet,' Curtis quipped. He looked around and grinned, inviting the others to join in.

Edna fixed him with a stare. 'Please stop thinking about yourself, it's most unbecoming. Most of us are here because we *want* to feel better. This is my project and you'll get your own turn to choose something.'

Curtis pulled the peak of his baseball cap lower. 'Okay, sorry Edna.'

'I've cut out some shapes to get you all started.'

Ginny examined a piece of fabric. It was pigeon-grey with tiny white flowers and didn't spark anything in her imagination. 'I've never really sewn anything before,' she said.

'Have you got anything more cheerful?' Heather asked. 'Perhaps something with sequins?'

Edna worked her jaw and her eyes turned steely. 'If you don't want to do this, just say so,' she snapped. 'I don't want to waste my time.'

Ginny placed a hand on her arm. 'We all want to do this, Edna. We're just inexperienced, that's all.'

'Quilting virgins,' Curtis added.

Edna's face remained sour. 'The extra fabric I bought in the village is in my room,' she said. 'You may retrieve it, if you wish.' She took her key out of her pocket and slapped it on the table.

Ginny picked it up and was glad to escape the spiky atmosphere.

On Edna's bedside table, she found a clear bag stuffed with remnants of fabric, including some brightly coloured pieces. It sat beside a photograph of two women and she couldn't help glancing at it. Edna was holding hands with a younger, much smaller woman who wore a grey dress printed with flowers. The words engraved on the photo frame read, *Daisy – Always in My Heart*, 1970–2020.

Peering a little closer, she saw the two women had similar eyes and smiles, and she recognized the floral print fabric from Edna's patchwork pieces. 'Edna and her daughter?' Ginny whispered to herself. Her throat tightened when she imagined how losing a child might feel and she hugged the bag of fabric to her chest.

She now understood the pieces Edna was sewing together weren't just random scraps. The older lady was crafting something full of history and emotion, in memory of her daughter.

It made Ginny think about her other guests, too. Maybe

hiking didn't cancel out Eric's grief, but helped him to reflect upon and live with it. Was Heather's cheerfulness disguising her pain? She supposed, in the past, she'd offered up one-size-fits-all solutions to solve heartache. As soon as she'd learned about people's problems on *Just Ask Ginny*, she promptly conjured up answers and didn't tap into her true empathy. It had become a job or habit, and it had taken Adrian walking out on her for Ginny to discover her true compassion again.

She didn't just want to help out Edna, Eric, Curtis and Heather in order to feel better about herself, but because she wanted to get to know them better and to hear their stories. Even if they brought on difficult emotions, it'd be better than the feelings of numbness and shock Adrian had thrust upon her.

Ginny carried the bag downstairs and sat back down beside Edna, seeing her in a different light, as deeply lonely rather than fussy. 'This is pretty material,' she said, picking up the grey floral piece from her pile. 'Where did it come from?'

Edna's eyes dipped and her voice was evasive when she spoke. 'It's from one of my daughter's dresses. She was called Daisy and she's departed now, as well as my husband, Desmond.'

Ginny swallowed. 'I'm so sorry to hear that.' She stroked the fabric, taking a few moments to ease Edna into their conversation. 'I've been here less than a week and already miss my daughter so much. I'd love to know more about Daisy. Did she like to sew, too?'

Edna moved a few fabric pieces around, her hand shaking a little. 'She struggled to do a lot of things,' she said, snipping off a length of cotton. As she began to stitch, the rhythm of the needle feeding in and out of the fabric seemed to make her breathing grow calmer.

Ginny watched patiently until Edna was ready to speak again.

'She liked to watch me sewing,' the older lady said. 'Daisy loved anything to do with fashion. One of her favourite pastimes was to look through magazines and circle the dresses she liked. We'd go shopping and choose fabric together and I'd try to recreate the patterns. She was attracted to grey things for some reason, maybe because pigeons, elephants and dolphins made her smile. I loved making her clothes and it kept me connected to the profession I had to leave behind, when she was born.

'Daisy could be rather difficult at times. Her food had to be presented in a certain way and she refused to eat anything green. She adored some people and vehemently took against others. When she died, I thought my life might return to normal,' Edna humphed. 'Except she *was* my normal. Losing her was like an eclipse of the sun. Everything fell dark and now my days seem never-ending. Sometimes, there doesn't seem much point in anything.' Her gaze drifted towards trees in the distance and stayed there.

Ginny silently gestured for Eric, Heather and Curtis to move closer. They huddled around Edna's small table to offer their support.

The elderly lady surveyed them warily at first before clearing her throat. 'You may think we're sitting here sewing for no reason, but it helps me to celebrate my daughter.' Her lips trembled. 'I have no use for Daisy's old clothes and can't bring myself to throw them away. They help me feel close to her. I once watched a TV programme about people making memory quilts to commemorate their loved ones and it seemed like a decent way to pass my time.'

Curtis rubbed the corner of his eye. 'Speck of dust,' he said.

Everyone listened intently as Edna continued to talk about her daughter while she sewed. The more she shared, the looser her shoulders became. Tension fell away from her face.

'If we all make blocks to represent the reasons we're here, it will give Daisy some company,' Ginny said.

Edna fell quiet for some time. She swallowed and her eyes grew glassy. 'I think she'd like that very much,' she whispered. 'I would like it, too.'

Curtis stuck out his tongue as he tried and failed to thread a needle.

'Pass that to me. I'll do it.' Edna took it from him and deftly pushed a strand of cotton through the tiny eye. 'You have the dexterity of a buffalo.'

Curtis laughed. 'You're not wrong there.'

They smiled at each other and a layer of tension seemed to lift.

Ginny stroked a piece of azure-blue silk. What could possibly represent the breakdown of a twenty-five-year-long marriage? She now understood Edna's desire to use muted colours.

Eventually, she cut out a red satin heart and then sliced it in two, using thick black stitches to sew the pieces onto the silk. Its meaning might be literal but it was how she felt. Adrian had sent her a wink, thinking it was to a stranger.

Eric took out his tin and used it to mark a semicircle on yellow fabric. After cutting it out, he attached it to a blue and green background, so it looked like the sun setting behind a hill. He painted a stick man and a dog on the top of it.

Edna embroidered a daisy, using white satin for the petals and a cluster of small buttons for the centre.

Heather cut out the word *MUM* in pink fabric and sewed it onto a piece of denim.

Curtis's effort had an air of punk rock. He cut out white rectangles and black letters that spelled STOP.

'It looks a bit like a blackmail letter,' Ginny said.

'Yeah, or a command.' He stared at it blankly.

'What does it mean?'

'Nada,' he said gruffly. 'Zero. It's just a word.'

Ginny could tell he wasn't telling the truth.

Nico joined in and made a block, too. He created the silhouette of a woman's side profile and used brown thread for her hair. He embroidered the name *Maria* under it.

Looking at it, Ginny felt envious that Adrian would never do anything so creative or romantic for her. His demonstrativeness was more practical, making sure her car was valeted and clean and that the MOT was up-to-date. Was it wrong to ache for more passion between them?

No one other than Edna spoke about their heartbreak as they worked, yet there was a new sense of purpose among them all, as if sewing was enough for now.

The beige dog they'd met outside the chapel on the hill appeared and settled down at Eric's feet. Eric tossed a whittled stick and the dog brought it back in his mouth.

Nico fetched coffee and small beige biscuits that were the same shade as the dog.

'What's the dog's name?' Eric asked Nico.

Nico shrugged. 'He does not belong to anybody.'

Eric picked up a biscuit. 'What are these called?'

'Biscotto for one, biscotti for more than one.'

Eric rubbed the dog under its chin. 'Hey, boy, do you like the name biscotti?'

The dog wagged its tail.

It was the most Ginny had heard Eric say and it was nice to see his eyes crinkling as he smiled. Perhaps the quilting was helping him after all. Or was it the dog?

They all sewed until the sun grew high in the afternoon sky and Ginny felt her skin tingle with the heat. Red patches formed on her shoulders and décolletage. She carried her completed block over to Edna who stitched it next to one of Daisy's. Curtis, Heather, Nico and Eric finished their pieces, too.

Eric continued to toss sticks for Biscotti. The dog bounded after them and returned, panting. Nico brought him a bowl of water and scraps of food.

Edna held up the quilt so they could all admire it. It had grown in size, big enough to become one side of a pillowcase. A sense of pride crept over Ginny and she noticed the others wore satisfied expressions, too.

There was a new brightness in Edna's eyes and a curve to her lips. A breeze started up, scattering a few reels of cotton and causing the quilt to flap in her hands. 'It needs a lot more work, but I think Daisy would love it so far,' she said.

'We've got over two weeks of the holiday left,' Ginny said. 'Plenty of time to make more blocks.'

'I will make the coffee,' Nico said, going back inside.

Eric threw a stick again. A gust of wind caught it and blew it in Edna's direction. Biscotti ran to retrieve it and caught sight of the fluttering quilt. He jumped up, sunk his teeth into the fabric and tried to tug it from Edna's hands.

'Hey, stop that.' Ginny reached out to grab it back.

Biscotti thought she was playing a game. He snatched the quilt from Edna's hands and ran across the courtyard, dragging it with him.

'Somebody stop him,' Edna cried out.

Eric stood up and held out a hand, walking very slowly towards his new friend. 'Hey, boy. Drop that. It's not yours.'

Biscotti came to a standstill and wagged his tail. His jaws remained clamped around the fabric.

'He probably speaks the Italian lingo,' Curtis said. 'We need Nico.'

Ginny sped inside and grabbed Nico's arm. 'Please, come quickly. We need you.'

'*Fermo*, sit,' Nico said, when he saw what was happening. '*Bravo cane.*'

He and Eric slowly approached Biscotti from opposite sides of the courtyard with their arms outstretched. '*Bravo cane, bravo cane,*' they chanted.

Biscotti looked from one of them to the other, until Nico made a lunge forward. The dog jumped and ran away at full pelt, dragging the quilt behind him.

Edna got to her feet and almost fell over in her haste. 'No. Stop him.'

Eric and Nico ran along the road after the dog, until all three of them vanished into the undergrowth.

The tendons in Edna's neck strained. 'Daisy . . .' she spluttered.

Ginny wrapped an arm around her shoulder. 'It's okay. Don't worry. We'll get it back.'

Edna jerked away from her touch. 'This is all your fault . . . I shouldn't have told you anything.'

'I'm sorry, Edna . . .' Ginny said. 'I thought it would help you to talk about things.'

'It's ruined *everything*.'

When Nico arrived back, he stood with his hands on his knees trying to catch his breath. 'Sorry Edna, we could not reach him.'

Eric's mouth was contorted so he looked almost as distraught as Edna. 'I promise to find your quilt,' he said.

Heather, Curtis and Ginny looked doubtfully at each other. Their own stories were part of the fabric, too.

Edna's hands shook as she gathered her thread and needles together. She stuffed everything into her bag and left the courtyard without saying another word.

Later that evening, Edna took her dinner in her room while the others ate together around Nico's dining table in subdued silence.

When the evaluation forms arrived under Ginny's door that night, Edna's heartache score had risen again, from a seven back up to a ten, and she hadn't written a single word.

CHAPTER 17

Costume

Stage Four. Depression, reflection, loneliness.

You may feel like you're in a boat on your own entering the Tunnel of Love at a fairground. You don't have a partner sitting beside you, so you feel deeply lonely. The darkness stretches ahead and you can only see vague reflections in the water. You can't get out, so you need to let the ride pull you along.

The morning after the quilt incident, Ginny sat on the edge of her bed and felt lower than she had in days. Just as Edna had begun to open up, she had closed back shut like a Venus flytrap. Ginny had only tried to be caring, showing an interest in her life, and now felt like she'd made things worse.

It made her miss Phoebe dreadfully and, wanting to hear a friendly voice from home, she gave her a call.

Phoebe didn't pick up and a few seconds later a text arrived.

> Hi Mum, sorry can't speak. Got an appointment. Call you
> later. Hope you're having fun xx

Ginny lowered her phone and wanted something else to lift her mood. She decided to listen to music and opened the Talk Heart FM website.

The message about Ginny taking time off remained, though her photograph had been replaced by the person hired to cover her show.

A smiling young woman with a mass of curls, wearing ripped jeans and a black PVC bra top, made a heart with her hands. The caption said *Kizzi Keeps it 100.*

A Twitter feed at the bottom of the page featured a tweet from Tam.

> Blessed for Kizzi Matthews to join the Talk Heart FM squad.
> Gotta problem? Kizzi keeps it real #advice #allthefeels
> #livecalls

Ginny's face crumpled. Her head and shoulders felt heavy and she crashed back onto the mattress, staring up at the ceiling. Her temporary replacement was prettier, younger and cooler than her. Who would her listeners prefer? Were they even missing her or wondering how she was?

She muttered to herself about her own years of experience and searched for more information about Kizzi. The younger woman had a degree in psychology and counselling, and certificates in sex education, healthy eating and personal training. She'd recently passed her motorcycle test.

Ginny ground her teeth. She imagined herself as a disused car in a scrapyard, whose only use was for spare parts, and a gloominess descended upon her that made her room appear darker. She was glumly scrolling through shopping sites on her phone when a message arrived.

It was from Adrian on ChainReaxions.

Ginny's heart began to pound and she sat bolt upright on the bed. A green dot on the website told her Adrian was currently online and available to chat. Her heart raced as she read his message.

Hi, Jenny. Thanks for the wink. How are you?

Ginny squeezed her phone so tightly her knuckles cracked. A range of emotions whirled around inside her, excitement and intrigue followed by an overwhelming sadness that her husband was chatting to her through a dating app. Although she wanted to reprimand him for not answering her calls and texts, she needed to remain undercover.

Fine thanks, she replied. Though I admit I have no idea what I'm doing on here. It's a new thing for me, kind of alien.

I like your honesty, Adrian said.

I feel the same way. Connecting used to start with a smile and coffee. Or does that make me sound old?

Honesty? Ginny sighed at the irony of his word. She moved over to the window and leaned against the sill.

It makes you sound like a human being, she texted back.

Good, because I am one. Well, the last time I checked ☺ Adrian said.

Glad to hear you're not a robot, Ginny replied.

So, how's your Sunday going? Do you kick-start it with waffles, newspapers or strong coffee?

Ginny wasn't sure what day it was. Her first week in Italy had whizzed by and she'd lost track of time.

All three served at once, please, she replied.

Actually, I think the word kick-start should be banned during the weekend. What's wrong with a leisurely pace?

Nothing. It should be obligatory.

A couple of minutes passed before Adrian messaged her again.

I need to be honest with you, Jenny. I'm still married, so understand if you don't want to talk to me.

Ginny frowned and considered his words. If she told Adrian it was okay to continue, was it like giving him permission to cheat? On the other hand, she didn't want to say no. She thought carefully before replying.

What would your wife think about it?

I think she lost interest in me some time ago, he said.

Ouch. Ginny's mouth dried instantly. She'd never grown bored of Adrian. Had she really given him that impression? He hadn't exactly made her feel desirable either. Her neck stiffened and she stared out of the window.

While she was considering how to reply, Adrian messaged again.

We split up very recently and I've moved out of our home, he said.

I'm feeling useless and unnecessary right now.

Ginny felt a weird mix of empathy and anger towards him that she struggled to contain.

Perhaps your wife feels the same way, too, she said.

Maybe. She's a good person and a great mother, but I've kind of lost myself as an individual over the years. What's your situation?

Ginny's face fell. Why hadn't she detected that Adrian felt

this way? Although he didn't tell her things like this, she prided herself on her ability to read people's emotions.

Now that she was in Italy, on vacation with strangers, visiting galleries, shops and gardens in Florence, eating gorgeous food, hiking and soaking up the beautiful scenery and learning to sew, her problems felt muted and further away. Even the low times were being bolstered by the sunshine. Perhaps it had taken Adrian leaving her to push them both out of their comfort zones.

I guess I'm in a similar situation to you, she replied.

Sometimes I feel like I'm wearing a costume, trying to be what others want me to be, rather than my true self. Or, is that too deep?

I totally understand! I sell cars for a living. I smile and talk about the weather and golf and new restaurants, anything to clinch a sale. It's like selling a piece of my soul.

Ginny nodded in agreement.

It's my job to help others and I'm happy to give them my all, but because I appear confident, people rarely ask how I'm feeling.

So, how are you? Adrian asked. Tell me.

Ginny closed her eyes, listening to the birds singing outside. Talking to her husband in this way was exactly what she'd wanted for a long time. It was what she needed.

You really want to know?

Yes

She inhaled deeply. They hadn't spoken to each other in this way for ages. They'd been together for over three decades and it was taking an ocean between them and anonymity to allow them both to open up. Perhaps if they'd *really* talked to each other properly and sooner, they wouldn't be in this mess.

I've devoted years of my life to someone I thought I'd be with forever. Now he says he wants to start afresh and the longer we're apart, the more confused I feel. It's making me rethink my entire life.

I can relate to that, Adrian replied.

The worrying thing is, I'm enjoying doing things without him. Do you have any regrets about leaving?

Some. I could have been kinder. (Told you I was human). I didn't want to hurt anyone. I just wanted to think about myself for once.

Ginny rubbed her neck.

Do you think you'll change your mind?

Things happen for a reason, he said. Perhaps we should change the subject?

She wanted to know his answer to her question, but didn't want to derail their conversation.

Sure. That's a good idea, she said.

Okay! What's the best thing in your life right now?

His words made memories appear in Ginny's head, about a game she and Adrian used to play when they'd first started dating. They spent hours asking each other about their favourite cheeses or films. Who was the best James Bond and who was the worst? Was Gorgonzola better than Edam? Would you prefer to have legs for arms, or a big toe for a nose? His question was something she could answer easily.

My daughter, she replied. She's getting married soon.

Hey! Mine, too. I miss her a lot. The house feels empty without her.

I know the feeling. It's like a chapter of my life has ended. Sorry if that sounds melodramatic.

It's because you care, he said. **We sound like similar people.**

Yes, we do.

Ginny rubbed her forehead, battling an urge to reveal her true identity. As the words queued up on her tongue, she mulled over the consequences, reminding herself how Adrian had treated her. When she thought about his pierced ear and his refusal to go on holiday, a vein in her forehead throbbed. What on earth was she doing, talking to him like this? What was *he* doing?

A knock on her bedroom door made her jump to attention. She cocked her head and her heart pounded. When the rapping came again, she messaged Adrian back.

Sorry, got to go.

Speak later? I like talking to you x

Me, too x, she said.

Ginny felt flustered, like a teenager who'd been caught with a boy in her bedroom. She smoothed a hand through her hair before she opened her door.

Nico stood on the landing with his hands clasped in front of him. 'Would you like coffee?' he asked.

'I'm okay, thanks. I have some water.'

Nico didn't move. His brow creased and he took a few seconds to speak again. 'This is not only about the coffee. I'd like to talk to you.'

As Ginny closed her door and followed him downstairs, she felt even more like an errant teenager. Had she been overly noisy or broken something?

Nico took forever to make two cappuccinos. He took the seat opposite at the dining table and held her gaze for too long. 'Are you happy with your holiday?' he asked.

Ginny wrapped her fingers around the cup. She'd read somewhere that Italians preferred to drink cappuccino before eleven o'clock in the morning so she was glad to be within the deadline. 'Yes, I'm having a nice time and I think the others are, too. Though it's a shame about Edna's quilt.'

'I hope we can find it for her.'

They sipped their coffees and Ginny heard a clock ticking.

Eventually, Nico leaned in. 'May I talk to you about something . . . sensitive?'

Ginny nodded, a little apprehensive of what it might be. 'Sure.'

He cleared his throat. 'It is about Loretta. She is now talking about going to the college in Milan, instead of Bologna, and I did not expect this. Milan is much further away and . . .' He let out a sigh. 'Sorry, I have no one else to talk to.'

'I'm guessing she still has plenty of time to decide. Do you want her to stay in Vigornuovo?' Ginny asked.

'Not if she does not want to. I want her to follow her heart. I had a dream that one day Loretta, Maria and I would run Splendido together, as a family again. Soon, there will only be me left.'

'It sounds like that's your dream and not Loretta's.'

He nodded. 'You are right and I have to let it go. If I ask Loretta anything, she will not tell me her full plans.'

Ginny could understand how he felt. Her own dream of spending the rest of her life with Adrian had shattered, too. She'd experienced Phoebe's sullen teenage years and knew they could be draining. She rubbed her neck guiltily when she remembered Loretta creeping across the landing in the early morning and pressing her finger to her lips. A moped had roared off into the distance and Ginny had kept hold of the secret. Could a new boyfriend be behind Loretta's plan to go to Milan? 'Is she dating anyone at the moment?' she asked.

Nico shook his head. 'There have been two or three boys – one of them still sends her flowers. Loretta broke their hearts,' he said. 'I want to know she is making good choices. She will be eighteen next week and I don't even know what she wants to do for her birthday.'

'What date is it?' Ginny asked, sipping her coffee.

'The twenty-eighth of June.'

The same day as my wedding anniversary, she thought to herself. Not that she'd be celebrating it. 'Have you asked her?'

'Each year, Loretta makes a joke and says she wants a slumber party. She had one with her mother once, before Maria left.' Nico flicked his hand. 'It is something for small children, an American thing.'

Ginny tried to think of a good way forward. 'I can speak to Loretta, though it may seem strange if I spark up a conversation out of the blue.'

'It could make her suspicious.'

'Maybe we could go to the village together, one day.'

Nico's eyes lit up. 'There is a market on Wednesday and I need tomatoes.'

'I can ask Loretta to take me.'

'This is a very good plan,' he said. 'Thank you. I'm sorry to ask you to do this.'

'It will be fun to go there with her,' Ginny said. 'I'm not sure if she'll open up to me though.'

'You are very good with people. I see why your friends like you very much.'

Ginny supposed that he meant Eric, Heather, Edna and Curtis and his compliment gave her a welcome lift. 'I haven't known them for long,' she said. 'We were all strangers before coming here.'

'You did not meet them before?' Nico frowned at her. 'You are paying for their holiday?'

'Yes.' Ginny couldn't think of an abbreviated version of her story, so she told him the full thing, starting with how Adrian had left her. She explained how she'd discovered his dating profile on a website, and that she'd invited strangers to join her in Italy, via her radio show. She wondered if the mysterious Miss Peach had any idea she'd been such a catalyst for change in the Splinter household. 'I was supposed to visit Italy with my husband instead.' She sighed.

'You have done a very kind thing.'

She gave an impromptu laugh. 'It is the silliest thing.'

'No.' Nico looked at Ginny as if she was an unexpected, lovely birthday present. 'You are a very special lady.'

And for the next few minutes in his presence, Ginny felt like she was.

CHAPTER 18

Tomatoes

For the next couple of days, Ginny felt as if someone had removed her brain and replaced it with mashed potatoes. She spent most of her time sitting and reading in the courtyard. Whenever she thought about her contact with Adrian on ChainReaxions, her emotions slid around. One minute she was angry and upset, and the next she felt more connected to him than she had in a long time. Hopefully their situation was a blip in their marriage rather than a roadblock. She reminded herself that no one was perfect and that good people made mistakes.

She just wished Adrian wasn't continuing to make them by confiding in a stranger. What if he hadn't selected Ginny to chat with and had connected with someone else instead? What if he was chatting to other women in addition to Jenny?

Ginny didn't know how to, or if she should, reveal her identity to him, and if he'd find it deceptive or funny. Hopefully he'd take it as proof they were made for each other and should get back together.

She hummed a song she remembered from her childhood,

about a bored couple who each turn to the personal column in a newspaper for some excitement. They talk about loving piña coladas, getting caught in the rain and making love at midnight without realizing they're liaising with each other. There was a happy ending to the song, and she hoped there'd be one for her and Adrian, too.

She tried to focus on Nico's kind words to her, about her being special. He was a thoughtful person and Ginny had started to see Splendido through his eyes. The tired parts of the hotel made it seem more charming, a nice escape from the modernity of her home and radio studio in England.

As she waited to meet Loretta in the courtyard, a message came through on her phone.

I've been thinking about you, Adrian said to Jenny.

Ginny's skin tingled all over. It was ironic that being far apart made the two of them feel closer than ever.

Me, too, she replied.

She lowered her phone when she saw Loretta striding towards her. The teenager had a hand stuck to one hip.

'Papà says I have to go shopping with you,' Loretta said with a pout. She wasn't wearing a scrap of make-up and her hair was pulled into a messy ponytail. She wore a loose beige dress and a tiny eye pendant shone around her neck. 'He has even given me a list.'

Ginny felt a little sorry for her. Loretta's frown was too old for a girl of seventeen to wear. She remembered Phoebe's own teenage years well, when anything she or Adrian said was met with a shrug and an eye roll. Things must be difficult for Loretta without her mother around. 'I'd love to see more of

157

the village and I bet you have insider knowledge,' she said. 'Your dad always seems very busy.'

Loretta flicked her ponytail. 'Yes, he is,' she said. 'I'm glad I'm not the only one who thinks this. Come with me.' She led the way around the side of the hotel where a shiny blue moped sat in the shade. She handed a helmet to Ginny and flung her leg over the vehicle.

Ginny stood there motionless. She hadn't been on a bike since Phoebe was a toddler, never mind one with an engine. She told herself that if Kizzi Matthews could ride a motorcycle, so could she.

'Come on,' Loretta said. 'Hold onto my waist.'

Ginny climbed on board and found it thrilling to feel every lump and bump on the road. She laughed out loud and clung on with the wind ruffling her hair. Loretta shouted out '*Ciao*,' and waved to people as they passed by.

'Thank you for not telling Papà about me coming home late,' Loretta shouted over her shoulder. She deftly swerved to avoid a cat.

'There's nothing to tell. I don't know where you'd been.'

'Papà wouldn't like it if he knew.'

They parked on a side street close to the town hall where Ginny could already hear chatter and smell delicious food aromas. She glimpsed rows of market stalls lining the square.

Loretta took off her helmet and shook her hair. 'Papà is protective. Sometimes I feel like a bird in a cage that isn't allowed to fly.'

'He only wants what's best for you, and to be sure that studying in Milan is the right option for you.'

'He has told you this?' Loretta raised both eyebrows. 'I will not know what is right or wrong for me until I try it. Has he asked you to spy on me?'

Ginny thought it was better to tell the truth. She pinched her thumb and forefinger together in the air. 'Maybe a little.'

The teenager twitched a smile. 'I am bored of living in the same place and doing the same things. Papà has to accept this. Splendido is stuck in time and I no longer want to study fashion. I try to explain this to him, but he does not listen.'

'You *are* only seventeen . . .' Ginny stopped herself from saying more. She'd only been a year older than Loretta when she'd told her mum that she was in love with Adrian Splinter.

Ginny's mum had tutted in response. 'You're too young to say things like that. There are millions of people in the world. Don't commit to one of them so quickly.'

'Love isn't a decision, like choosing a library book,' Ginny had argued. 'It's a chemical reaction.'

'That's the voice of youth, right there,' her mum had said with a sharp laugh. 'You'll live and learn.'

Ginny was certain that loving someone for a lifetime was possible, and she'd been proof of it until Adrian had stamped on her heart.

She followed Loretta towards the bustling market. Vigornuovo village square had become a community gathering space. The stalls all had white canopies and there was much laughter and sharing of recipes. All the fruit and vegetables looked plumper and more vibrant than in any English super-market and loaves were the size of small pillows. Ginny could smell fresh herbs and the sharp tang of vinegar.

Loretta chatted with a stallholder in Italian and pointed to a red pepper. 'Has Papà told you about my mother?' she asked Ginny.

'Only a little.'

'She left three years ago, yet Papà still waits for her to come back. He won't change anything, about the hotel or himself, until she returns. It's like he needs her permission to move on.'

Ginny didn't want to pry but wanted to understand. 'Why did she leave?'

'Work.' Loretta's face clouded. 'Mamma wanted Papà to renovate the hotel and Nonna wanted him to keep it exactly the same, so Papà was caught between them. Mamma said my nonna acted like Papà's wife, not like his mother.'

'And what did *he* want?'

'To please them both. It was an impossible task. How can you please others until you please yourself first?' She headed towards another stall. 'After Nonna died, Mamma soon realized she and Papà couldn't afford to transform Splendido. She took up a job as a hotel manager in Naples, a long way away, vowing to return when she'd earned enough money to update our hotel. I stayed with her a few times, and she kept in touch with Papà, but when the pandemic came it meant we could not see her for many months and our calls grew fewer. I think Mamma liked her new life alone and decided to stay in Naples. It is like she has forgotten she has a family at home.

'Papà blames himself and hopes she will return to Vigornuovo one day, but I know she never will. I wish she would tell him the truth and I have taken down photographs of her from the hallway. Papà keeps them in his room instead.'

Ginny wanted to give Loretta a hug but the teenager's eyes were defiant. She weaved her way around the shoppers in the market and Ginny struggled to keep up.

She noticed young men coyly glancing at Loretta, while others were more obvious with their stares. However, the teenager was oblivious to their attention. Loretta bought some big juicy tomatoes and they ate them as they walked.

Ginny sensed she should change the subject. 'Your dad told me it's your birthday soon and he doesn't know what you want.'

Loretta finished her tomato. 'I want to celebrate with my friends, perhaps a nice lunch at Castello Bella Vista. When Mamma was here, we once had a slumber party, watching films in our pyjamas and eating pizza. It was fun.'

A man selling olives said something to Loretta in Italian and winked. She shook a finger at him and held up Ginny's hand, showing off her wedding ring. 'Tsk.'

'What did he say?' Ginny whispered.

'He said you are beautiful and ripe, like the grapes used for finest wine.'

Ginny didn't know whether to be flattered or offended. She felt her cheeks burning.

Loretta nudged her arm. 'Come on, we have lots to buy,' she said.

They strolled around the market armed with Nico's shopping list, buying bread, strawberries, cherries and carrots. Ginny didn't know how they'd possibly carry everything back on the moped.

Loretta pushed her purse into her bag and fixed her eyes

on a boy leaning against a red moped. '*Un momento*,' she said to Ginny. 'There is someone I want to speak to.'

Ginny rearranged her shopping bags while Loretta and the boy chatted and laughed together. Could this be a boyfriend the teenager didn't want Nico to know about? They looked very close.

'There is somewhere I need to go,' Loretta said when she returned. 'Can you make your own way back to the hotel?'

Ginny looked around her blankly. It would be a long walk back in this heat, carrying all their shopping. She doubted Nico would be impressed if she returned without his daughter.

'A bus stops outside the town hall in five minutes,' Loretta said. 'It will take you close to Splendido.'

'What shall I tell your dad?'

Loretta walked backwards and performed an exaggerated shrug. 'Tell him I need to live my life and he should start to live his, too.'

The bus Ginny caught was packed so full of people she had to stand in the aisle and couldn't see her whereabouts through the windows properly. She got off too soon and had to walk a third of a mile back. By the time she reached Splendido, her back and forehead were sticky and her arms felt stretched from carrying the shopping.

She set the bags down in Nico's kitchen, hoping he wouldn't worry when he saw she was alone. The hotel was strangely quiet for lunchtime, though Ginny could hear a man talking. Curtis was lurking around at the end of the hallway on his own. He didn't notice her and stood in front of Nico's family photos while speaking into his phone. He moved along the hallway into the dining room, picking up and examining Nico's pink vase and cushions and making more voice notes.

Something felt amiss and Ginny stepped back so he wouldn't see her. She couldn't make out his words and he eventually made his way outside. He stood in the courtyard looking up at the hotel with his phone still pressed to his lips.

As Ginny watched him through the window, she felt like she was witnessing a crime taking place without knowing what it was. What on earth was he up to? She waited until Curtis left the courtyard before she went outside, too.

A bark interrupted her thoughts and Biscotti appeared from behind the minibus. He had a stick in his mouth and scampered past her, disappearing around the corner. She followed him towards a field with grass so dry and yellow it looked like a sandy beach. Several colourful rugs were laid out like towels.

Ginny saw a gorgeous array of food spread out on plates. Juicy purple grapes shone in the sun, and there were two loaves of bread and an array of cheese. She noticed Curtis approaching with a walk so nonchalant it made him appear guilty.

Nico stood up to greet Ginny. 'Where is Loretta?' he asked.

Ginny swallowed. 'She saw a friend at the market and wanted to stay to talk to him.'

'*Him*?' Nico asked. 'Is she okay?'

'She's fine. I caught the bus back.'

He looked crestfallen. 'I have been making a small picnic to celebrate some good news and now Loretta will miss it.'

'We bought some lovely tomatoes and fruit, should I bring them outside?' Ginny asked.

'I will get them. You stay here, so Edna can tell you her good news.'

Edna held up a clump of fabric. 'Eric followed Biscotti this morning and found my quilt,' she called out.

Ginny sat down on the rug next to Edna and slipped off her sandals. She took the quilt from the older lady and examined it. Ginny's block was missing, the one made by Curtis was hanging by a thread and others were torn. The entire thing looked grubby and tattered, but Edna's eyes were shiny.

'We can all make new pieces,' Edna said loudly, making it sound like a command rather than a request.

'I will clean the quilt with soap and water,' Nico said, reappearing with more food. 'The washing machines at Grand Hotel Castello Bella Vista will surely ruin the delicate fabric.'

'Thank you kindly,' Edna said.

They all ate in the sunshine and Ginny could sense their moods lifting once more. She laughed at Eric and Biscotti running around together in circles.

Heather shuffled a pack of tarot cards, drawing different ones from the pack and referring to a book. She seemed to be willing certain ones to turn up. 'I bought them in Florence,' she said, noticing Ginny's interest.

'Do you believe in fortune telling?'

Heather cocked her head. 'I never used to. I mean, how can random cards predict your future? They're interesting though, supposed to have originated in Northern Italy during the late fourteenth or early fifteenth century. People have used them for years, so there *must* be some reason they're enduring,' she said, her voice full of hope.

Ginny didn't really believe in them, but she did wonder about her future. 'Can you do a small reading for me?' she asked.

'I'll try. I'm not totally au fait with them yet.' Heather handed the deck to Ginny. 'Shuffle them and think of a question.'

Ginny moved them around a little and handed them back.

Heather slid three cards off the top of the deck: the King of Pentacles, the Fool and the Lovers. She referred to her book and tapped on the King first. 'He's supposed to be an inspirational man who offers you good counsel. He is a faithful provider and represents security. The Fool is the next card and I think that's you.'

Ginny barked a laugh. 'Thanks.'

Heather shook her head. 'The Fool means you're on the path of an exciting, unexpected new venture. You will need to make a leap of faith to benefit from this new experience. The Fool has the potential of a new-born baby.' She picked up the third card and read her book again. 'The Lovers represent love, harmony, aligning values and choices. It's all there waiting for you to embrace it.'

'Do the cards refer to my husband?' Ginny asked, thinking there was no one else they could possibly relate to.

'I think that's for you to interpret.'

The truth was, Ginny just didn't know. The three cards had left her feeling more confused. 'Have you done your own reading?'

'The tarot hasn't been very obliging.' Heather drew the Four of Swords out of the deck for herself. 'It usually means rest, relaxation and recuperation,' she said.

'Usually?'

Heather grimaced as she returned the card. 'It was upside down so its meaning is reversed. It represents exhaustion, burnout and deep contemplation. It indicates that it's time to retreat to face challenges.' She puffed out her chest, and raised her voice so everyone could hear her. 'It's probably all nonsense and not correct. I'm all about positivity and strength. In fact, I've been organizing our next activity. I've chosen something that will soothe our souls and warm our hearts.'

'Sounds like we're making soup,' Curtis quipped.

When Eric laughed at his joke, Curtis's cheeks flushed with pleasure.

'You'll need to wear loose clothing and keep an open mind. We're all going to the Grand Hotel Castello Bella Vista for gong therapy on Friday. The soundwaves are supposed to cleanse your body of negative energy.'

'Wha—?' Curtis started to say.

'You should come, too, Nico.' Heather nodded at him.

Nico brusquely gathered some of their plates and glasses together, making a din. 'I am very busy,' he said.

'I think Loretta would like you to go,' Ginny said. 'She mentioned having a birthday meal there with friends and you could check the place out.'

Nico's knuckles whitened as he gripped the crockery. He appeared to wrangle with his thoughts, until he gave a short nod. 'If my daughter wants this, I will go, too.'

That evening, Ginny returned to her room to find that Adrian had sent her another message.

Rum and cola, or vodka and orange? he asked. **Would you**

rather be invisible, or be able to fly? Would you jump one year forward, or a year back in time?

Rum please, but I never drink and fly, Ginny replied.

She pondered over his next question for a while. Would she go back in time, to try to turn things around with him, or would she speed forwards twelve months to see how everything turned out?

Before she could reply, Adrian got back in touch.

Great answer, he said. Want to meet up for that rum one day? No flying required.

Ginny pressed a hand to her chest, thinking about the Lovers tarot card.

I think that would be very interesting, she said.

Great. Looking forward to it.

Me, too.

Let's make it soon, he said.

Good night, Adrian x

Sweet dreams, Jenny x

CHAPTER 19

Gongs

Nico

Nico stood outside Grand Hotel Castello Bella Vista and toyed with a coin in his jacket pocket. It had been two days since Heather announced they were coming here and he'd struggled to sleep since.

He'd only entered the hotel once before, on Gianfranco's opening day. It had been a few months after Maria left him and Nico had felt glum, surrounded by all the gold balloon arches and champagne chilling in silver buckets.

A Glorious Escape had just premiered in cinemas worldwide and Gianfranco had hired a multitude of singers and dancers to perform numbers from the film as he opened his hotel doors for the first time. He'd insisted that he'd seen Tim Vincenzo among the guests and Nico had scowled at the thought of the actor staring at Loretta again.

Nico was proud of his friend's achievements, so he hated how his envy took over when Gianfranco gushed about his sauna and whirlpool baths, his massage tables and the fluffy white robes he'd personally sourced from Rome.

Nico's mamma had vehemently opposed Gianfranco's renovation, writing objection letters from her bed. She could see the building work from the window of her bedroom. 'You must never ruin Splendido in this way, my son,' she'd said.

'I give you my promise,' he'd replied.

Nico's thoughts were brought back to the present by Gianfranco dropping an arm around his shoulder. 'I would love you to see my new spa,' his friend said. 'In my humble expert opinion, it is the best in Bologna, maybe even the whole of Italy. I want your blessing more than anything.'

Nico battled with his conscience. He pictured himself closing his mamma's curtains after she'd passed away. 'Your hotel is truly magnificent,' he said. 'No one would believe you used to kick a football around in the dirt with me. You are now a VIP.'

'The building is grand, not me. Inside, I'm the same small boy who wants to score lots of goals.' Gianfranco's bulldog eyes grew watery. 'I helped to collect your guests from the airport, and picked up the lost suitcase. I offer you advice on Splendido to support you, and my son worked on your website. Please do this one thing for me.'

Nico clicked his tongue. He looked up and saw that a castellation on the roof was missing. It assured him that not everything about the hotel was perfect. 'Yes, I will look at the spa,' he said.

Gianfranco beamed and punched the top of Nico's arm. The two men walked towards the revolving door together. 'I saw you looking at my roof,' Gianfranco said. 'Do not worry about it. My builders will repair it tomorrow.'

When Nico entered the hotel lobby, his eyes widened. Tiny silver specks glittered in the white marble floor and huge Murano glass chandeliers glistened overhead. Cream leather sofas were resplendent with gold cushions and a glamorous lady tinkled tunes on a piano. It all made Nico feel small and inadequate, reminding him again why Maria had left him.

'Tasteful bling,' Gianfranco whispered to him.

Guests floated around wearing handmade leather shoes and designer handbags. Others walked around sporting only white robes and slippers. Nico watched his own guests from the corner of his eye. Like him, they didn't seem to fit in here.

Heather was taking the lead today, bounding about like she was in charge. Ginny reminded him of a small bird, twitchy and glancing around nervously. Eric's walking boots left crumbles of dried mud on the floor that Gianfranco's staff discreetly swept away with silver dustpans and brushes. Curtis's eyes roamed everywhere. He squinted at the label on a cushion and dropped to his knees to examine a rug.

'Do you love my lobby?' Gianfranco asked Nico.

'It reminds me of the *Starship Enterprise*. Remember how you used to pretend to be Captain Kirk and I was Spock?'

Gianfranco choked back a tear. 'There is no bigger compliment,' he said. 'Thank you.'

They walked across the lobby and Nico frowned at a sign.

Massage Envy — Verona Room, Back Lobby Far Right

*Breastfeeding and Feminism International
Conference — Venice Suite, Far Left*

'My workshops and conferences are very popular,' Gianfranco said. 'You should consider hosting them, too.'

'What would I offer?' Nico shrugged.

'You could give cooking lessons, and Loretta could do photography or a fashion masterclass ... .'

'I think she has lost interest in Splendido, just as her mother did.'

'Don't be too sure about that . . .'

Nico halted and stared at his friend. 'What do you mean by *that*?'

Gianfranco clamped his mouth shut. He hurriedly picked up a bowl of oranges off the counter of a bar, tipping them into a machine. Seconds later, fresh juice gushed out and he handed a glass to Nico. 'No peeling or squeezing is necessary,' he mumbled.

Nico sipped his drink and the juice tasted so fresh. When his wife returned, he would buy one of these machines for her. He was about to repeat his question, but noticed his friend was eyeing him intently.

'Are you thinking about Maria again?' Gianfranco asked.

'No,' Nico said, then let out a heavy sigh. 'Yes. I can now see that your hotel is the picture she had in her head. She tried to describe it to me and I couldn't see it.'

Gianfranco patted his shoulder. 'The gongs might help you to feel better.'

'How? What happens?'

'A man hits the gongs and the noise makes you relax . . . I think.'

Nico was none the wiser, but he was willing to give it a try.

★

Ginny, Heather, Edna, Eric and Curtis changed into slippers and white robes for a tour of the spa. Edna's robe reached her ankles and she lifted it, gathering it in her hands as if it was a ball gown.

After a light scalp and hand massage, they sipped glasses of champagne before a member of Gianfranco's team escorted them towards the sound healing room. 'Please wait in the corridor until the session is ready,' she said.

Heather closed her eyes and pressed her hands together. 'I'm getting into my zone,' she said.

Ginny meandered up and down the corridor, looking at the posters for workshops. Ben and Ally Prince had hosted a session here several weeks ago, as part of their *The Power of Two* book tour. A photo showed the couple gazing lovingly into each other's eyes.

Ginny would have loved the opportunity to meet them, to ask the experts about her situation with Adrian. Should she carry on dating him incognito from afar, or should she come clean? Should she give him more space, to decide what he wanted from life, or try to persuade him to come back to her? Advice was so easy to dole out to others and so difficult to give to herself.

She sighed and turned to find Nico standing behind her. 'Are you waiting for the gongs?' he asked.

It sounded so ridiculous they both laughed.

Ginny wasn't sure why she felt so nervous about someone banging shiny circles of metal around her.

The door to the room opened and a man with a topknot and silver beads in his beard bent his head low. 'Namaste,' he said.

Heather repeated his greeting and bowed, too. She bounded into the room with her shoulders back, as if she was running the class.

The corporate grey-carpeted room had been transformed into something resembling a harem. Colourful mats, pillows, blankets and eye masks were strewn on the floor and gongs of many various sizes hung from wooden frames. They reminded Ginny of the gold disks that pop stars used to receive for selling lots of records. There were around twenty people in the room in total.

Heather sat cross-legged on the floor and pulled her feet into the Lotus Pose. Edna allowed Eric to help her settle onto a pile of cushions.

Loretta entered the room and lay on her side with her head resting on her hand. When Nico selected the mat closest to her, she flicked her hand until he moved next to Ginny instead.

Ginny lay down and crossed her arms over her chest like an Egyptian mummy. There was no way Adrian would ever accompany her to anything like this. She was lucky if she could get him to take part in a bar quiz on holiday.

'Namaste. Welcome, my name is Gong Master Leo,' the man with the topknot said. 'The organs and emotions in your body have unique frequencies, working like the strings of a guitar. Over time, factors like stress can cause them to become out of tune. Sound can bring your frequencies back into harmony and get rid of emotional blockages. The vibrations can have a lasting and profound change on your body and mind.'

Loretta giggled and Curtis said something into his phone.

'No electronic devices please,' Leo said. 'It interrupts the energy.'

Heather turned her head to face Ginny. 'I've heard that sometimes people experience visions,' she said. 'Don't worry. It's your energies releasing into the wild.'

Ginny swallowed. She pictured her emotions like a herd of wildebeest rampaging across the carpet and it wasn't pretty.

'Make yourself comfortable and close your eyes,' Leo continued. 'Feel your fingers growing heavy as you start to relax. Today I'm going to be using the gongs, quartz singing bowls, an ocean drum, Peruvian rattles, seed shakers and bamboo rattles. Put your hand on your belly, draw down air to the pelvis and release it slowly through your mouth. Enter a state of stillness and sink into the earth.'

Ginny put on her eye mask and listened to the epic sounds. It was like lying down in an IMAX cinema with noise booming all around her. One gong sounded like an airplane taking off over her head, whereas other ones were gentler, like the tinkle of wind chimes. Leo's instruments conjured up the swish of the ocean and rain tapping against windows.

Gradually, she felt the strangest of sensations overtaking her, a combination of exhilaration and weightlessness, as if she was floating upwards. If the ceiling wasn't there, she would surely drift into the sky. She tried to think about Adrian, picturing him at their dining table eating dinner. His face wouldn't appear in her head and she saw trees and blue skies instead. Losing all track of time, she felt like she was flying above the earth with her arms outstretched. Her body seemed to pixelate and disappear, until she became a wisp of air.

Ginny found herself consumed by uncontrollable laughter and then hot tears streamed down her cheeks, dribbling into her ears.

Five weeks ago, Adrian had told her he wanted a divorce, and now she was surrounded by strangers on the floor listening to gongs. She had no idea where she was headed next in her life, and she was being accompanied on her journey by a tarot-reading teacher, a monosyllabic hiker, a quilt-making widow, and a secretive man-child. It made her laugh and cry even more. Her feelings were a messy jumble, clamouring to be let out, and she emitted a low howling noise.

The gong sounds eventually dispersed and the room slowly came back into focus. Ginny wondered if her guests had been affected in a similar way to her, too.

She removed her eye mask and felt like everyone was staring at her. Leo cast her a knowing smile. Oddly, she was the most concerned about what Nico must think of her behaviour. She stood up and wiped her eyes on her sleeve, her tears still pouring.

A hand touched her shoulder and there he was, with his chocolate-brown eyes and kind smile. 'Are you okay?' Nico asked.

She appreciated his concern and the others gathered around her, too.

Ginny shook her head, wanting to disappear. 'No, I'm not okay,' she sniffed, her emotions still releasing. She needed to be strong for the others but was failing miserably, letting them all down. 'My husband has left me and is cheating on me. I thought we'd be together forever.'

'There, there.' Heather handed her a tissue. 'I'm so sorry.'

Ginny balled the tissue in her fist and was unable to stop her words from flooding out. 'I'm dating him online and he doesn't even know it's me.'

Curtis stared at her in bewilderment. *'For real?* How does that work?'

Heather nudged him in his ribs.

'We're both liaising on a dating site and getting along well, rediscovering our connection. But it's all built on lies. I've been pretending to be someone else, but I want Adrian to love me again for *me*,' Ginny said.

Heather pulled her closer and made soothing noises. 'Oh, honey, you deserve better than this. Hang on in there.'

Edna pursed her lips. 'You should never settle.'

Ginny caught Eric's eye, expecting him to look away, but he smiled at her sympathetically.

They all edged closer together, until they formed a clump of white-robed, broken people. Hesitantly, they wrapped their arms around each other to form a protective circle.

Only Curtis loitered on the outskirts, circling his bald spot with a finger. He opened his mouth, as if considering what to say next. 'Looks like we all need to get a grip,' he said eventually.

When no one laughed and Edna glared at him, he tightened the belt on his robe. He stepped forwards, reaching past Heather, and placed his hand on Ginny's shoulder. 'Let's be honest here,' he said solemnly. 'Your husband sounds like a right douchebag.'

Everyone froze until Ginny broke the silence with a chortle.

'I think you're right. He wasn't always like this,' she said, starting to cry again. But this time her sadness was mixed with laughter. She didn't feel so alone with her problems any longer. In fact, her shoulders felt much lighter. 'I'm so pleased you're all here with me.'

Between a gap in the bodies around her, Ginny saw Gianfranco take Nico's arm and lead him away. She overheard his next words.

'If you charge higher prices, you will get better guests,' Gianfranco told his friend. 'Ones that are less strange.'

CHAPTER 20

Roses

After leaving the gong room and the security of the group hug, Ginny's head felt floaty. Gianfranco led her and the others towards an area with white leather sofas arranged in a circle. Cups of mint tea awaited them, and a huge bowl of fruit sat on a wooden table that looked like a log sawn in half.

They each sat down, sipped their teas and smiled meekly at each other while Gianfranco and Nico hovered around in the background. Now that Ginny had revealed her heartache and her subsequent liaison with Adrian in full, the atmosphere between them all felt warm and close. 'Does anyone else want to talk about why they're here?' she asked.

Heather nursed her cup to her chest and took a long, deep breath before speaking. 'Now that you've opened up, Ginny, I feel able to share my story, too.' She gnawed her lip a little. 'My mum has dementia and doesn't recognize me most of the time. I've tried therapies and positive thinking, but they're failing and so am I. Mum's turning into a different person and I just feel so helpless to do anything about it . . .'

Edna nodded with understanding. 'A couple of my friends have dementia and it's so difficult to cope with. Please don't punish yourself, it sounds like you're doing the best you can.' Her voice trailed away and her knuckles whitened as she clasped her hands together in her lap. 'I just feel so terribly lonely and afraid. I'm at the age where I might not wake up one morning, or even know if I want to. Would anyone even notice or care that I'd gone? What do I bring to the world any longer?'

'Many wonderful things, Edna,' Ginny said firmly. 'Including creativity and great wisdom.'

Heather nodded in agreement.

Eric gave his beard an awkward rub. 'I really miss Bess,' he murmured.

'Pets are family,' Edna assured him.

Curtis leaned down and readjusted the cuff of his sock.

Gianfranco broke the moment with a cough and he hurriedly handed out price lists for treatments. 'What do you want to do next?' he asked. 'Any friend of Nico's is a friend of mine. I will give you all fift— um, thirty-five per cent off any spa activities.'

He fixed his eyes on Heather. 'For you, madame, I recommend our yoga classes, or maybe Pilates. You, sir,' he nodded at Curtis. 'I think you would enjoy our signature manicure.'

Eric shrank back in his seat until Gianfranco pointed at one of the windows. 'A walk in the extensive grounds of my hotel is good for the soul.' He turned to Edna next. 'In my ballroom there is a live band playing music, accompanied by tea and cakes.'

While they all browsed the treatment lists, Nico whispered

to Gianfranco. 'How do you know what my guests will like? It's as though you can read their minds.'

Gianfranco shook his head. 'It is not magic. I just look at the people. The man with the long blond hair has tanned skin and his hands are rugged, so I can tell he will enjoy being outdoors. The elderly lady has fine bone structure and a genteel manner so she will like elegant entertainment. The man with the black hair and thick eyebrows dyes his hair so he will probably enjoy a manicure.' He nodded towards Heather. 'She has the word *peace* on her necklace, so I think she will like spiritual activities.'

'This is very clever,' Nico said.

'It is something I can teach you.'

'I want to do things my own way.' Nico's gaze settled upon Ginny. 'You didn't mention the other lady.'

Gianfranco surreptitiously looked at her and frowned. 'She is more difficult to read, like a book when you don't quite understand the story.' He cleared his throat to address her. 'Do any of my treatments interest you?' he asked.

Ginny stared at the list. 'There are so many things,' she said. 'Maybe too many.'

'Impossible.' Gianfranco laughed heartily.

Ginny shivered when she thought about the wedding vow renewal ceremony she'd hoped to share with Adrian. Perhaps seeing the venue would help her finally accept it wasn't going to happen. 'I believe you host weddings and celebrations here,' she said tentatively.

Gianfranco nodded. 'Would you like to see the room? It is truly magnificent.'

'Please. I'd like that.'

Ginny felt like she was betraying Nico by showing interest in another man's hotel. She didn't meet his eyes as she exited the room.

Her nerves jittered as she followed Gianfranco along endless corridors. He pointed out his swimming pool and main restaurant, conference rooms and a souvenir shop like a proud parent boasting about his child's exam results.

'This is my celebration room,' Gianfranco announced, when they reached the top floor. 'It is the most romantic place in Italy for weddings.'

Ginny tried to mentally prepare herself before she peeped around the door.

A red-carpeted aisle led to an arch covered in white silk roses that framed a bird's-eye view of Vigornuovo through a floor-to-ceiling window. White muslin hung in swathes around the room and chairs were tied with powder-pink chiffon ribbons. There was an Instagram-worthy wall full of pastel silk flowers.

Ginny's stomach knotted with regret. She'd already decided what to wear for the ceremony: a white suit with a slightly flared trouser that made her look taller and slimmer. She'd imagined that Adrian would wear a navy suit, similar to the one he wore on their wedding day.

Ginny didn't entirely believe that marriage vows were something that needed to be renewed. A promise was surely a promise. However, a ceremony would have been a time to pause and celebrate something precious between them. She felt a lump swelling in her throat and couldn't swallow it away.

'Come inside and see,' Gianfranco said, heading along the red carpet.

Ginny's ankles felt weak as she followed him. This wasn't supposed to be the way she walked down the aisle. Adrian should be at the end, waiting for her under the floral arch. He'd be wearing a goofy grin, ready to take her hand and gaze into her eyes. They'd giggle like the teenagers they once were.

Ginny suddenly felt wretched and empty. Gianfranco's description of his ballroom became a droning noise in her head and her body felt like it wasn't her own.

She edged underneath the arch and stood in front of the window. The hills and sky were vast and seemed to draw her towards them. She could still hear the chime of gongs in her head and found herself swaying like bulrushes in a breeze. Her head became light, so light she felt herself falling. Then falling even deeper.

Until everything went blank.

The next thing she knew, Ginny was lying on the floor, looking up at the rose-covered arch. She could feel carpet beneath her fingertips.

'Ginny, Ginny?' a voice sounded, as if from space.

Her eyelids flickered as she tried to work out if she was in heaven or not. 'Adrian?'

'No. It is Nico. I have brought you some water.'

She felt a hand grip her elbow, and another one on the flat of her back. They eased her into a sitting position. 'What happened?' she rasped.

'You fainted,' Gianfranco said. 'This has never happened in my hotel before. Perhaps you didn't drink enough water before—'

Nico patted his friend's arm. 'Will you bring Ginny some fruit or bread? She should eat something.'

Gianfranco nodded. '*Prego*. My chefs make fresh pastries each day,' he muttered as he left.

Nico helped Ginny into a chair. 'Please take your time,' he said. 'The others can take a taxi back to Splendido, if they like. I'm sorry, they overheard Gianfranco telling me about your fall. They are all worried about you.'

Ginny sipped her water. She'd usually feel self-conscious about everyone knowing her business, especially when she was supposed to be the strong one in the group. She reminded herself that they'd all seen each other at their worst, and wearing only hotel robes. And they now knew each other's problems, too.

Gianfranco returned with a plate of food. He beckoned Nico to the corner of the room and the two men spoke for a few moments.

'Gianfranco says you can use one of his bedrooms,' Nico said when he rejoined Ginny. 'You can stay here until you feel well.'

'My rooms are luxurious with the finest cotton sheets from Rome . . .' Gianfranco started.

Nico held up his hand to stop him. 'We know about your rooms, thank you,' he said. 'This is about Ginny.'

There was part of her that wanted to pad along the corridor, open a bedroom door and slip into a sumptuous king-size bed. She could experience the luxurious accommodation that she and Adrian should be enjoying. A hot bath and sampling cute toiletries might help her feel better. Yet a bigger part of her wanted to return to Splendido, to be with Nico and the others. They'd been going through so much together, she could now call them friends.

Ginny didn't know if the gong vibrations had actually

cleansed her body, or if her fall had knocked some sense into her, but her thoughts now appeared much clearer.

She was almost halfway through her holiday and had to stop yearning for her husband. Adrian wanted a divorce and was confiding in Jenny. What more evidence did she need that her marriage was ending? Perhaps the passion she was searching for was something she could find for herself.

Glancing around the room, she spotted a couple of fallen petals on the carpet and specks of bird poo on the corner of the window. Ginny suddenly knew she had to go cold turkey, breaking all contact with her husband until she got back to England. Taking her phone out of her robe pocket, she deleted their conversation from ChainReaxions. 'I'd like to go home, back to your hotel,' she told Nico. 'I'm feeling better already.'

Her words made him glow with pride.

Gianfranco jingled keys in his hand. 'I will drive you to Splendido. My minibus has both air-conditioning and a sunroof.'

'Thank you, but I have my own vehicle.' Nico topped up Ginny's glass of water and sat down beside her. 'Are you really feeling okay?' he asked.

Ginny could feel warmth radiating from his body and his heart. 'Yes. And I need to start looking after myself better from now on.'

He gave her a small smile. 'I think that is easier for you to say, rather than to do.'

'I'm determined to give it a go,' she said.

★

When Ginny woke up the next day, she felt somehow different, as if her skin had been scrubbed clean. Birds chirped outside and through a gap in the curtain, she could see the sun was already high. There wasn't a cloud in the sky and she chuckled to herself when she checked her phone and saw it was almost noon. She'd slept through the night and most of the next morning, too.

She was actually looking forward to seeing Edna, Eric, Heather and Curtis today. All their problems were edging out in the open, no longer hidden away.

Well, all except for Curtis.

Ginny still didn't know what he was doing here. Maybe his heartache needed more time to emerge from the shadows. Perhaps his way of dealing with things was to record stuff on his phone. Why did he need to prowl around Splendido and Grand Hotel Castello Bella Vista to do it? Maybe there was nothing actually wrong with him.

Ginny didn't have her usual urge to check for messages from Adrian. She wasn't sure she needed the advice from *The Power of Two* any longer either, but she picked up the book anyway.

Stage Five. Welcome to your upward turn.

You're stepping out of a cold dark room into the sunshine.
It may take a while until it heats your skin, so take it easy
and enjoy feeling part of the world again. You're on the
right path, so keep on walking.

'Hallelujah,' Ginny said out loud.

She saw heartache sheets had been pushed under her door while she slept and she gathered them all together. All the scores had fallen, finally proving to herself that she'd made the right decision to invite strangers on holiday.

Curtis had even partially completed a form, writing, *Sorry for laughing after the gongs. I just know some things won't work.*

Ginny wondered what he meant.

There was one extra sheet, making five in total. She pressed her fingers to her chest when she saw the name at the top, Nico.

He hadn't completed an evaluation scale, but he had put forward an activity. In neat handwriting at the bottom of the page it said, *Venice, the city of love.*

Perhaps Nico wanted help with his heartache, too.

CHAPTER 21

Bridges

The beauty and romance of Venice made Ginny feel breathless. Her loose hair danced in the wind and her pulse raced with excitement as she sat with the others on board the *vaporetto*, a water taxi that took them along the Grand Canal towards Piazza San Marco. Because Venice was a car-free city, Nico had parked his minibus on the outskirts near the train station. Since fainting in Gianfranco's hotel, Ginny had taken a couple of days to recuperate and now felt back to her full strength.

The water rippled as the boat swept past crumbling buildings in shades of peach, dusky pink, ochre and white. Many of the ground floors had been vacated due to the rising water that reached halfway up some of the doors. Gondolas bobbed on the waves beside striped wooden mooring posts. Reflections danced under the oldest bridge that reached over the canal, the triangular white limestone Ponte di Rialto.

As the vaporetto neared the end of its thirty-minute journey, Ginny spied the orange and white structure of the Campanile, a tall bell tower overlooking Piazza San Marco.

The magnificent Doge's Palace (or Palazzo Ducale, as Nico called it) was petal pink with tapestry-like brickwork and hundreds of intricately carved stone windows. The building was topped with a row of structures that looked like the heads of spears. Heather took lots of photos on her Polaroid camera, shaking the shots and watching as images appeared.

When the water taxi came to a stop, the waves lapping against its side sounded like applause.

The sight ahead made Nico stand taller and he placed an arm around Loretta's shoulder, pulling her closer. When he leaned in to kiss his daughter's forehead, she didn't pull away.

Edna wore an orange scarf tied around her hair, and a swathe of turquoise silk, worn as a sarong over her black skirt. With her large sunglasses, she looked like an extra from the set of *A Glorious Escape*. She got off the boat next to Ginny. 'Are you okay, my dear?' she asked. 'I've been fretting about you.'

'I'm fine now. I got a bit overwhelmed by everything.'

'Tsk, young women take on so much responsibility these days, working, raising children, and looking after all and sundry. Something has to give and it's usually themselves.'

'Oh, it wasn't that—' Ginny started to say then stopped herself. A few weeks ago, she'd have insisted that women *could* have it all, even though she often felt like a circus performer keeping plates spinning on top of thin poles. She mustn't have been managing things very well if her marriage had broken down. 'You're right, Edna,' she admitted. 'I'm beginning to see the light.'

'Good girl,' Edna said. 'Me, too.'

When they all stepped off the boat, the sky grew greyer and

fat drops of rain started to fall. Ginny flicked up the collar on her blouse. She'd read somewhere that Venice had a similar amount of rainfall to Manchester. Even in the drizzle, the city looked enchanting and she felt like pinching herself, to make sure she was actually here.

'Don't worry. It is only a summer shower,' Nico said. He'd brought a pink umbrella with him and held it aloft so it was easy to follow him.

Other umbrellas opened around them like flowers in a meadow. Plastic rain macs shone wet and Ginny concentrated on her feet in case the pavement was slippery.

Nico stopped on a corner of Piazza San Marco and waited until his hotel guests gathered around him. He nudged Loretta, prompting her to tell them about the building with domed roofs like piped meringue that dominated the square. On top of a granite column stood a bronze lion with wings.

Loretta merely glanced over her shoulder. 'This is the Basilica di San Marco,' she said, as if the magnificent structure was a new charity shop that had opened in the city.

Ginny didn't know how she could be so blasé. The Romanesque carvings around the central doorway of the Basilica and the four horses presiding over the piazza were so beautiful they brought a lump to her throat. There were so many statues and small towers she couldn't count them all and luminous gold mosaics glistened wet in the rain.

She instinctively reached out to hold Adrian's hand and wriggled her fingers through thin air. She could barely hear Loretta's sparse commentary above all the tourists talking around her.

Nico bent his head and spoke into Ginny's ear. 'The church was originally built in the ninth century to house the remains of Saint Mark, the patron saint of the city. The building has been remodelled several times over the centuries so is a stunning mix of architectural styles. It has five domes, four thousand square metres of mosaics and over five hundred columns,' he said. 'Today, the square is also famous for luxurious restaurants, floods and many pigeons.'

Ginny found it difficult to concentrate when Nico's hair brushed against her cheek. She could feel his breath on her neck and found it oddly erotic. She felt like she should inch away from him, even though she didn't want to.

Nico continued his narration, this time addressing the whole group. 'Venice is built on a group of one hundred and eighteen islands separated by canals. Over four hundred bridges link them together,' he said. 'The city is built on a muddy lagoon with inadequate foundations. People say the city is sinking, but really it is flooding because of the rising sea levels.'

'Climate change has a lot to answer for,' Heather said. 'We've been studying it in class.'

Ginny looked around her. Everything looked beautiful and solid, yet beneath her feet, invisible erosion was taking place.

'I'd like a nice sit-down and a coffee,' Edna said. 'I believe the stylish people go to Caffè Florian and Harry's Bar.'

Nico shook his head. 'They are very expensive and charge many euros for a coffee.'

'You only live once,' Edna said, flicking the ends of her orange scarf over her shoulders.

Ginny performed a double take, surprised at her new breezy attitude.

'I'll join you, Edna,' Eric said, scrunching his shoulders at the number of people swarming around the square.

'That would be delightful. It's a long time since I had a handsome young man on my arm,' Edna said.

Eric laughed.

Nico looked at his watch. 'You will have to do these things later. I have booked the gondola ride for us.'

'A gondola?' Curtis raised a finger. 'Seriously? We've just got off a boat.'

Nico led them towards a row of them, rising and bumping against each other on the tide. Each had red quilted seats that looked like small thrones. The gondoliers stood waiting on the sterns, wearing black and white striped T-shirts, black trousers and straw boater hats with trailing ribbons.

Whenever Ginny thought of Venice, she pictured the curved black boats that glided through the city. She'd dreamed of a sail with Adrian where she nestled her cheek against his chest while a gondolier crooned Italian love songs. Sharing a boat ride with the others wouldn't have the same romance.

Heather lifted her camera. 'Let's get a photograph of us all together before we get on board, so I can show it to Mum,' she said. She handed her camera to a stranger and ushered their group closer.

Curtis stood in the middle, draping his arms around Heather's and Ginny's shoulders and pulling them towards him.

Heather shook the photos, watching the pictures emerging. 'Something light coming out of the dark,' she said.

They sailed along the narrow back canals of the city where the decaying buildings were the colour of verdigris and rust. The gondolier's oar swished through the olive-green water and the sun broke through the clouds, making the ripples sparkle.

'I told you the sunshine would find us,' Nico said, pointing to the brightening sky.

Afterwards, they arranged to meet back at the vaporetto stop at 4.00 p.m. Nico gave Eric and Edna his umbrella, in case it rained on their way to a café. Heather wanted to spend time alone taking more photos and Loretta wanted to shop. Only Curtis, Nico and Ginny remained.

'I'll take a hike.' Curtis jerked a thumb over his shoulder. 'I know when I'm a gooseberry.'

'Don't be silly—' Ginny started.

Curtis gave her a look that stopped her in her tracks. For a moment, his cocky bravado was gone, making him appear smaller and more vulnerable. His eyes looked bleary, as if he hadn't slept properly in days.

As if realizing his facade had slipped, Curtis twisted his cap back to front. 'Enjoy yourselves,' he said and strolled away.

'What does he mean by the *gooseberry*?' Nico asked.

'It's an English saying. It means he feels like the odd one out.' Ginny didn't add that it usually meant being with two people who'd prefer to be alone together.

'This is not true,' Nico said. 'I am worried about him.'

Ginny was more concerned about Heather, Eric and Edna. Their problems (from what she knew about them) seemed bigger than anything Curtis had going on. 'Why is that?' she asked.

'I see him talking into his phone a lot and making notes about my hotel. I am worried he is a hotel reviewer. Splendido has gone through a difficult time. What if he writes something that isn't good?'

Ginny would be angry if that was the case. She'd invited Curtis on holiday because he was supposed to be heartbroken, not so he could critique the hotel. 'I hardly know anything about him,' she mused, watching as he disappeared into a crowd. 'The others are opening up while he's still very secretive. I'll try to speak to him alone.'

'*Grazie*,' Nico said.

They continued their walk through the city, heading inland where the hordes of people dwindled. Ginny strolled languidly, taking in all the details of her surroundings. Nico didn't seem to mind her slow pace and pointed out *mascaroni*, stone faces adorning the keystones of arches, bridges and water wells that Ginny might not have noticed on her own. Most had deformed faces and looked frightening. 'They are supposed to scare away demons,' Nico said.

Ginny stopped when they came to a mask shop. The hundreds of hollow-eyed faces looked beautiful and also eerie. There were Pierrot clowns with teardrops on their cheeks and other masks had huge hooked beaks like prehistoric birds. Some were topped with jester-style hats with gold bells on their peaks.

They were the kind of thing Adrian would grumble about, saying they'd gather dust. Ginny thought they looked theatrical and she was the one who did most of the housework anyway. 'Can we take a look?' she asked.

'*Sì*,' Nico opened the door, gesturing for her to step inside first. A lady appeared behind the counter and smiled.

'The Venice Carnival began in 1162 to celebrate Venice's victory over its enemy, the Patriarch of Aquileia,' she told them. 'People gathered in Piazza San Marco to dance and play games. Ever since then, the victory has been celebrated in the streets of Venice each February. It was once the only time that lower and upper classes mingled together, aristocrats and peasants, and they wore masks to conceal their identities. They could carry out their fantasies, such as gambling and partying. There were affairs and even political assassinations. Three million visitors still attend the carnival each year.'

'Wow,' Ginny said, wondering what things she'd carry out behind the guise of a mask. Probably nothing illegal; she'd be too worried about being caught.

She picked up a mask and turned it over in her hands, wondering if she'd been donning a metaphysical one by pretending to be Jenny.

This one was white and painted with delicate red and gold flowers. When Ginny saw other customers were holding their purses, ready to make purchases, she experienced her familiar urge to whip out her credit card.

'That mask is one of my favourites,' the shopkeeper said with a smile.

Ginny gritted her teeth, fighting her impulse to buy it. If there were any gaps in her life, pretty objects wouldn't fill them. 'It is beautiful, but no thank you,' she said, congratulating herself on her restraint. She handed the mask back to the shopkeeper.

Nico said something in Italian to the shopkeeper who nodded. She vanished into the back of the shop before re-emerging with two packages wrapped in brown paper and tied with string. Nico paid and tucked them under his arm.

'Birthday presents for Loretta?' Ginny asked him.

Nico smiled enigmatically. 'Come, we should eat something,' he said.

They bought slices of pizza from a small street café and sat at an outside table, cheese strings trailing on their chins. Eating in the sunshine was one of Ginny's little pleasures. She loved feeling the warm rays on her face.

Nico handed one of his parcels to her. 'This is for you,' he said.

Ginny stripped off the paper to find the mask she'd admired in the shop. Nico had bought one, too. It had a wide black stripe across the eyes and a three-cornered hat attached.

'Oh, gosh. Thank you,' Ginny said. She slipped the ribbon behind her hair and the mask felt cool against her skin. She glanced around, feeling conspicuous until she noticed a few other people wearing them, too. She glanced at Nico and thought he looked mysterious and handsome in his mask. It was good he couldn't see her face and tell what she was thinking.

Nico led the way towards a tiny bridge with uneven paving stones. Ginny stumbled a little and he reached out for her hand to steady her. His fingers were slim and rough, so different from Adrian's fleshy digits.

Holding another man's hand felt wrong but, at the same time, Ginny welcomed the closeness of Nico's skin.

They walked across the bridge together with their fingers

linked for mere seconds, but it felt like much longer. The delicious sensation that trickled through Ginny's body made guilt stir inside her. *If it wasn't for Adrian's foolish actions, I wouldn't even be here*, she told herself.

'Where are we going?' she asked Nico.

He faced her and she could see his eyes shining behind the mask. 'Come with me,' he said.

Ginny's stomach flipped as she followed him towards a small wooden door in a wall. She looked up at the inauspicious building with its tiny windows and unkempt window boxes. 'What is this place?' she asked, her intrigue hampered by a touch of worry.

'You will see,' he said.

An ornate bell hung on the wall and Nico rang it.

They stood together and waited for the door to open.

CHAPTER 22

News

The door parted to reveal a slice of greenery beyond it. Nico took off his mask and gestured for Ginny to step over the threshold first.

When she saw the beautiful oasis that awaited her, she also removed her mask and took in the view. Water trickled in a scalloped stone fountain held aloft by cherubs. Low curated boxwood hedges, set in squares, contained white rose bushes. As Ginny walked alongside Nico, she spotted hydrangeas, snapdragons and irises among the pomegranate and olive trees. A balcony fit for Romeo and Juliet brimmed with window boxes, and a sweet, floral perfume hung in the air.

'There are over five hundred gardens in Venice, many of them hidden behind the tall walls,' Nico said.

Ginny spun around on the balls of her feet. 'You'd never know they were here, tucked away. It reminds me of a book I had as a child, *The Secret Garden* by Frances Hodgson Burnett.'

'I think Loretta has this book,' Nico said. 'Maria gave it to her.'

'My mum bought it for me, too. I loved the illustrations of the girl wandering through the overgrown plants and flowers.'

Ginny's thoughts took her back in time to her tenth birthday. Most of her childhood birthdays had become a jumble in her head, but this one stood out for all the wrong reasons.

She'd woken with butterflies in her stomach because her dad had promised to come home and spend the day with her. He'd missed many important events throughout her early life, school plays, birthdays and Christmases, so this was going to be special.

'Are you okay?' Nico asked, noticing her thoughts had flitted elsewhere.

'Talking about *The Secret Garden* made me think about my mum and dad,' Ginny admitted. 'Some of my memories are a little sad . . .' She tried to fix her mind on the sound of trickling water and an aeroplane soaring overhead, instead of on her parents. 'The sun is very hot,' she said. 'Can we sit down for a while?'

'*Prego.*' Nico led the way towards a white marble bench in the shade, surrounded by red roses.

They sat together quietly for a few minutes.

'If you want to talk,' he said. 'I am a good listener.'

Ginny knew that people contacted her show to reveal their worries because their words wouldn't stay inside them. And now she found her own story was pushing her to set it free, too.

She bit her lip, sensing Nico was a good man that she could trust. She slipped her mask back on, finding it easier to talk to him from behind it.

'My dad was in the military which meant he travelled a lot,' she explained. 'Mum was very supportive of his career, but things became more difficult when they had me. Dad was absent for months at a time and Mum and I had to follow him around the country, living in a series of different houses that never felt like home.

'Whenever Dad returned, it felt like Christmastime and I used to run and fling my arms around his waist. He'd swoop me off my feet and swing me from side to side. He always brought presents for me, a doll, T-shirt or a bracelet. I didn't care what they were, the gifts proved to me that he loved me. They made me forget that he'd soon have to leave us again.'

Nico made a sympathetic noise. 'Did you also have to attend different schools?' he asked.

Ginny nodded. 'I found it very tough,' she said with a sigh. 'I was always the new girl and had to learn to fit in quickly. I created a role for myself as a good listener, offering other girls a friendly ear and a shoulder to cry on. That was my thing. Dad also bought me a dog, a Jack Russell, as a companion.

'As I grew older, I began to notice how Dad's job made life difficult for Mum. She was very bright and had passed all her exams at school, but the short-term jobs she had to take on didn't utilize her skills fully. I think she squashed her potential so that Dad could reach his and she started to resent it.

'Constantly moving was a chore and I noticed Mum growing quieter and wearier, especially when she reached her forties. She lost her sparkle and I overheard her talking to Dad on the phone, pleading with him to keep our family in one place.' Ginny stopped speaking for a while, also remembering her mum mentioning her struggles with an early menopause. It was something she didn't share with Nico.

'I remember my tenth birthday because Dad had promised to be there, to watch me unwrap my presents and to sing when I blew out the candles on my cake. I think Mum was just as excited, too.

'We decorated the house we were staying in with banners and balloons, to make it look cheerier, and I spent ages making a "Welcome Home" sign.' Ginny paused and lowered her chin, disappointment creeping over her. 'But then Dad phoned and said his plans had changed. He wasn't coming home and would be working away for a further few weeks.

'Mum started yelling at him and it was the first time I'd heard her so angry and upset. She told Dad that she'd finally had enough and she thumped her hand down on the table so hard a vase toppled over. I remember water pooling on the table and tears streaming down her face. Their row on the phone meant that Dad didn't even have time to wish me a happy birthday.

'Me and Mum ate my birthday cake together in silence and she ripped down the welcome home banner. She gave me *The Secret Garden* and made it clear that she'd bought it for me, not Dad. I watched her defiantly apply pink lipstick.

'During the night, I couldn't sleep and I wanted to check Mum was okay. I thought I could hear voices in the kitchen, so I crept downstairs to see her.

'I saw her standing by the back door, in an embrace with a man who wasn't my dad. I couldn't see his face but he was holding her tightly, whispering into her hair and caressing her back. It looked very . . . intimate.'

Ginny dug her fist into her stomach, recalling the slug of shock she'd felt. The memory of her mum with someone else still made her want to scratch her skin. 'I wanted to run away but I froze to the spot. I was sad and furious and confused, yet I also understood. I could *feel* what Mum was going through with my dad and I wanted her to be happy. All she wanted was a normal, stable family life and I wanted it, too.'

'I am sorry,' Nico said quietly. 'What did you do?'

'Nothing. I left them alone and went back to bed. I let Mum have her moment of comfort and I never mentioned it to her, then or since. I still don't know if I made the right decision . . .

'In the weeks that followed, it was like someone had waved a magic wand, making Mum smile again. She seemed to dance when she walked and I guessed it might be because of this man. I convinced myself she wasn't having an affair, but I never knew if that was true or not.

'We moved again soon afterwards and this time Mum gave Dad an ultimatum. She told him she couldn't live this way any longer, that their marriage was dedicated to his needs and she wanted to think about her own, too. She threatened to leave him if things didn't change.'

Nico's fingers edged closer to Ginny's hand, to console her and she flashed him a watery smile.

'I think Dad finally realized that marriage was about two people being satisfied, not just one. He found a home and a job that kept us all together in one place,' Ginny said. 'Mum and Dad tried to make things work but, by then, Mum had been left on her own for too long. Dad missed his career and resentment from both sides made their marriage rot.

'I tried to be the glue that held us all together, always pointing out Mum and Dad's good points to each other and suggesting things we could do together. But I used to hear Mum crying at night and Dad pacing around downstairs. The weight of responsibility I placed on myself was crushing.'

Ginny took off her mask again. She cradled it in her lap and glanced at Nico, appreciating how his eyes were so caring and calm.

'You were a child and they were adults,' Nico said. 'It wasn't your responsibility.'

'But, still. . .'

'And now you keep doing the same thing, trying to help other people fix their lives?'

Ginny paused and blinked hard. She hadn't made the connection before and it was perceptive of Nico to notice it. 'I suppose I give out advice to strangers, to try to stop a situation like mine from happening again. My biggest regret is that I couldn't stop my own parents' marriage from disintegrating. They now live at opposite ends of the country with their new partners.' She sighed. 'Perhaps people are better off without my input.'

Nico placed a hand on top of hers. 'Everyone needs kindness,' he said.

'When Mum and Dad split up, I promised myself that if I ever got married, I'd make it work,' Ginny said. 'I looked for a partner who shared the same values as me, and I thought Adrian did.'

'People can change,' Nico said with a small sigh.

Ginny thought how being with him felt so familiar and secure, even though she hadn't known him for very long. She liked how he smelled of sunshine and citrus, so different from Adrian's musky scent. It was comfortable to sit beside him, even in silence.

When her phone suddenly rang, piercing the serenity of the garden, Ginny fumbled in her bag and saw Phoebe's name on the screen. 'Sorry,' she told Nico. 'My daughter's calling.'

She didn't get to the call quickly enough and it ended.

A text message arrived within seconds.

Mum, can you talk?

Ginny messaged Phoebe back.

It's a little tricky right now. Can I call you later? X
Now's better ☺ x

'My daughter.' Ginny smiled apologetically to Nico.

He stood up and indicated that he'd look around the garden. He walked towards a display of roses and bent down to smell them.

Ginny phoned Phoebe back. 'Is everything okay, sweetheart?' she asked.

Phoebe's voice had an unusual waver when she spoke.

'I'm not sure ...'

Ginny frowned. 'What do you mean?'

'Mum,' Phoebe whispered hoarsely. 'I'm pregnant.'

Ginny slow-blinked and her surroundings seemed to evaporate into thin air. Her heart felt like a helium-filled balloon that might make her body float away. 'Gosh,' she said, trying to absorb her daughter's news. She wriggled her toes to try to ground herself. 'Congratulations, darling. That's brilliant.'

'I'm in shock . . .'

'I'm *delighted* for you. Are you pleased?'

'Well, yep. I mean, I wanted kids one day, but this is . . . unexpected. Right in the middle of our wedding plans, too,' Phoebe said. 'We had the first scan today and everything looks fine.'

Ginny closed her eyes, and tilted her face towards the sun. Was it possible to feel any happier than she did now? 'That's great to hear. How far along are you?'

'Fourteen weeks! *That* was a bit of a shock. I thought I was more like eight. You'll be a gran in less than six months' time.'

'Wow, I'm so pleased for you both.' Ginny paused for a second. 'Um, does your dad know?'

'I wanted to tell you first.'

Ginny felt a shot of smugness about hearing the news before Adrian. It was soon overtaken by her guilt about being so far away from her daughter. 'Thanks, that's sweet of you.' She blew up into her hair. 'I wasn't expecting *this*.'

'We didn't either. We're thinking of tying the knot sooner, so I'm not waddling down the aisle.'

'Do whatever makes you both happy. Your dad and I will support you. Are you feeling well?'

'It sucks being sick each morning, and moving the wedding forwards sounds stressful.'

Ginny found it easy to slip back into *Advice Angel* mode. 'Have you tried nibbling on raw ginger? And bland food like rice and toast is easier to digest. Make sure you keep well hydrated, especially if you're sick. Choose a wedding that suits you both, and there's no rush to go on a honeymoon straight after you get married.'

'I knew you'd give me some good advice.' Phoebe laughed then hesitated. 'Will things be okay with you and Dad?'

Ginny wanted to cough and she held her fist to her mouth. She glanced at Nico who was still strolling around the garden. 'Yes, of course,' she said. 'There's nothing to worry about. You just think about yourself, Pete and the baby. If there's anything I can do to help, let me know.'

'Thanks, Mum. Love you.'

'Love you, too, Phoebes.'

After her daughter hung up, Ginny clasped her phone to her chest and allowed the news to sink in. All her senses came alive as she walked towards Nico. She could suddenly smell lavender and hear the faint hiss of a water sprinkler. She could taste a hint of tomato from the pizza she'd eaten earlier and her skin felt tingly from the sun.

'Is everything okay?' he asked her.

Ginny wrapped her arms around herself and felt like bursting into song. 'I'm going to be a grandmother,' she said. 'My daughter's having a baby. She called to tell me.'

Nico broke into a smile. 'This is great news,' he said. 'Congratulations.'

They stood facing each other, and he held out his arms.

It felt natural for Ginny to sink into them for an embrace.

She wasn't exactly sure what happened next because one moment she was hugging Nico, and the next their lips seemed to find each other and press together. It was a congratulatory kiss that lingered for a second or two too long and made her toes tingle.

Ginny hadn't kissed another man for thirty-one years and it felt clumsy and unexpected, and yet it was also tender and full of promise. She was Ginny Splinter and at the same time she wasn't, like a character performing behind a mask on stage.

She pulled away abruptly when she thought about Adrian. She also couldn't help picturing her mum in the embrace with a stranger. Ginny couldn't believe she'd done a similar thing. 'I'm s–sorry,' she stuttered with her cheeks heating. As her surroundings shot back into sharp focus, she pressed her fingers to her mouth. 'I didn't mean to . . .'

'It is my fault,' Nico said.

'I was excited about the baby.'

'I was happy to see you happy.'

'It was a silly moment and I got carried away,' Ginny said, trying not to think about how soft and welcoming his lips had been.

'Yes,' he said. 'Me, also.'

They stood awkwardly together until Nico looked at his watch. 'We should return to Piazza San Marco.'

Ginny nodded. 'The others will wonder where we are.'

Ginny and Nico walked together towards the door that led back into the street, keeping a few feet apart. They forgot about their masks and left them lying on the bench.

The bell jingled as they closed the door behind them, shutting out the flowers and the beautiful view.

CHAPTER 23

Bingo

The weather turned again as Ginny and Nico jogged through Venice towards the vaporetto stop. Splats of water hit the pavement and a drop dribbled down Ginny's back, making her shiver.

Edna, Heather, Eric and Curtis stood huddled together, waiting for them on the pavement. Loretta's hair was damp and plastered to her forehead and she tapped her watch when she saw her papà. The seven of them hurried on board the boat.

Ginny felt her stomach rolling as she took a seat next to Edna, who seemed in an upbeat mood.

'I discovered some beautiful silk handkerchiefs in an antique shop,' she said. 'I might sew them together to make a waistcoat.'

Ginny tried to feign interest and caught sight of Nico from the corner of her eye. She was sure her face was shining scarlet and she hoped Edna hadn't noticed. Her kiss with the hotelier had been a spur-of-the-moment thing, a reaction to Phoebe's pregnancy and Adrian leaving, that had left her reeling. She tried telling herself it had only been a friendly embrace, yet the buzz it had given her was like internet shopping, multiplied by ten. She felt sure she was radiating shame.

'Has the cat got your tongue?' Edna tapped her knee. 'That makes a change.'

Ginny hugged her belly. 'I feel a little seasick.'

'The water's flat,' Edna said, rooting in her handbag anyway. She handed Ginny mints and a packet of travel sickness tablets. 'Daisy wasn't a good traveller either. Where did you, Nico and Curtis get to?'

Ginny performed an uncomfortable shuffle in her seat. She swallowed a travel tablet then popped a mint in her mouth. 'Nico took me to see a beautiful garden,' she said, not mentioning Curtis's early departure. 'My daughter phoned while we were there, to tell me she's pregnant.'

'Oh, that's excellent. Congratulations.'

Ginny thought Edna's tone sounded a little dry. 'It's going to be great,' she told her. 'I can't wait to push a pram and read stories to a little one again. We'll bake cookies, sing nursery rhymes together and have lots of cuddles.'

'That sounds wonderful.' The older lady's lips were so straight they almost vanished. She knitted her fingers together in her lap. 'You must make sure you still take time for yourself. It's very important.'

Ginny thought it was a strange thing to say. Her new role as a grandparent was going to be exciting and might plug the gap in her life. If Phoebe had discovered her pregnancy sooner, Adrian might not have made such unwise decisions. 'I appreciate your concern,' she said.

Edna stuffed the mints and tablets back into her bag. 'I'll tell you a little tale,' she said. 'I gave up driving a car when I turned seventy years old, even though I have twenty-twenty vision.'

Ginny frowned, trying to work out how this was relevant.

'I'd never had a car accident in my life,' Edna continued. 'Then, one day, I drove Daisy to the hospital for an appointment. She had to go there a lot, always something or other that needed assessing or treating. It was rush hour and the motorway was horrendously busy but I navigated it with ease. All was fine until I came to park the car. I checked all around me as usual before I reversed. And then . . . crunch. I heard the crumple of metal. I was so busy concentrating on everything else that I didn't see a huge tree behind the car. It seemed to appear from nowhere.'

'Were you and Daisy okay?'

'She was asleep and didn't notice a thing. I *couldn't* believe that I hadn't seen the tree. So, what I'm saying to you Ginny, is this: when you're busy navigating life, thinking you have your eye on everything, there's sometimes an unseen obstruction that stops you noticing something glaringly obvious.'

'Are you saying that a grandchild or Adrian could be my weak spot?' Ginny asked, still confused.

Edna patted her leg. 'You cared for me and the others by inviting us here. You give out advice to strangers on the radio, and now I'm giving it to you.' She cleared her throat and paused. 'I can see that you and Nico like each other.'

Ginny coughed out her mint. It rolled around on the deck of the boat until she stamped her foot on it. She felt like Edna had been spying on her and Nico in the garden. 'That's ridiculous. I hardly know him.'

'Hmm,' Edna said. She pointed at each of her eyes in turn. 'Don't forget, twenty-twenty. Take time to notice and enjoy *all* the things in life. It's what I'm trying to do now.'

Ginny noticed that on Edna's other side, Curtis had cocked his head, as if listening in to their conversation. He nodded as if agreeing with Edna's advice.

Ginny felt too flustered to say anything to him and stared at the horizon instead. The sky and canal were almost the same shade of grey, difficult to see where one ended and the other began.

Edna prodded Ginny's arm to break their scratchy silence. 'Look what Eric found for me in a shop,' she said, opening her bag to reveal a vintage English game of bingo.

'That's nice,' was all Ginny could manage to say.

'Daisy and Desmond hated the game,' Edna said. 'It's terribly sad they're no longer here, but I need to make the most of things. I have you to thank for my renewed joie de vivre.'

Rather than being pleased for Edna's new zest for life, and her own role in it, Ginny felt like she'd been jabbed all over with a sharp stick. She took her bag and set it down on the seat, slowly leaning over sideways to use it as a pillow. 'Please wake me up when we reach dry land,' she said.

Back in her hotel room, Ginny curled up on her bed and tried to stop Edna's words about parking, surprise trees and Nico from circling in her head. Her moment with Nico had left her nerves on edge, a similar feeling to when Miss Peach had asked how well she really knew her husband.

Adrian had made a mistake and, now, so had she. They'd both been tempted by others. Was that a big enough reason to throw away their life together?

To distract herself, Ginny picked up her phone and looked at online baby boutiques. A soft roaring lion toy was so cute, and she'd have to buy a cot, changing mat and blankets. The tiny outfits were gorgeous and new shopping possibilities were endless.

She opened an unread WhatsApp message and found Phoebe had sent her a photo of the scan. The baby looked like a kidney bean with tiny arms and legs and Ginny already felt a rush of love towards it.

Dad says it looks like him, Phoebe said.

Adrian obviously now knew the good news and Ginny's compulsion to speak to him was like an itch from a rash. To chase it away, she forced herself to look at his dating profile again.

While she was on ChainReaxions, a new message arrived from him.

Hey, Jenny. It's been a while. Do you still fancy meeting up? x

The temptation to call him back, to yell at him, consumed her. Their daughter was pregnant and he was still thinking of someone else, but mainly about himself.

Ginny let out a growl and tossed her phone across the bed. After all the hurt Adrian had caused, that he was continuing to stir up, she wanted to catapult him out of her head. She paced around the room but couldn't stop thinking about her husband. There was only one thing she could think of that might dull her senses.

Ginny jogged downstairs to see if Edna fancied a game of bingo.

Edna was delighted and insisted that the others should join them, too. She sat down at the dining table and doled out yellowing numbered cards to everyone, smiling as she placed faded pink plastic balls into a bag and gave them a shake. When she plucked one back out, she held it delicately, as if it was a Fabergé egg.

Curtis stared at his bingo card. He lifted his baseball cap and scratched his head. 'This wasn't in our schedule. How will it make us feel better?'

'It's a game,' Ginny said. 'We're trying to have fun.'

'Fun? Yeah, right.' Curtis reluctantly reached out for a pen. 'Don't tell anyone I'm doing this. It'll spoil my reputation.'

'Reputation for what?' Edna asked, her grey eyes growing narrow. 'Skulking around the hotel surreptitiously making notes?'

The room fell quiet and Ginny pursed her lips. 'I've noticed you doing it, too,' she said, remembering she'd promised Nico that she'd speak to Curtis about his snooping around. 'You're the only one who hasn't shared with us why you're here.'

Curtis folded his arms tightly. 'Eric hasn't said much either,' he said.

Eric lifted his eyes. 'I've lost my dog. Everyone knows that. We don't know anything about *you*.'

Curtis raised both hands as if being arrested. 'Hey, don't gang up on me. Let's have a little trust around here.'

Edna hadn't finished with him. 'How can you expect to feel better if you're not fully involved or committed?' She rapped the dining table. 'You haven't even suggested a heartbreak activity yet.'

Things were getting a little heated and Ginny felt the need to play devil's advocate. 'Maybe Curtis needs more time to—'

'Shh, enough with the advice,' Edna said. She turned and pointed a finger at Curtis. 'Come on, young man. We're waiting for an explanation.'

He looked a little scared. 'I've got nothing to confess. All's good.'

Edna plucked a bingo ball out of her bag and threw it at him, hitting him on the nose.

'Ouch,' Curtis yelled. He caught the ball and held it in his fist. 'My business is none of your business, okay?'

Ginny slowly became aware that Nico was standing behind them.

He pressed a hand to his chest and nodded solemnly at Curtis. 'I have also seen you searching around Splendido. My hotel can never compare to the luxury of the castle hotel. What I offer here is good food, comfort and friendship. It breaks my heart to think you might want to criticize that.'

Loretta stood alongside her father, her eyes shining with tenderness towards him. 'Papà is right,' she told Curtis. 'This is our family home and you should respect that.'

'Thank you, Lolo.' Nico hitched an eyebrow, instantly regretting using Maria's nickname for his daughter.

Loretta nodded, assuring him that it was okay.

Everyone stared at Curtis, waiting for him to talk.

He bounced the bingo ball despondently on the table. Sweat beaded on his forehead. 'I kind of like to keep a private diary.

Nothing wrong with that.' He glanced at each of them in turn and his right eye twitched. 'Hey, don't look at me like that. I'll explain everything, before you beat it out of me,' he said.

'We need to trust you,' Ginny said. 'Perhaps we can also help you, too . . .'

'Doubt that,' Curtis said.

A hush fell upon the room.

'I promise I feel just as lousy as you guys. He took off his cap and circled a finger on his bald spot. 'I've got a brain tumour, okay? It's the size of a marble with the capacity of a wrecking ball.'

Heather let out a gasp. 'Oh, my.'

Edna frowned at him. 'I hope this isn't one of your jokes.'

Edna, Ginny muttered in her head. *Let the poor guy speak.*

'It's called a glioblastoma.' Curtis shrugged. 'It might sound like a superhero with a laser gun, but it's a stage four demon. It's going to steal my life away and there's no stopping it. So, that's why I'm here.

'I made a bucket list of things I've always wanted to do and Italy was numero uno. I watched all *The Godfather* films during my chemo downtime.'

Ginny closed her eyes, trying to let Curtis's situation sink in. She could still imagine him breaking into a grin and admitting he was kidding. 'Why have you been making so many notes?' she asked him.

'I've got a blog. I make notes of my thoughts and ideas, putting them online when I'm in the mood.' He turned to Nico. 'I'm not criticizing your hotel, man. I *love* a bit of shabby chic. When I get home, I'm going to frame up some photos like the ones on your wall and buy some copper pans. The castle hotel is too sterile for my taste. Reminds me of my hospital visits.'

Curtis took out his phone to scroll through all the selfies he'd taken in Venice. There were also shots of Splendido's courtyard, Nico's dining room and other interior decor highlights. In a photo he'd taken in Gianfranco's hotel, Curtis held up a gold cushion and made a thumbs-down sign. Another shot showed him lying in a hospital bed with a shaved head. His eyes were bloodshot and his face was deathly pale. He showed some of them to the group.

'I call it *Curtis's Brain Blog*. Before coming here, I ticked off a few things on my bucket list, like skydiving, going to a footie match at Old Trafford, etcetera. I'm getting tired now and my time on earth is running out.' He tapped his watch for effect. 'Going to support groups just reminds me the end is nigh. Friends don't know what to say to me, and being on my own sucks. If it's any consolation to you guys, I've been happy hanging out with you here, and our trips have been cool.'

Ginny didn't know what to say. Her own problems with Adrian paled in comparison to Curtis's illness and a lump formed in her throat.

Curtis unfurled his fingers and stared at the plastic ball. 'Number five, man alive. That's me,' he said wryly. 'My mum knew all the bingo nicknames.'

An uncomfortable silence lingered until Edna reached out and gently took the ball from him. 'We're going to need that,' she said, popping it back into her bag. 'We can't play the game with a ball missing.'

Curtis nodded. He lowered his eyes and stared at his hands for some time. 'Sure can't, Edna,' he said.

Ginny, Heather, Curtis, Edna and Eric played several rounds of bingo. At first the games were awkward and reluctant, but they gradually grew livelier. Edna treated her role as games master very seriously, which made the others act like school children, teasing her and messing around.

Heather captured the game on Polaroid, including when Curtis triumphantly punched the air and shouted, 'House.' Nico presented him with a small copper pan as a prize and Curtis held it aloft like a trophy. 'Oh, man, I love it,' he said, kissing the shiny metal.

After the game came to an end, they all sat around the dining table, talking until midnight. They didn't discuss their issues, only stories from the holiday. Nico opened a bottle of red wine and they nibbled on bread and olives.

Eventually, Ginny patted a yawn with her hand. 'We've all put forward heartache cures, so there's only yours left, Curtis,' she said. 'Is there anything you'd like to do?'

He thought about it for quite some time. 'There is one thing.' He put his baseball cap back on and tugged on the peak. 'Do you guys fancy going to a nightclub?'

Ginny's eyes widened in surprise. The last time she'd been to a club was for her fortieth birthday. The music was so loud it made her ears ring and she spent the night shouting, 'What? I can't hear you,' to her friends. She glanced at Eric, who had shrunk his head into his shoulders. 'Is clubbing on your bucket list?' Ginny asked.

Curtis nodded. 'When I'm dancing, I can forget about everything.'

Edna packed up her bingo game. Her lips were pinched, as if she'd eaten lime pickle. 'You'll have to count me out,' she said.

'Why's that, mate?' Curtis replied.

She tossed her head. 'I may have the physique of someone half my age, but jostling on a dance floor with scantily clad young folk is not my thing.'

'It's a chance to dress up in your finery and be among people having a great time. That's what you want, right?'

'Not in this way—'

'You all said it was my turn.' Curtis huffed. He leaned forwards on both elbows as if about to share a secret. 'I've seen photos of a beach bar where they serve amazing cocktails while you watch the sunset. There's DJs and they play cool beats. Nico might even attract some new customers . . .'

'Where is this place?' Nico asked.

'Rimini. That's not too away far, right? Maybe you can sweet-talk Gianfranco into driving us there, so you can take a night off.'

Heather, Ginny, Edna and Eric wore a variety of expressions ranging from blank to terrified.

'Sounds fun,' Loretta said, mischievously. 'It's my eighteenth birthday in two days' time. Time to celebrate.'

'Come on,' Curtis pleaded. 'Make a poorly guy happy. I'll foot the bill. My treat.'

And the thing was, after they'd all pushed him into revealing his heartache, how could anyone refuse?

CHAPTER 24

Rooftops

Curtis

Curtis perched on the edge of his bed and spun his cap in his hands. Spilling his guts hadn't been on his agenda. He'd had a firm handle on things and didn't need anyone's sympathy. He'd had enough of that from hospital staff to last a lifetime, and he didn't want any chance of his insurance company finding out he'd travelled overseas with a terminal illness.

His plan had been to chillax in Italy, soak up some sun and eat great food. If Ginny was offering to provide it for free, that was even better.

Throughout his life, Curtis had never been averse to taking advantage of folks' generosity. He'd had to forge his own way in the world after losing both his parents in his early twenties. They were in their mid-forties when they had him, having given up on being able to have children, so it had been like a miracle when he was born. He supposed they'd spoiled him throughout his childhood, doting on him like he was a little prince.

Because of their ages, Curtis had always expected to lose them sooner rather than later in life, but nothing had prepared him for such an early loss and how hard it hit him.

As an only child, he'd had to clear out and sell the family home on his own, whittling down his parents' furniture and belongings until there were only a few photos, his dad's fountain pen and mum's wedding ring left. He'd put the house on the market at a ridiculously high price and learned how to charm prospective buyers. The rush he got when he sold the house, at well above market value, was like no other and selling houses became Curtis's thing.

He hadn't earned many qualifications at school and learned his trade on the job. His easy manner and chatty way with words meant he could befriend anyone from any walk of life, from bank managers to plumbers. One of his ex-girlfriends described him as a rough diamond and Curtis was fine with that. He was happy doing what he did without being all polished.

He set his sights on the outer areas of the city, where housing was run-down and cheap. If owners fell on hard times, he offered to pay cash for their properties. He installed budget kitchens, basic bathrooms and carpets and resold the houses pronto, making a profit. Curtis moved into more prestigious areas, too, developing a neat property portfolio. Wheeling and dealing were his way of making a living and getting things done. Although they weren't here any longer, he wanted to make his parents proud.

Curtis's business quickly grew. He bought a fancy office but didn't occupy it much, preferring to get out and about, checking out properties and sealing deals. He celebrated his bigger triumphs with a bottle of champagne in his outdoor Jacuzzi with a view of the city rooftops. If a pretty girl agreed to join him, even better.

One day, he wanted one of those prestigious blue plaques on the wall of his apartment to signify historical importance – *Curtis Dunne lived here.*

As Curtis reached his mid-thirties, he watched his friends settling down, buying houses in the suburbs and having kids. He noticed the people dancing in clubs were getting younger. His life of working, partying and hooking up suddenly seemed like a sandwich with a lack of filling and he started to think about the future. A nice wife and a couple of kids suddenly appealed to him.

But then he'd developed headaches that made his head feel like a huge church bell, with the clapper continually striking the bronze rim. Sometimes the pain in his skull was so great he crouched in the corner of his bathroom with his arms cradling his head, dizzy and nauseated.

Curtis initially attributed it to the amount of booze he consumed. He was rarely without a bottle of lager, pinot noir or champagne in his hand. He cut down on the demon drink but still fell over in his kitchen, scoring a black eye when his forehead hit the worktop, when he was totally sober.

He'd laughed when a doctor had first told him about the tumour. It couldn't be true. Curtis didn't even believe it when he saw the results of his MRI scan. A grey-white mass on the image looked like a small floret of cauliflower, so harmless. Surely, it couldn't be *that* serious.

He told himself he was invincible, that the docs would be able to zap the cancer and decimate it.

Except the bad news kept coming. The words *months not years*, *chemotherapy* and *prolonging life* came at him like army tanks with their guns pointed in his direction.

He'd initially dealt with his diagnosis by throwing himself into work, going out at night and sleeping with too many women, until he realized it was making him feel worse.

Going in the opposite direction, he started to drink coconut water and introduced kale into his diet. He grew nostalgic and bought clothing brands he used to wear in his teens: Reebok, GAP and even a G-Shock watch. He revisited his favourite hip-hop tracks from the nineties and bought an iPod on eBay.

Each time Curtis went to a hospital appointment, he convinced himself his condition would have improved. The doctor would scratch his head and say, 'My word, this is incredible. Your tumour has completely vanished.'

And Curtis would raise his finger and blow on the end in victory.

But when the news grew ever graver, Curtis tried to cheer up the doctors and nurses. 'Come on guys, it could be worse. I'm still standing and looking good.'

His words didn't raise any smiles.

Eventually it dawned on Curtis that there was no holding back the inevitable. His diagnosis was a mix of bad luck and biology, nothing he'd personally done wrong.

It was difficult to accept he'd never meet someone to read newspapers and enjoy a cup of tea with, like his parents had done, something he'd once thought was lame. He'd never get married, or take his child to play football in the park. His thirty-eight years on earth would be snuffed out like a candle flame between damp fingers, with a small hiss and a wisp of smoke.

Curtis tried not to think about his funeral, then couldn't think of anything else. How many people would even attend it or miss him? What did life mean? What was his legacy? There *had* to be some reason he'd been put on earth and why he was exiting it so early.

A counsellor suggested that Curtis start a blog, to deal with his thoughts and emotions.

He'd initially rubbished the idea, until one night he started to type on his phone and couldn't stop. *Curtis's Brain Blog* was born, a series of random musings, photos and videos that kept him busy and helped him to express himself. It made him feel in control of his brain, instead of the other way around.

On the gong day in the castle hotel, it finally dawned on Curtis that life wasn't all about him. Seeing Ginny, Edna, Eric and Heather clinging together like barnacles on a rock made him recognize he wasn't the only one with problems. Although his were definitely bigger, he felt guilty for the first time at viewing his time in Italy as a free ride.

In offering up the holiday, Ginny had shown him there were good people in the world, and Curtis no longer wanted to take advantage of them. He wanted to *be* one of them instead, even if it wouldn't get him a blue plaque.

Curtis lay back on his hotel bed and scrolled through the photos he'd taken on his phone, pausing at one of him holding Nico's copper pan in the air. In Vigornuovo, he didn't need to try to be cool or flash his cash. He was just a man with time running out, having a strangely nice time with people he'd usually cross the road to avoid.

Acceptance of his lot was bringing with it a calmness Curtis hadn't anticipated. But before he completely resigned himself to the quiet life, the petering out of his days on earth, Curtis wanted to have a bloody good dance. One last big hurrah.

One day, someone, somewhere might read *Curtis's Brain Blog* and take some kind of inspiration from it. For now, though, it was just him and his words.

He flipped onto his side and started to write a new entry.

Number five, man alive. Today I played bingo and it was fun . . .

CHAPTER 25

Maze

Ginny lay dreaming in bed. She pictured opening a door in a wall to find a maze stretching out before her. She entered and tall green hedges rose up on either side of her, so she couldn't see where she was going. With each corner she turned, and each dead end she encountered, the more she got lost. She began to run and her body flooded with panic. A hedge crashed down on top of her, felling her to the ground, and everything went dark. As she struggled beneath the weight of the branches, she could hear a ringing noise.

The sound of her phone jolted Ginny awake. She held a hand to her eyes against the bright daylight and tried to acclimatize, her heart still pounding. She could hear laughter and the chink of cups and saucers outside. Nico must be serving breakfast in the courtyard.

Ginny grabbed the phone from her bedside table and struggled to breathe when she saw Adrian's name on the screen. Remembering that he'd messaged Jenny again, yesterday, her first instinct was to cut him off.

'Hello,' she answered curtly.

'Hi there. How's your holiday?'

She frowned, taken aback by how casual he sounded, like everything was fine between them. She didn't feel like rewarding his question with an answer.

'Are you still there?' he prompted.

She took a gulp of water from a bottle. 'Yes, I'm here and having a great time, thanks for asking.'

Adrian didn't react to the coolness in her voice. 'Phoebe said she'd told you her news. I've tried calling you several times this morning. Didn't you see my missed calls?'

Now you know what it's like, she thought.

'I've only just woken up,' Ginny said, performing a yawn for effect.

'Um, what time is it in Italy?' he sounded confused. 'It's two in the afternoon here.'

Ginny glanced at her watch and saw it was 3.00 p.m. Perhaps Edna's travel tablets had knocked her out. Nico must be serving afternoon coffee and cake outside, not breakfast. 'I must have overslept,' she said with a groan.

'That's some lie-in.' Adrian laughed, not unkindly. 'It sounds like you're making the most of your break.'

Ginny's mind flashed back to the previous day, recalling the beauty of Venice, the gondola ride, the mask shop and her walk in the garden with Nico. Her armpits grew damp when she remembered *that* moment. She'd definitely felt a crackle of electricity between them. Then there'd been bingo and Curtis's shocking revelation. It felt like she and Adrian had been apart for six years rather than six weeks. 'The holiday has been very . . . eventful,' she said.

'Anything fun you want to tell me about?'

Ginny was about to share a few snippets then clamped her lips shut. 'I've been doing *all* kinds of new things,' she said mysteriously.

A few thorny beats passed between them.

'So, we're going to be grandparents,' Adrian said. 'I'm really excited and proud.'

'Me, too. It was a big surprise.'

The mention of their daughter allowed their conversation to warm and flow.

'You should see Phoebe. She looks different already. She's glowing and has a little rounded belly. I invited her over for tea last night,' Adrian said. 'Can you believe she couldn't face eating the cheese sandwich I made for her? She's always loved cheddar.'

Ginny's face fell a little. She wanted to see the curve of her daughter's stomach, too, and her chest tightened with homesickness. The distance away from her family suddenly felt like a chasm. She rubbed her tautness away and tried to process her husband's words. 'So, Phoebe came over to Dave and Linda's house?' she clarified.

'Well, no, not exactly.' Adrian hesitated. 'I offered to make her a sandwich in our kitchen. I, um, moved back into our house a couple of days ago.'

His revelation felt like a karate chop to her throat and Ginny propped herself upright in bed. '*Really*?' was all she could manage to say. Picturing him sitting in his home office to message Jenny made her feel angry and queasy. 'Are you trying to rub salt into my wounds?' she asked.

226

'I thought you'd be pleased. You said it's what you wanted.'

'Maybe I'm not so sure any longer . . .'

'Oh,' he sounded crestfallen. 'I know we have lots to discuss, but I felt like a spare part living with my friends, and our house was just sitting there empty. It made sense for me to come home.'

Ginny couldn't argue with his logic, but where was his emotion? Where was Adrian's grovelling apology? He'd made a huge assumption about moving back home without asking her if it was okay first. Did he expect things to return to normal between them, as if nothing had happened? Or was his coming home a temporary thing?

'It's our anniversary tomorrow,' Adrian said quietly, plugging the gap in their conversation. 'It'll be weird not celebrating it with you. Will you be doing anything to mark the occasion?'

It was a strange question, after he'd *left* her. Ginny had lost track of her days on holiday and hadn't thought much about it, other than noting her anniversary was the same day as Loretta's eighteenth.

'Are there any nice bars where you're staying?' Adrian added, before she could answer. 'Are the people you're holidaying with nice?'

It sounded like he was trying to pry or organize her, and Ginny didn't like it. Though, she supposed it was how she used to treat him. 'Oh, don't worry about me,' she said, not caring if she sounded petulant. 'My only plan is to have fun with my new friends.'

Adrian was silent for a while. 'Look, I know I owe you a big apology, for the way I've treated you,' he said, letting out a sigh. 'I'm really sorry.'

Ginny gritted her teeth. 'I think you mean a *gargantuan* apology.'

'Yes, yes I do. I've been under lots of pressure at work, just like you said, and I didn't realize it. Taking some time apart, staying with Dave, and hearing Phoebe's lovely news has brought things into perspective. I don't want us to live separate lives when the baby arrives. We're a family and should be together.'

Ginny screwed up her eyes, trying to decipher what he was saying. His apology was a long time coming and it made her feel numb. Was Adrian saying he wanted to work on their marriage? Or did he just want to put on a united front for their daughter's sake? Things couldn't just slot back to how they were previously. There'd have to be great change between them.

Ginny felt like she was trying to flee the maze in her dream again. She needed time to think about her relationship with Adrian and do things on her own terms. 'Perhaps you should have thought about all this before you joined a dating site,' she said.

'I understand I've hurt you—' Adrian started.

'That's the understatement of the year.' Ginny slid out of bed and carried the phone into the bathroom. She put Adrian on speaker while she cleaned her teeth.

'Phoebe's talking about moving her wedding forwards and I think we should be together for that,' he said. 'Please give it some thought. I'm sorry I messed up. Twenty-five years of marriage is too good to throw away.' He paused and cleared his throat. 'I still love you,' he said.

Ginny gripped her toothbrush at his use of the L word. She

hadn't heard him say it for a long time. It was a word some people threw around like birdseed, whereas others treated it like a precious gift. Adrian was one of the latter.

When they'd first dated, they used to whisper it to each other between kisses, reassuring each other, treating each other. Over time, it had morphed into a habitual addition to the end of phone calls, or as they left the house, 'Love you, bye . . .'

When Phoebe was born, Ginny and Adrian had bestowed the word on their daughter, so it took on a different meaning yet again. This wasn't a romantic love, it was one of protection and all-encompassing pride.

Although Ginny could admit to herself that she still loved Adrian, she didn't know what shape the word took for him any longer. Saying *I love you* back to him would sound like forgiveness that she wasn't ready to give. It would mean excusing his presence on the dating site or pretending it never happened. It hadn't been long since he started to message Jenny, sparking up an online relationship without knowing it was with his own wife. If Ginny admitted her ruse to him, right now, she didn't know if Adrian would laugh it off or be angry with her. And if she didn't know *that*, how well did she really know *him*?

Ginny looked at her reflection in the bathroom mirror, at her messy hair and toothpaste on her chin, and she wondered if Adrian would still say those words if he could see her like this. Perhaps he was saying them out of habit, or even as a bargaining tool.

She quietly spat out and rinsed her mouth, feeling frayed around the edges. She thought about Curtis again and how life was so short and what she'd do in his situation, with time literally ticking away. Would she try to get back with her husband? Or not?

'I really am sorry,' Adrian repeated. 'It's difficult talking on the phone. You'll be back home in a few days' time and we can work everything out then. We've always been there for each other and I know it's what *I* want . . .'

Ginny turned away from the mirror. She leaned her back against the sink and placed a hand against it, feeling the cool smooth ceramic. Several weeks ago, she would have jumped through a burning hoop to have him back. But now? She wasn't so sure.

By walking out on her, Adrian had opened a door in their marriage, allowing her to peek through into a different world she hadn't known existed. It was one full of colour and possibility. Ginny felt like she was hovering on a threshold, scared though intrigued to step over it. 'This isn't about you and what you want any longer, Adrian,' she said. 'I need to think about what *I* want.'

'I didn't really mean some of the things I've said to you. I haven't been thinking straight.'

'You've allowed me to picture my life without you, and it looks okay. Pretty good, in fact.'

Adrian's breathing grew hoarse. 'You've been calling me and texting . . .'

'Yes, and you haven't replied for weeks. You even wanted to take someone else on holiday.'

'I didn't mean it,' he mumbled.

Ginny walked back into her bedroom and all the thoughts in her brain were too big and too confusing to contemplate. They spun around as if caught in a whirlwind.

At this moment in time, she didn't want to think about her future at all. She wanted to ignore Adrian and their personal circumstances, and to take her mind and body somewhere else.

'I don't want to talk about any of this right now,' she said. 'I'm going to hang up.'

All Ginny really wanted to do was dance away her heartache.

CHAPTER 26

Cocktails

Ginny felt sassy in her new zebra-print dress, heels and her hair piled on top of her head, as she waited for the others in the courtyard. She refused to think about her conversation with Adrian and couldn't wait to sip cocktails, dance and laugh in Rimini.

The evening was sultry and Splendido took on a dusky, magical quality, like an Edward Hopper painting, as the sun fell. The air was rich and sweet from the smell of garlic and olive oil from Nico's kitchen, complemented by the flowers and fruit trees surrounding her. She could hear Nico singing inside the hotel and imagined him whirling around, using a pan as his dance partner.

Curtis came out of the hotel with Eric and let out a long whistle when he saw Ginny. 'Mamma mia,' he said with a grin.

Ginny cast him a chastising look, while simultaneously concealing a smile. '*Really?*'

'I meant that comment for Edna, not you,' Curtis said,

full of mock innocence. He nodded towards the doorstep where Edna and Heather had just appeared. 'See, she looks pure class.'

Edna had handstitched a simple waistcoat out of the vintage handkerchiefs she'd bought and wore it over her black clothes. At the bottom of the garment was a piece of fabric that didn't match the rest, grey cotton with a white daisy print. 'Your flattery means nothing to me,' she said, but the flush of her cheeks revealed that it did.

'What about my outfit?' Eric asked. He lifted one leg and then the other to show off his cream cargo trousers. He'd trimmed his beard and wore his hair down so it flowed over his shoulders.

'You look fine, too,' Curtis said. 'Like Thor having an off day.'

'At least I don't look like a reject from the Beastie Boys,' Eric fired back.

Ginny and Edna laughed. The men's blossoming bromance was bringing Eric further out of his shell.

Only Heather appeared subdued. Her curls were mussy and she was the only one who hadn't bothered to dress up, still wearing her yoga pants and a T-shirt. 'I've just taken a call from the care home,' she said. 'Mum's been asking for me and I feel guilty going out while she's stuck in there.'

Ginny's eyes softened with sympathy. 'Is she okay?'

'Yes, apparently she's fine. But . . .' Heather let out a sigh.

'There are only a few days of our holiday left,' Ginny said. 'I bet your mum wouldn't want you to miss out on anything.'

Heather took a moment to rally herself. 'She probably

doesn't even remember I'm on holiday, although I've told her many times. I suppose I just have to get on with my own life,' she said, not sounding convinced.

'You don't have to put on any kind of act with us. Just like you said, we're all friends here.'

Heather closed her eyes and nodded, taking a moment to think. 'Thank you. I *do* want to go to the beach bar tonight to support Curtis. Have I got time to change my clothes?'

'Of course. We're happy to wait for you.' Ginny smiled.

Gianfranco stood polishing the wing mirrors of his minibus. It looked pristine and shiny next to Nico's battered old vehicle. He'd agreed to drive everyone to Rimini, partly because he'd forgotten it was Loretta's birthday the next day and he hadn't bought her a present yet. He swept a cleaning cloth over his bonnet with a flourish and stood back to admire his handiwork. 'Remember, this is not a party vehicle,' he announced. 'If you feel ill please say so immediately, so you can get out.'

Curtis waved both hands as if directing air traffic. 'Gather around,' he shouted. 'The master plan is to arrive at the bar around eight p.m. for drink and food. We'll catch the sunset as the beats kick in and then dance until we drop.'

Loretta performed an excited twirl.

Nico's movements were twitchy when he joined them all. He twisted a napkin in his hands.

'Nico? Are you coming with us?' Curtis asked.

'I have important things to do, so I will stay here.' His eyes settled on his daughter. 'What time will you be back?' he asked her.

Loretta folded her arms and lifted an eyebrow.

'Before midnight?'

'*Papà!*'

'Twelve thirty?'

'I am nearly, officially, not a child any longer,' Loretta said with a teasing smile. 'I will turn eighteen at midnight and can do whatever I like.'

'Maybe not *everything*,' Nico said. 'And you will want to feel good for your birthday tomorrow. Do you still want to go to Castello Bella Vista with your friends? I will arrange this with Gianfranco.'

Loretta stared at him in surprise. 'Yes. Do you really mean it?'

Nico nodded. 'So, perhaps be back by two a.m.'

'*Grazie, Papà.* I will message my friends on the way to Rimini.'

Curtis bent his head to speak into Nico's ear. 'Not sure *I'll* last until two in the morning,' he said. 'We'll probably be back sooner.'

'That is a good idea,' Nico said. 'I am trusting you all to look after my daughter.'

Gianfranco pulled up outside the beach bar and Curtis jumped out of the minibus first. He strode inside to locate the manager and the two men talked for a while. Curtis gestured towards the group and the manager nodded, escorting them to an area with low cream sofas cordoned off with a red rope overlooking the white sandy beach. Big straw umbrellas above them were strung with fairy lights. The sun was sinking quickly in the sky, making it bloom violet with streaks of lemon.

'I told him it's Loretta's eighteenth tomorrow, so he's given us the best seats in the house,' Curtis said. 'It's also thanks to my considerable charm.'

'Ha–ha,' Loretta said.

The bar was full of gorgeous young people wearing flimsy outfits that showed off their bronzed skin. Ginny sensed that she and the others weren't the usual type of clientele. She felt a bit antiquated even in her glamorous dress and she nervously spun her wedding ring around on her finger. Tomorrow was her wedding anniversary and she was questioning if she'd been wise to reject Adrian's efforts on the phone.

Her melancholy musing was interrupted by the appearance of cocktail glasses filled with red liquid and adorned with straws, umbrellas and sparklers.

'*So* pretty,' Loretta said, snapping a photo on her phone.

'Nonalcoholic,' Curtis said, almost poking himself in the eye with a paper umbrella when he took a drink.

'*What?* Is that Papà's rule?'

'My rule,' Curtis said. 'You're not quite eighteen yet and I'm not drinking either. It gives me a headache.'

Edna eyed everyone. 'My capacity for alcohol is surprisingly large and I could probably drink you all under the table,' she said. 'Tonight, I shall also abstain.'

Ginny thought it was a good idea not to end up drunk and crying on a sun lounger.

Loretta gingerly sampled her drink and nodded. 'Hmm, *buono*,' she said.

Ginny enjoyed chilling out and chatting with the others, eating small plates of food and watching as the setting sun made the clouds look like they were on fire. The music grew louder until she could feel the bass thumping in her chest.

Curtis stood and performed an elaborate bow in front of Edna. He proffered his hand and she took it, standing up with a curtsy.

'The sunshine has loosened my joints and I bet I can dance like Margot Fonteyn,' Edna told him. 'Please don't feel intimidated by that.'

'Who?' Curtis asked, striking a *Saturday Night Fever* pose.

The two of them headed to the middle of the dance floor.

At first, other people in the bar stopped and stared at the man dressed twenty years too young who was boogying with an elderly lady dressed in a patchwork waistcoat. But soon they became impressed by Curtis's and Edna's stamina and exuberance. A small crowd gathered around them, joining in with their dance moves.

Loretta peeped over the top of her mocktail and blew out her cheeks. 'Curtis is making a fool of himself,' she said to Ginny. 'Please stop him.'

Ginny laughed. 'Somehow, I don't think he cares, and Edna looks the happiest I've ever seen her.'

Curtis noticed Loretta was looking at him and made even more exaggerated movements, until she burst out laughing. 'Ridiculous,' she mouthed and shook her head.

Eric hunched over in a corner seat, trying to make himself look as small as possible. Two girls eyed him from across the dance floor and whispered to each other. They made their way over and persuaded him to join them.

Heather sat with her drink untouched in front of her. Even

though she'd changed into a T-shirt and linen skirt, she looked like she wanted to be somewhere else. 'Please go and enjoy yourself,' she urged Ginny. 'I'm fine here on my own.'

'Are you sure?'

Heather nodded. 'I just need a little time out.' She made a T shape with her hands.

Ginny got up to dance, posturing to songs from the eighties and nineties she hadn't heard for a while and a few tunes she didn't know. She only got to dance at weddings, or shimmied in her chair while playing tracks on her radio show, so she took the opportunity to bop and spin until she felt giddy and her feet hurt. Whenever thoughts of Adrian appeared in her head, she danced even more furiously to shake them out. A mirror ball flecked her face with light and she felt like a teenager again. The music reverberated through her body and all the happy people around her made her feel invigorated and free.

When her mouth grew dry, she headed to the bar to get another drink. She saw Loretta talking to a boy and girl of a similar age to her, on the other side. The boy pointed towards Curtis and Edna, and Loretta shook her head, as if to say, *No, those people definitely aren't with me.*

Ginny bought a cola and waited until Loretta sat down next to her. 'Would your friends like to join us?' she asked.

Loretta smoothed down her dress with her hand. 'No, it's fine. They are just some people I know from work.'

Ginny sipped her drink and tried not to react. 'I didn't know you had a job, other than working with your dad.'

The teenager quickly averted her eyes. 'It is only a little thing,' she said with a wave of her hand. She chewed on the end of her straw for a while, thinking. 'Actually, Papà doesn't know about my job and I'm worried he will find out soon. Perhaps you can help me out?'

Ginny shrugged a shoulder. 'How?'

'I have been working at Castello Bella Vista in secret, helping out with weddings, parties and other events, to make some money for college,' she said.

Ginny tried not to gape at her. '*Oh*. Does Gianfranco know about this?'

Loretta nodded. 'Of course, it's his hotel. I've decided I want to study event management, not fashion, so I want experience of working in a proper hotel. I begged Gianfranco to give me a job and not to tell Papà. He understands what he is like . . .'

'Splendido is a prop—' Ginny started to say.

'It is small and traditional,' Loretta interrupted with a curl of her lips. 'Nothing ever changes there and I know Papà doesn't have any money to pay me a real wage. At Castello, I have already learned and experienced many new things and saved some money.' She lowered her gaze. 'I know Papà will be angry with me.'

'So, when I saw you creeping around in the early morning, you'd been working?'

Loretta nodded. 'A friend gave me a lift home, the boy we saw in the village. I'd been working at a party that went on for a long time. There was a lot to tidy up afterwards.' She picked up a napkin and folded it several times. 'You are friendly with Papà, and you like to solve problems. Will you speak to him for me?'

The back of Ginny's neck prickled at the thought of Loretta

and Gianfranco in cahoots behind Nico's back. Nico might be more upset than angry when he found out, and Ginny had also hoped for a fun evening without any problems to solve. 'Your dad is a good man and does his best for you,' she said. 'You need to be grown-up and sort this out for yourself. Not telling him will only make things worse, for *both* of you.'

Loretta twirled her straw between her thumb and forefinger while she thought. 'I want him to understand that I am not like Mamma. I do not want to leave forever, I only want to spread my wings. I am learning things that will help him.'

Ginny smiled and leaned in a little closer. 'I think you've put it perfectly yourself,' she said. 'Now all you have to do is tell your father.'

'It is not possible. I can explain things to him, but I can't make him listen.'

'Sometimes you just have to try,' Ginny said.

CHAPTER 27

Waves

Later that evening, when Ginny, Edna, Eric, Curtis and Loretta were all exhausted from dancing, they took off their shoes and carried them down to the beach, accompanied by Heather. The sea looked like a shimmering grey satin sheet and the swish of the waves offered a welcome respite from the distant hum of music. They found a line of sun loungers and Eric and Edna lay down to look up at the constellations in the sky. Heather sat on the end of her lounger with her fingers knitted together. Laughter sounded further along the shoreline as people splashed and swam in the sea.

Curtis handed his phone to Ginny. 'Will you film me for my blog?' he asked, signalling for her to follow him down to the water's edge.

Ginny watched through the screen as Curtis picked up a pebble and tried to skim it across the surface of the sea. After one tiny bounce, it disappeared into the waves.

For his next throw, he showed off by curving his arm behind his back but his stone didn't even reach the water. He lost his footing and toppled backwards so he lay sprawled on the sand. Jumping back up to his feet, Curtis grinned and wriggled his backside for the camera, displaying a damp patch on his shorts.

Ginny giggled and then clamped her lips together, trying not to record her laughter on the video.

Curtis picked up more pebbles and hurled them into the water with increasing force. The tide was coming in and waves soon lapped against his toes. They crept in higher until his feet were surrounded by water.

Ginny jumped back when a wave crashed higher onto the beach. It crawled and fizzed until it reached the end of the sun loungers, and the others stood up and pulled them higher up on the beach. Curtis didn't notice and stood with his eyes fixed on the horizon.

Ginny paddled closer to him, filming as the water swilled around their ankles.

He reached down and retrieved yet another pebble. This one had a hole in the middle and he held it up to his eye like a monocle. He turned around to survey Ginny through it and spoke to the camera. 'This stone is like me,' he said. 'It looks solid, but is defective. No one will notice it when it's gone.' He lobbed it as far as he could, watching as it flew through the air until it plopped quietly down. He stared after it numbly.

Ginny zoomed in on him, inadvertently capturing his trembling lips and glistening eyes on film. Something rolled down her cheek and she realized she was crying. She tried to do it quietly so the video wouldn't pick up the sound.

Recording Curtis suddenly felt like an intrusion, so she

ended the video. She waded towards him and placed a hand on his shoulder.

He turned to face her and managed a weak smile before his face crumpled. He dropped his chin to his chest and his tears fell into the sea.

Ginny reached up and gently cupped the side of his head, pulling it towards her until it rested on her shoulder.

'Sorry, mate,' Curtis said between sniffs. 'Don't know what came over me. Didn't mean to get all maudlin.'

'It's okay,' she whispered. 'We're all here to look after each other.'

They stood together while the sea swept further in, reaching their calves and hypnotizing them with the swirl of white foam around their legs. The sky was now navy blue and the stars looked like crystals.

After some time, Ginny looked around her and saw they had company. Edna and Eric stood a few metres away and Loretta kicked her feet, splashing until her dress was wet and clung to her knees. Even Heather joined them, standing at the shoreline with her arms wrapped around her body.

The hem of Edna's skirt billowed on the waves. 'I used to be able to swim like a dolphin,' she called, above the swish of the waves.

Curtis forced a smile. 'Is there anything you can't do?'

She mused on this for a while. 'No, I don't believe so,' she said. 'Not if I put my mind to it.'

He woofed a laugh and the old, fun Curtis reappeared. 'Film this,' he told Ginny. Pulling away from her, he spread his arms wide then let himself fall back into the sea. A big splash enveloped him.

Ginny's mouth dropped open. '*Curtis.* You're drenched.'

'Yup. I know.' He flipped himself onto his front and

breaststroked his arms in the air while walking along the bottom of the sea. He circled Edna and hummed the theme tune from *Jaws*.

Edna's mouth twisted into a mischievous smile. She lowered herself into the water, too, sitting down so the sea lapped around her torso. She let her arms bob up and down on the waves. 'I won't be able to do *this* in Shady Pines,' she said.

Ginny shook her head at them both in disbelief. She filmed Curtis and Edna and then zoomed in on Eric as he performed a neat dive headfirst into the waves. He bobbed back up with his hair covering his face like a curtain.

'You have all lost your minds,' Loretta shouted. She shrieked as she waded in further until the sea reached her thighs.

Heather paddled tentatively in the shallows. 'I can't swim very well. Be careful, everyone,' she said. 'No being silly.'

'The sea's nice, not too choppy,' Curtis called back to her.

Ginny filmed the silver clouds drifting across the moon and lowered the phone to capture everyone splashing around. She focused on the expanse of sea until she saw a thick band of white water approaching. It looked to be rising and travelling towards them with speed. She lowered the phone, so she could view it with her own eyes. None of the others seemed to have noticed it and Ginny's ribcage contracted.

The wave grew taller so it soon looked like a wall of water. She heard it roaring and she numbly tucked Curtis's phone into her bra for safekeeping. Cupping her mouth with her hand, she shouted to get everyone's attention. 'There's a big wave coming. Get out of the sea . . .'

Ginny tried to drag herself through the water, heading

towards the shore. The sea sucked her back in, as if trying to tug her into its midst. She could hear the wave bellowing behind her and then there was an eerie second or two of quietness. The wave reached her and seemed to hang over her head for a few moments like the wing of a giant bird, before it crashed down on top of her. It knocked Ginny off her feet and she thrashed around, coughing and spluttering. Her eyes, nose and throat were clogged with sea water and when she broke to the surface, the sky was so dark she couldn't get her bearings.

Through stinging eyes, she saw Eric and Loretta helping Edna up onto the beach and she felt a brief rush of relief. Trying to wade ashore again was like moving through mud. Her ankle buckled and she slipped, immersed in the water again. She fought against it, thrashing and trying to claw her way back out, her limbs growing weaker and her breath shorter.

Just when she thought the sea was claiming her for itself, something firm circled her waist. Ginny heard Curtis's muffled shout, 'You alright?'

She shook her head furiously, not able to see him properly.

'Hold onto me.' He pulled her close and she felt herself being towed along beside him.

A rumbling sound came again and another big wave broke against their backs, sending them both reeling. Ginny gasped and tried to right herself, unsure what direction she was facing. Again, she felt Curtis beside her, strong and solid. He helped to pull her out of the water and they both staggered up onto the beach.

Ginny coughed until her chest hurt. Droplets of water ran

down her back making her shiver. 'You saved my life,' she wheezed.

'Nah,' he said, patting her on the back. 'No drama.'

'But you did.'

'It was only a puddle.'

Ginny looked at him, full of gratitude. Underneath all Curtis's bluster and bluff, there was strength and vulnerability. She discreetly pulled his phone out of her bra and looked at it. 'Sorry, I tried my best to save it.'

'It's only a phone,' he said, then inched back with astonishment. 'Did I really just say *that*?'

A towel landed around Ginny's shoulders, and she watched Loretta handing them out to Eric and Edna. They each dried themselves in a state of shock.

Ginny's dress clung to her like a shroud and she rubbed her hair. She looked around her and a lump lodged in her throat like a swallowed sweet. 'Where's Heather?' she asked, her voice sounding echoey.

The others looked around them, too.

'I think I saw her in the sea when I got out,' Edna said. 'Only briefly,' she added.

Ginny felt like a mannequin, stiff and fixed to the spot. Everyone stared at the sea that now looked pewter and innocent.

'She said she couldn't swim very well,' Eric said quietly.

A fraction of a second passed before a rush of activity broke out and everyone searched around frantically for their missing friend.

Curtis patrolled around the sun loungers, crouching on the

sand to look under them. Edna called out Heather's name and Loretta ran up and down the shore.

'Where is she . . .?' Ginny asked. 'She can't have drow—'

'*No*,' Loretta cried out.

'She didn't go in deep . . .' Edna said. 'Is there a lifebelt around?'

'What should we do?' Loretta asked.

'It's all my fault,' Curtis's voice cracked. 'I went in there first. I messed around in the sea.'

The waves rolled in calmly as if mocking them.

Panic made Ginny's temples throb. She was the one who'd invited Heather on holiday. She'd persuaded her to come to the beach bar and now she'd vanished. She looked around her, and at the others searching helplessly. Were they all too late?

'Can someone give me a hand?' a woman's voice said from behind them.

Ginny turned to see Heather treading tentatively along the sand holding a tray full of cups.

'I thought you might all need warming up,' Heather said. She halted and frowned. 'Um, why are you all looking at me like that? Have you seen a ghost or something?'

'Oh, god,' Ginny gulped. 'We thought that you'd . . . gone.'

'*What?* You mean, drowned?' Heather lowered her tray. 'Don't be silly, I went to get drinks. *Cioccolata calda*, Italian hot chocolate.'

'You didn't get hit by the wave?' Edna asked. 'I thought I saw you . . .'

Heather shook her head. 'I didn't stay in the water.'

'I usually have magnificent vision . . .'

'The salt water must have got into your eyes, Edna,' Curtis said.

Loretta hugged her towel around her. 'Papà is going to kill me when he sees me like this.'

'It's my fault,' Curtis repeated. 'I'll take full responsibility.'

Ginny couldn't believe they'd done something so foolish, but along the coast she could still hear people playing in the waves.

Eric pulled all their sun loungers closer together so they could huddle and drink their hot chocolate. Ginny's shoulders shook and she gripped her cup with all her might. She caught sight of her watch and saw it was just before midnight. It was almost her wedding anniversary, and she allowed herself a few moments of self-pity. What if *she* had drowned? Adrian would have been left without a wife, and Phoebe without a mum. She'd never have met her grandchild. All because she'd wanted to escape her life at home for a while. Her head suddenly felt too heavy for her neck to support.

'Perhaps we should go home,' Loretta said, looking down at her sodden dress. 'Is that okay, Curtis?'

He nodded meekly.

'I'll go find Gianfranco.'

Ginny, Heather, Edna and Eric agreed to go with her.

Curtis dried his phone with a towel and played around with it. 'It's still working,' he called out, as the screen lit up his face with a silver glow. 'I'll follow you all in a mo. I want to jot some stuff down.' He watched the video of himself hurling pebbles into the sea and his face grew stern. Without looking up, he started to type.

Before she left him alone, Ginny picked up a towel and draped it around his shoulders.

CHAPTER 28

Fireflies

The atmosphere in Gianfranco's minibus was downcast as it approached Splendido. Edna had fallen asleep with her face resting on Eric's shoulder and she emitted small rhythmic snores. Curtis was still typing on his phone and Heather's thoughts were elsewhere. Ginny didn't have a clue what to feel. Her emotions were all over the place, ranging from relief at escaping the waves, to sorrow about the state of her marriage, to lingering giddiness from dancing.

'I hope my seats are not damp,' Gianfranco muttered as he drove through the gates of Splendido. 'They are made from the finest leather.'

'They are fine. We're sitting on towels,' Loretta said glumly.

Curtis finished writing up his blog. His movements were jerky as he put his phone away. 'What are you going to tell your dad?' he asked her.

'The truth,' Loretta said. 'We were paddling in the sea, there was an unexpected wave and you saved Ginny's life.'

Ginny turned to gape at her. 'Please don't tell him that,' she said. 'We don't want to worry him.'

Loretta fixed her with a stare. 'You tell me to be honest with Papà about my job, and then ask me to keep a secret from him,' she said. 'Make up your mind.'

Gianfranco kept jerking his head around, listening to their conversation. He pulled on his handbrake in the courtyard and spoke to Loretta in Italian, so Ginny couldn't understand.

When the teenager raised her voice back, Ginny shrank into her seat.

From the cool glances Gianfranco and Loretta gave her, she felt sure she was the topic of their discussion. 'Um, what did you both just say?' she asked, when Loretta stopped talking and folded her arms.

The teenager puckered her lips. 'Gianfranco is worried that Papà will blame him for giving me a job when he finds out I've been working at Castello. I reminded him I'm earning money and gaining valuable work experience. I told him *you* think I should reveal *everything* to Papà.'

Gianfranco cast Ginny a chastening glare and made a claw with his hand. 'Nico will go *wild*,' he said.

Ginny slumped and a chill rippled down her backbone. She opened her mouth to defend herself but Loretta wrenched open the minibus door and jumped out.

The others reluctantly followed her.

A light came on in the kitchen and Nico walked out into the courtyard with Biscotti trotting at his side. The hotel owner's body language was relaxed until he saw his daughter's straggly hair and crumpled dress. 'What has happened?' he asked, his brow furrowing. 'Why are your clothes damp?'

Curtis stepped forwards, taking charge. 'We went for a little wade,' he said. 'Not my best idea . . .'

A bead of sweat bobbled on Nico's chin. 'You went in the sea? At night?' he asked. 'And Loretta, too?'

Curtis lowered his eyes and nodded.

Loretta placed a hand on Nico's arm. 'I am fine, Papà. The sea was . . . um, unpredictable and we all got wet.'

'*All* of you?'

'Curtis was a hero tonight. He saved Ginny from the water,' Loretta said.

Ginny felt her face flush up to the roots of her hair. Nico bored his eyes into hers, making her squirm.

'You were in the sea, too?' he demanded.

She gave an apologetic nod.

Nico stared at everyone's crinkled clothes and glowered. 'You were *all* supposed to look after my daughter. It's her birthday and I trusted you.'

'We're all okay,' Loretta said, reaching out for him. 'There is nothing to worry about.'

Gianfranco got out of the minibus and Nico immediately strode towards him. 'What do you know about all this?'

Gianfranco's eyes darted, unsure what his friend was referring to. 'I thought I was helping out you and Loretta with money . . .'

'*What?*' Nico's forehead creased even more. 'What do you mean by *money*?'

Gianfranco rubbed the back of his neck. 'Um, Loretta's job at my hotel,' he said. 'I was trying to help her out.'

Loretta glared at him and expelled a huff. 'We were talking about swimming in the sea,' she said. '*Not* my job.'

'*Oh*,' Gianfranco melded his lips shut. 'Sorry.'

Nico's eyes flashed as he glared at them all in turn. 'There is a lot of explaining to do here. We will all speak in the morning,' he said. 'Loretta, go to bed.'

'But Papà!'

'Inside, *now*,' he snapped. 'And do not think you are going to Castello Bella Vista for your birthday. It is cancelled.'

Loretta's face fell. She opened her mouth to speak then thought better of it. She ran towards the hotel with a sob.

Gianfranco stepped forwards with his palms upturned. 'Nico, *amico mio*. It is not her fault. I should have told you about—'

'Stop.' Nico pressed a hand flat against Gianfranco's chest and turned to face his guests. 'I do not want to speak to *any* of you.' He scowled. 'I don't even know if I want you to stay in my hotel any longer.'

'Nico. We're so sorry . . .' Ginny started. She stopped speaking when he fixed her with a look that might turn her to stone.

He spun around and marched back into his hotel.

Ginny watched him, feeling hopeless. Her insides felt like they were shrivelling up. She wanted to run after him to explain, but suspected it was best to let his fury subside. They'd all been through an emotional time and she couldn't help blaming herself. If only she'd agreed to speak to Nico about Loretta's job, like the teenager had asked her to, she might have prevented this row from happening. If she hadn't been busy filming Curtis, she could have stopped Loretta from going into the sea.

Not only was her own wedding anniversary lying in ruins, but now Loretta's special birthday had imploded, too, and the guilt felt like a boulder in Ginny's stomach.

Eric patted his leg and Biscotti slunk to his side. 'I need a walk,' he said.

'It's late, man,' Curtis said. 'Too dark for hiking . . .'

Eric shrugged and walked away anyway with the dog by his side.

'I'm ready for bed,' Heather said, rubbing her eyes. 'I'll escort Edna to her room.'

For once, Edna didn't object.

Gianfranco remained standing in the courtyard with Ginny. 'Do not worry about Nico,' he said. 'He doesn't get angry often. When it happens, it's over quickly.'

'He's disappointed with us all.' She looked down at her feet. 'That's worse and will last a lot longer.'

'Yes. He finds it difficult to trust anyone since his wife left, and now I have let him down also.' He let out a regretful sigh.

Ginny's jaw felt tight after all the upset. 'You should go home and get some sleep. Thanks for driving us this evening.'

'I wish I had taken Nico's minibus, then I might have broken down and not reached Rimini,' Gianfranco said. He got back inside his own vehicle and drove away.

Ginny's legs shook as she entered the hotel. Her hair was brittle from sea salt and she could still taste it in her throat. A light was on in the kitchen and she glanced around tentatively, making sure Nico and Loretta weren't around. She could hear their muffled voices, raised and coming from Loretta's room.

A homemade cake sat on the dining table adorned with eighteen unlit candles. There was a small box wrapped in floral paper and tied with a pink bow.

Ginny's heart sank even further, imagining how she'd feel if Phoebe had gone out with friends and returned in such a state. She'd be furious, distraught and unhappy. Just thinking about all the emotions made her miss her daughter and home life more than ever.

Knowing the adrenaline still pumping through her body wouldn't allow her to sleep for some time, Ginny tidied up the dining room. She found a globe of dough and some tomatoes on the worktop, as if Nico had planned to make fresh pizza for everyone when they got back from the beach bar. She guiltily placed the ingredients back in the fridge.

Several photos of Nico's relatives had been removed from the wall and sat stacked on the table, leaving behind ghostly grey rectangles. It looked like he'd started to make changes to the hotel and Ginny cursed herself for being part of any setback.

'Happy anniversary, Ginny,' she whispered to herself, feeling like a failure in *all* areas of her life.

She closed her eyes and flashed back to flailing in the sea. She really had thought she wasn't going to survive. Struggling to catch her breath, she stumbled towards the back door with tears in her eyes, needing some fresh air. Flinging it open, Ginny took in several deep gulps. The moon had turned the sky a milky blue and she wrapped her arms across her chest for comfort.

She watched as a figure headed in through the gates and towards the courtyard, probably Eric returning from his walk. Ginny looked out for Biscotti and couldn't see him. There were many shadows in the courtyard to conceal the dog.

She was deliberating whether to go back inside when she saw something glinting in the figure's hand.

As the person drew closer, she saw the man didn't walk with Eric's usual purpose. Perhaps Gianfranco had returned, or a new guest was arriving at the hotel. Ginny frowned into the darkness and waited.

The person gradually moved forwards until she could see his features in the moonlight and she let out a gasp.

'Hello, Ginny,' Adrian said, holding out a present wrapped in shiny paper. 'Happy silver wedding anniversary.'

CHAPTER 29

Photograph

Ginny stood frozen, trying to comprehend that her husband was really standing in front of her. Since she'd last seen him, his face looked slimmer than usual, as if he'd lost weight. He wore cord trousers and a sweater that looked too formal for Italy, even at night. Still, it was a relief to see the old version of him, not the one wearing shades and skinny jeans. Part of her wanted to throw her arms around him, so he could comfort her after the evening's events, but she also wanted to shove him away. 'W-what are you doing here?' she spluttered.

'It didn't seem right to spend our anniversary apart.' Adrian shrugged, as if the last few weeks hadn't happened.

'Couldn't you have called or texted first?'

'I wanted to surprise you. My flight here was delayed, so I've only just checked into my hotel. I didn't want to wait until breakfast to see you, in case you set off somewhere early. So, I took a taxi here.' He stepped forwards and looked all around him. 'This place looks . . . rustic.'

Ginny pursed her lips. 'I'm guessing you didn't come here to discuss Italian architecture.'

Adrian nodded. 'Can we go inside to talk?'

She glanced over her shoulder. Nico and Loretta might still be awake and she didn't want either of them to find a stranger sitting in their dining room. She could hardly sneak Adrian upstairs to her bedroom without anyone hearing. 'No, it's too late,' she said.

'*Too late?*' he asked, with fear rising in his voice.

Ginny reassessed her words. Adrian must have assumed she was referring to their marriage, and she welcomed his worry.

'I'm sorry, you're right,' he said with his shoulders sloping. 'I should have told you I was coming, or waited until later to see you. Do you want me to leave?'

Yes, Ginny thought without saying it. Then she reconsidered. Hadn't she been longing for some kind of big gesture from him? Didn't this show he really cared? 'We can sit outside, at one of the tables for a while,' she said. 'There are blankets if we get cold.'

'Thanks. I left my jacket at the hotel.'

They sat down opposite each other, both of them unsure who should talk first. Ginny wrapped a blanket around her shoulders and looked up at the fairy lights hanging from a tree. They looked like clusters of fireflies and speckled their faces with a golden glow.

Adrian smiled tentatively. 'You look beautiful,' he said.

Ginny brushed salt dust from her forearms. Something tingled inside her at his compliment, even though she didn't feel attractive at all. 'Thanks,' she said.

He cleared his throat. 'I've bought you something for our anniversary,' he said, passing the present to her.

Ginny hesitated. 'I didn't get you anything . . .'

'That's understandable.'

She took the gift and peeled off the paper to reveal a simple silver photo frame. Angling it to get a better view, she saw the photo was of her and Adrian sitting on their sofa at home, laughing together.

'The frame's sterling silver,' he said. 'I tracked down the photographer who did our magazine shoot and asked to see the shots he didn't use. I thought you'd like this one.'

Ginny studied the picture and wondered if she and Adrian had been truly happy when it had been taken, or if they'd been acting like that for the camera. It was difficult to tell and she hated how his recent behaviour had forced her to put their relationship under a microscope.

'And you look really hot in the picture,' he added.

A surprised laugh escaped from Ginny's mouth. Adrian's sense of humour was one of the things that had attracted her to him in the first place and it had been missing for quite some time. 'You don't look too bad yourself,' she said.

He pulled a face. 'I look rough and have for some time. You're the one who still looks great. You have a good job and lots of friends . . . I envy you sometimes.'

It was rare for him to open up to her like this. Ginny's first instinct was to deny it all, to tell him she'd been replaced at work by Kizzi and felt superfluous, in a bid to make him feel better. But why should she, after what he'd put her through?

Adrian wriggled his shoulders and relaxed back into his

chair. 'I think this time apart from each other has been good for us,' he said. 'We both needed it.'

Ginny's feelings towards him had been thawing, but then blew away in an instant, as if a snowstorm had blasted in on a sunny day. She blinked at him hard, questioning if she'd heard him correctly. 'I think you mean it's what *you* needed,' she said, lowering her voice to a hiss. '*I* was happy as we were.'

He surveyed her for a few moments before leaning forwards. 'Were you honestly *really* happy?' he asked her. 'Or did you feel the same way as I did, like you were always running for a train that was pulling away from a station, leaving you feeling stranded? We've been married for a long time, we live together, and eat and sleep together, yet it feels like there's been a big gap between us for a long time.'

Although his words stung, Ginny knew he was right. She could admit to feeling unsettled and unsatisfied, but she hadn't resorted to joining a dating site. Their conversation suddenly felt too heavy for this time of the morning and she wanted to crawl upstairs to bed. 'You've had plenty of opportunities to discuss this with me,' she said stiffly. 'I'm on holiday and I'm tired. We all went out to a beach bar in Rimini this evening and I'm—'

'*We?*' Adrian chimed in. 'Do you mean the strangers you invited on holiday? What are they like?'

There was a hint of jealousy in his voice and Ginny gave it a silent cheer. She decided to tell him about her new friends. 'Edna's eighty and has been feeling lonely since losing her daughter and husband. She's been springing to life since showing us how to sew. Curtis is a property developer in his late thirties who's been hiding a heart of gold. Heather's a bouncy primary school teacher who's struggling with her mum's health issues, and Eric's a shy carpenter mourning the loss of his dog.'

The corners of Adrian's mouth twitched upwards. 'His dog? I thought you'd invited people with broken hearts.'

Ginny narrowed her eyes at him. 'Bess was Eric's best friend, just as much as you *were* mine,' she said.

Adrian sat back as if she'd punched him in the chest. 'Ouch,' he said. 'I suppose I deserve that.'

'Yes, you do.'

'Sorry, I stand corrected. They're all lucky to have you sorting out their problems.'

'We've been helping out each other.' Ginny set the photo frame to one side. 'I'm not trying to be the Patron Saint of Problems any longer.'

Adrian digested her words. 'When I said *that*, I didn't mean it as a bad thing. Maybe I've felt left out, because you're always helping others . . .'

'I've tried to help you, too, and you didn't like it.'

Adrian ran a finger around the collar of his sweater. 'I *know* I've been thoughtless and unreasonable. I know you've deserved more from me. Lots of people lock their problems away and I'm one of them. I can't expect you to be a mind reader.' He reached out and smoothed his thumb across the back of her hand. 'It *is* really good to see you.'

Ginny couldn't deny that she felt the same way, too. Adrian was the person she'd thought of when she was tumbling in the waves and coughing up salt water on the beach. He was her partner in life, her friend and soul mate. His touch raised a flutter in her stomach.

'I miss our life together,' Adrian said. 'Nearing fifty years old feels like the curtain coming down halfway through a play. You shuffle off to the bar to get a drink and then forget what's just happened on stage. I'm sorry it took Phoebe's pregnancy to make me appreciate what we had, what we do *have*, together.'

They both fell quiet so the only sound was the chirrup of crickets in the undergrowth. Ginny curled her fingers away from him. The hurt Adrian had caused her was so deep it would take more than just words to heal it. 'Showing up with a present doesn't mend the things you've said and done,' she said.

'That's just the start . . .' Adrian paused. 'There's something else, too.'

A metallic taste appeared in Ginny's mouth and she swallowed it away. 'What is it?'

'I'm staying at the castle hotel on the hill and have spoken to the owner, Gianfranco. He says we can still renew our wedding vows, just like you wanted to. We can have a fresh start, look to the future and leave everything behind us.'

Ginny felt like she'd been pushed off a high diving board and was bracing herself for a belly flop. Her head floated upwards as her stomach plunged to the depths of her body. Adrian was saying all the things she'd wanted to hear, so why did his suggestion sound like white noise in her brain? She *couldn't* renew her wedding vows with him. She was on holiday with Eric, Edna, Heather and Curtis and had to think about them. She had to make amends with Nico and make sure Loretta was okay.

Her pulse quickened when she pictured herself with Nico in the Venetian garden, his lips pressing softly against hers. She wished she had a fan to waft her face.

'Come back to Castello Bella Vista with me tonight,' Adrian said. 'I've got a suite with an enormous bed and a whirlpool bath. You only have a few days of your holiday left and we can spend it together in style.'

'I can't leave my friends, just like that . . .'

'Surely, they won't mind. You've only known them a little over two weeks. Please say yes.'

Ginny shivered and hugged the blanket around her. 'This is all too sudden. I need to stay here tonight.'

Adrian gnawed his lip, thinking to himself for a while. 'I have something else to tell you . . . it was going to be a surprise.'

Ginny was now so tired she felt like flopping her head forwards onto the table, to go to sleep. 'What is it?'

'Phoebe and Pete are here with me,' Adrian said. 'They can join us for our vow renewal.'

Ginny's mouth hinged open and she rubbed between her eyebrows. 'What? They're here, in Italy?'

Adrian's smile was a little self-congratulatory. 'I wanted to do something special for you and invited them along. I knew you'd love to see Phoebe.' He took hold of her hand again. 'We can renew our wedding vows at two o'clock this afternoon, and then Phoebe and Pete can get married afterwards.'

Ginny shook her head, trying to take this in. 'Can they do it so quickly?'

'It will be a symbolic ceremony, before the baby arrives. They can marry afterwards in England, to make it official, when they're ready.'

Ginny was sure her body was shaking, but when she looked

down, she was sitting still. She knew their daughter wanted to get married sooner and with less fuss, but this seemed *too* quick and more complicated. 'Is this what Phoebe wants?'

'It was my idea to invite them to the renewal, and Pete's idea for their ceremony at the same time. We can all cement our futures together, as a family.'

Although Adrian's grand gesture was full of the passion she'd yearned for, a spate of dizziness overcame her. 'You hurt me so much . . .' Ginny whispered.

'I know and I'm truly sorry.' Adrian stood up and walked around the table. He kissed the top of her head and pulled her close.

Ginny pressed her cheek to his chest and felt his heart beating. The events of the last few weeks slipped away, replaced by memories appearing in her head, of her first kiss with Adrian, getting the keys to their first house, and kissing baby Phoebe's tiny fingers. They'd had so many wonderful times together and some tough ones, too. There were probably more of each to come, that they could embrace and face together.

It seemed the older you got, the more life picked up speed, and she and Adrian might be halfway through it by now, or even three-quarters. Or perhaps even nearing the end. Life was impossible to predict.

'Give me the chance to make things right,' Adrian said, crouching down beside her. 'I'm happy to arrange everything and you can even invite your new friends. I've already been thinking about what to say in our vows. I love you and always will.'

Ginny willed herself to echo his words, so things could slide back to how they were previously. She screwed her eyes shut and found she couldn't do it. She stood up stiffly and dropped her blanket onto the chair. 'I need to sleep and have time to think.'

Adrian hesitated. 'Okay, I understand.'

Ginny walked towards the back door and Adrian accompanied her. They stood facing each other in the shadows, and it was easy to imagine him as a young man again. She was about to say good night when he suddenly leaned in and kissed her.

His mouth felt so familiar and inviting that Ginny melted into him. The kiss was like sitting in front of the fire on a cold day, wrapped in a fluffy blanket. It felt like a welcome home.

After pulling apart, they glanced coyly at each other like the teenagers they once were.

'Sorry, I couldn't help myself,' Adrian said, pressing his forehead against hers. 'Please call me when you wake up, whatever your decision is. Phoebe and Pete will go ahead with their ceremony anyway.'

Ginny swallowed. 'Okay.'

'I hope you say *yes*.' Adrian kissed the tip of her nose. He picked the photo frame up off the table and passed it to her before walking away. He paused to wave when he reached the hotel gates. 'See you later,' he called out.

'Shh.' She giggled back at him.

Back inside Splendido, Ginny stood with her back against the door, hugging the frame to her chest. Her heartbeat sped as she walked across the empty dining room towards the stairs. Had this *really* just happened?

She jumped when she caught sight of someone standing at the end of the hallway in the darkness.

'Ginny,' Nico said. 'Are you okay? I thought I heard voices.'

Her fingers stiffened around the frame. She felt strangely guilty about talking to her husband and was glad it was too dark for Nico to see her face properly. 'I'm just going to bed. Sorry if I woke you,' she said. 'And sorry again about this evening.'

She had the strongest desire to tell Nico about Adrian's arrival and to ask him how he'd feel if Maria returned, begging for his forgiveness. Would he welcome her back with open arms? However, Ginny's eyelids were sore and swollen and she saw Nico stifling a yawn, too. They'd both gone through enough emotional turmoil for one evening and she needed to sleep. 'I should go to bed now,' she said.

Nico moved closer so Ginny could hear his breathing. Something about his presence always made her feel safe and secure.

'I must also apologize for the way I spoke to you earlier, the way I spoke to everyone,' he said. 'Loretta has explained everything and things will look better when we all wake up.'

'I hope so,' Ginny whispered. 'Good night, Nico.'

As she crept upstairs in the dark, she concentrated on each step and thoughts whirled in her head. Phoebe was here to get married, and Adrian wanted to renew their wedding vows. Wasn't this exactly what Ginny wanted, what she'd hoped for?

And then there was Nico. Lovely Nico who had stirred up feelings inside her that had lain dormant for a long time, who was kind and caring and . . . new.

What on earth was she going to do?

CHAPTER 30

Ribbons

Ginny slept surprisingly well, considering she'd almost been swept out to sea and her husband had shown up in Italy unannounced. When her eyes opened, later that morning, she turned to see Adrian smiling out at her from the silver photo frame, proving he really *was* here. There was a tickly sensation in her stomach when she remembered their kiss.

He had displayed all the spontaneity, interest and, yes, passion she'd been looking for. And yet, his presence on the dating site and his conversations with Jenny speckled in her head like tarnish spots around the edge of an old mirror.

Ginny recalled how she'd fought hard to hold her own parents together. Today, she had an opportunity that had evaded her back then. She could glue back the pieces of her own relationship, to fix it and make it strong again. Phoebe wouldn't have to experience the turmoil of her parents' marriage breaking down, like Ginny had.

She sat up in bed and reminded herself that out of all the potential matches on ChainReaxions, Adrian had been attracted to the photo and profile she'd created. He'd replied to her wink. They'd both rekindled their connection and the ceremony would seal that. It would be amazing if Phoebe and Pete said their vows, too, a real family affair.

Ginny told herself that Nico had been a distraction from her troubles, a shoulder to cry on, a fantasy figure who'd been there when she needed him. Adrian's unwise actions had sent her looking for comfort from strangers and her magnetic pull towards Nico was just a reaction to the rejection from her husband. After all, how well could she possibly *know* someone after only a couple of weeks?

She picked up *The Power of Two* for reassurance that she was making the right decision and flicked towards the back of the book.

Stage Six. Reconstruction and working through.

Imagine dropping jigsaw pieces onto the floor without having a box with a picture on it to refer to. At first it feels impossible to fit them together, and you need determination to try. You know things have changed for you, because you're looking for solutions. Take things step by step and you'll soon be looking at a pretty picture again.

Ginny liked how that sounded and she made her decision, one that was the best for her and her family.

Instantly, a weight seemed to lift from her body and she pulled back the curtains to let the daylight kiss her face. The sunshine had bleached the hairs golden on her arms. She sang as she showered, and padded lightly downstairs to the dining room to share her good news.

She was met by a heavy contemplative air hanging around the dining table.

Heather peeled a banana in slow motion. Eric yawned and Edna sipped her coffee as if it was poisonous. Curtis slumped in his chair and toyed with his phone. They all looked bleary-eyed after their shortened sleep.

Nico's eyelids were lilac and he didn't perform his usual fussing around. The table was half set and the food options were sparse. 'I didn't know if you would all want breakfast or not,' he said with a thin smile. 'Loretta is staying in bed, so she is not tired when she meets her friends.'

'So, she's not grounded?' Curtis asked hopefully.

Nico shrugged a shoulder, not understanding him.

'You told Loretta that she couldn't go to Gianfranco's hotel,' Ginny said. 'You were going to cancel her birthday lunch with friends.'

Nico straightened a spoon and then the bread basket. 'Last night, I said things I should not have.' He lifted his eyes. 'Loretta has explained what happened and I am sorry for my words. You are all welcome to stay at my hotel. Being worried made me upset.'

'We're sorry, too, man,' Curtis said. 'Things got out of hand.'

Ginny, Heather, Eric and Edna echoed his words.

'Thank you. I appreciate and accept this,' Nico said.

When they started to eat, the atmosphere gradually lifted.

'I'm happy doing nothing today,' Curtis said with a yawn. 'Don't know about you guys.'

Ginny glanced furtively at Nico, wondering whether to take him aside, to tell him about Adrian. He flitted between the dining room and kitchen so it was difficult to catch his eye. Each time Ginny prepared to speak to him, he ducked his head and disappeared again, until she became convinced he was avoiding her. She decided it would be too conspicuous to follow and corner him in the kitchen.

The longer she waited, the more her announcement threatened to burst out of her.

When Nico brought in a jug of fresh orange juice, Ginny couldn't wait any longer. She cleared her throat and addressed the table. 'Um, I have a suggestion to make for today. My husband and daughter arrived in Italy late last night and they're staying at Gianfranco's hotel. Adrian's asked me to renew our wedding vows this afternoon, and Phoebe is getting married, too.'

Edna shot her an astonished stare.

Nico nudged the bread basket onto the table and a couple of pieces slid out. He quickly gathered them together in a napkin, folded it up and whisked it away. He returned a moment later and topped up everyone's coffee so it almost spilled over the brims of their cups. 'Congratulations,' he said, too brightly.

'Yeah, that's cool, Ginny,' Curtis said. 'Well done.'

'The ceremonies will start at two this afternoon and I'd love for you all to join us,' Ginny said.

She was met with a wall of pained expressions, making her feel like the first member of a pop group to announce they were going solo.

'I suppose you're proof that broken hearts really can mend,' Heather said.

Edna sipped her coffee and didn't speak. Her eyes were as small and steely as ball bearings.

Back in her bedroom, Ginny curled the end of her ponytail and applied her make-up. She changed into the cream linen dress she'd bought in Florence, trying to look casual and elegant, rather than pristine and polished. Her feet were sore after dancing in Rimini, so she wore comfortable flat ballet shoes.

She'd hoped the others might have greeted her news with more excitement. It was great her life had taken this upwards turn and she wanted them to be part of it and be happy for her. Perhaps they just needed more caffeine and time to wake up properly.

When a knock sounded on her door, Ginny thought Nico might have come to speak to her in private and her spine stiffened. Thoughts of their kiss in the Venetian garden popped into her head, and her body flooded with nerves. Was he standing on the other side of the door, thinking about their kiss, too?

She smoothed down her dress and her stomach leaped as she twisted the door handle. She opened it to find Edna standing there instead.

'Well, you've done a U-turn,' the elderly lady said. 'Are you sure about this?'

Ginny's lips flattened and she felt her spirits shake. 'I thought you might say something like that. Come inside.' She opened the door further and gestured for Edna to sit down on the bed.

'I just want to make sure you've not been brainwashed,' Edna said. 'You came here because you were heartbroken.'

'Adrian's my husband, not a kidnapper.'

'For the last few weeks, he's been your enemy.'

Ginny's shoulders fell and she sat down on the mattress beside Edna. The older lady had a way of offering advice that was both practical and challenging at the same time. She was probably the closest thing Ginny had to a confidante in Italy. 'Things have been really tough,' she admitted. 'Adrian's really sorry and wants to make a go of our marriage.'

'And what do you want?'

'When you promise to spend your life with someone, it's an intention rather than a guarantee. You said yourself that measuring heartbreak isn't an exact science, and marriage isn't either. You must have gone through ups and downs with Desmond, too.'

Edna sucked in her cheeks as if she'd tasted something sour. 'We're talking about *you*, not me.'

Ginny stared at her, waiting for something more. 'I'm kind of expecting a story about cars or trees, or super skills you might have . . .'

Edna shook her head and glanced at the framed photo of Ginny and Adrian. 'It's your life. You must make your own decisions . . . and mistakes.'

Ginny chose to focus on the first option and to ignore the second. She'd grown fond of Edna and knew she had her best interests in mind, even if it didn't always come across that way. 'Will you be there this afternoon?' As she asked the question, she was surprised by just how much Edna's

271

presence meant to her. She also really wanted Eric, Heather and Curtis to be there, too.

'Yes,' Edna nodded. 'We'll *all* be there to support you. Well, everyone except for Nico. I think he's . . . busy.' She cleared her throat. 'It's Loretta's birthday, after all.'

'Of course.' Ginny understood that Nico might not want to see her remarry her husband, though she felt sad he wouldn't be there.

Edna reached into her bag. 'I know it's not *exactly* your wedding day, but I've brought along a few things to bring you luck. There's something old, something new, something borrowed and something blue. Heather wants you to have a new scarf she bought and Curtis only has one blue item to give you, a baseball cap. Eric says you can borrow his penknife . . . again.' Edna held it out and flipped open the blade.

The two women blinked at it. 'I'm not sure I'll need it,' Ginny said. 'Or the cap.'

'You never know,' Edna said. Her hand shook when she reached into her bag again and took out a necklace, a simple silver daisy pendant on a chain. She looked at it for a while and swallowed. 'This is old and belonged to my daughter. I'd like you to have it.'

'Me? Oh, gosh.' Ginny pressed her fingers to her collarbone. 'It's beautiful . . . I really can't . . .'

A tear shone in Edna's eye as she fumbled to unfasten the clasp. 'Yes, you can,' she said firmly. 'I don't wear it and have no one else to pass it on to. It'd be nice to give a new lease of life to something that belonged to Daisy.'

Ginny turned around and allowed Edna to fasten it around her neck. Emotion swelled in her throat. 'Thank you,' she whispered.

Edna went quiet for a few seconds. 'It suits you,' she said.

The two women sat together for a while without talking.

'How will you get to Castello?' Ginny eventually asked. 'Shall I book a taxi for you all?'

'You just worry about yourself for once and leave the rest to us.' Edna stood up and headed towards the door. 'Good luck today.'

Ginny placed the cap and penknife in her handbag and tied the scarf around the strap. She applied lipstick and looked out the window to see Gianfranco pulling up outside in a shiny grey Mercedes. He'd fastened a wide cream ribbon to the bonnet.

The car looked like something from a fairy tale and Ginny was briefly transported back in time to her wedding, twenty-five years ago.

She and Adrian had chosen something classy and simple, holding the ceremony in their local church and hiring a nice room above a pub for their reception. Ginny had worn a vintage cream silk dress and a fresh floral crown and Adrian had been handsome in a cobalt-blue suit. They were in love so there was no need for showiness, an ostentatious cake or chiffon bows on chairs because they had each other.

'This is about you and me getting married, and having our friends and family with us to celebrate. Nothing else matters,' he'd said. And she'd felt the same way.

This time she and Adrian were going to do things in more luxury, but it didn't quell her worrying urge to run away.

Gianfranco gave a small beep of his horn outside, breaking her thoughts. Ginny grabbed her handbag and went downstairs to meet him.

'It's your special day,' Gianfranco exclaimed as he helped her into his car. 'Are you happy?'

'Yes, but I'm nervous, too.'

'Do not worry,' he said. 'In my humble expert opinion, everything will be fantastic. I have also spoken to Nico and we have fixed our differences.'

'That's great,' Ginny said with a relieved sigh. 'I'm so pleased.'

'Our bond is unbreakable. We are very different people who have been through many troubles together and we always work things out.'

Ginny sat thinking how his words could also relate to her and Adrian.

Gianfranco set off and Ginny toyed with her wedding ring. Her stomach jittered as they drove along the road towards Vigornuovo village then turned right, climbing up the hill to the Grand Hotel Castello Bella Vista.

A moped horn tooted at the car and a cyclist waved at her. Ginny smiled and waved back. *This is what you want*, she told herself.

The car pulled up outside the grand entrance to the hotel and a flash of auburn hair made Ginny's spirits soar. Phoebe stood waiting on the entrance steps to the hotel. She looked gorgeous in a long cream lace dress with sheer sleeves that gracefully curved over her stomach. She wore a pale pink gerbera in her hair.

Ginny carefully stepped out of the car and sped towards her, finding it hard to believe her daughter was here in Italy. She held Phoebe gently in her arms and breathed in her scent of rose petals, sun cream and home. She'd missed her so much.

Phoebe stood back to admire her outfit. 'My god, Mum. You look amazing.'

'You, too.' Ginny was finally able to reach out and place her hand on her daughter's belly. She felt the greatest rush of love. 'How are you feeling?'

'Excited. Pleased to see you. Happy to see the sun. It's like some kind of dream.'

'I'm so pleased for you both,' Ginny said. She looked all around her. 'Where's your dad?'

'With Pete, upstairs. I know things have been tricky between you and Dad . . .'

Ginny wondered how much Adrian had told their daughter, and if he'd put a spin on things. *Tricky?* She rolled the word around on her tongue. It sounded insubstantial and even a little cute. Things between them had been the complete opposite, and she'd borne the brunt of it. She reminded herself this was a chance to draw a line under everything and to start over. To forgive and try to forget. The only doubt still niggling in her mind was Adrian's presence on the dating site and his liaison with Jenny.

'Are you ready, Mum?' Phoebe asked.

Ginny heard a car pulling up and looked around to see Eric, Edna, Curtis and Heather arriving in a taxi. As they got out, she felt a twist in her chest that Nico hadn't changed his mind to join them.

She curled her fingers into her palms, taking a few final moments to try to leave all her upset and worries behind her. 'Yes, I'm ready,' she said.

She walked inside the hotel with her daughter, and up the stairs to greet her husband.

CHAPTER 31

Bouquet

By the time Ginny reached the top of the stairs, her chest was aflutter. The doors to Gianfranco's celebration room were closed and she guessed Adrian and Pete were already inside. Edna, Eric, Heather and Curtis must have taken the lift because they were already waiting at the end of the corridor. Biscotti was with them wearing a bow tie and, strangely, Heather had a suitcase by her side.

Ginny fixed her eyes on it, wondering why she'd brought it with her. 'I just need to speak to my friends for a minute,' she told Phoebe.

'I'll come with you. I'd *love* to meet them.'

Ginny made her way towards the group. 'Thanks for coming,' she said. 'This is my gorgeous daughter, Phoebe. It's her special day, too.'

Everyone smiled, shook hands and said congratulations.

'A double whammy,' Curtis said.

Heather inched forwards. 'I'm sorry, I have to dash away straight after the ceremony. I've booked an earlier flight home.'

'Oh,' Ginny said, feeling a little disappointed. 'Why?'

Heather gripped the handle of her suitcase, as if needing its support. 'Last night's events made me think a lot about things. I know it might sound odd, but I actually felt lucky for the first time in ages.'

'*Really?*' Edna asked.

Heather nodded. 'I counted my blessings and can see that I'm healthy, have lots of good friends and I love my job,' she said. 'I lay in bed this morning and decided that I can choose to see Mum's illness as darkness setting in at night, or I can try to focus on the stars in the sky. The more you look for them, the more you see.'

She puffed out her chest, trying to summon more bravery. 'Mum's still here and although she's different, we'll always be mother and daughter. I have to learn to embrace the new version of her, rather than mourn the old one. And feathers and fortune telling aren't going to help me or her one bit. I'm ready to face the future, even if it keeps flinging custard pies in my face.

'I don't know what Mum's outcome will be and I can't predict how things will turn out. Even if she can't remember who I am, I want to show her my photos of Venice. We can still look at the canals and buildings together. I can tell her about my new friends.'

Ginny felt like she'd swallowed a rock. Tears sprang to her eyes and she could see Phoebe's eyelashes shining, too.

Heather took hold of Ginny's hand. 'Thanks for everything,' she said. 'I couldn't have found this peace of mind without you, and I hope you find it, too.'

Ginny thought how it was a strange thing to say before

her ceremony. 'You're a superstar,' she said, using Heather's teacher language.

'It's all down to terrific teamwork.' Heather winked, pulling Ginny into a hug.

Gianfranco broke their moment by rushing along the corridor waving his hands. 'Dogs are not allowed in my establishment,' he called out.

'He's a good boy,' Eric said. '*Seduto*, Biscotti.'

The dog sat down and lifted his paw.

Gianfranco hesitated and crouched down to shake it. 'Ha, he is a clever handsome beast.' His big eyes shone and he spoke directly to Biscotti. 'You are very welcome at Castello Bella Vista, *bravo cane*.'

The double doors to the celebration room swung open and Adrian stepped into the corridor. He looked surprised to see all the people gathered there and he nodded hellos until his gaze settled on Ginny. Breaking into a grin, he nodded approvingly. *Gorgeous*, he mouthed.

Ginny blushed.

'There is a little paperwork to sign before the ceremony. Please follow me,' Gianfranco said. He escorted Adrian and Ginny into a small room and showed them a couple of forms. 'I will be back in a few moments,' he said.

'Phoebe and Pete have already signed theirs,' Adrian said, wrapping his arms around Ginny's waist and pulling her close to him. 'It looks like you've invited the entire village.' He laughed. 'You did say your new friends were a random bunch. The old lady looks familiar somehow . . .'

Even though his description was apt, Ginny prickled. 'You

said it was okay for them to come,' she said. 'I think you'd remember Edna if you'd met her before.'

'It's great they're here to support you. They can stay for a drink afterwards, then I've booked a meal for me, you, Phoebe and Pete in the hotel restaurant.'

'Oh, great,' Ginny said, a little dismayed the others wouldn't be a full part of her day.

'I'm so glad you're here,' Adrian said.

'Me, too.'

They kissed and it helped to quash some of the doubts that still wriggled in her mind. One question still rolled around, growing bigger until her only option was to let it out. 'There's something I need to ask you, before we go ahead with our vows,' she said. 'We didn't have a chance to discuss it last night . . .'

'Sure, go ahead.'

She ran her tongue around the inside of her mouth and the magnitude of her question gathered momentum. 'I want to know if you met anyone on the dating site.'

Adrian's jawline reddened. 'Let's not talk about that now,' he blustered. 'It didn't mean anything and we don't want to spoil our special day.'

Ginny stood her ground. 'It means something to *me*,' she said, pausing for a few beats. 'Some people would say it was cheating.'

'Well, that's an exaggeration. It was a silly thing to do, but it wasn't like I was unfaithful.'

'Why did you do it?'

'I thought I told you already,' he said a bit tetchily. 'I was feeling low and I was looking for some kind of . . . validation, to feel interesting and attractive again.'

'And did you find it?'

'I didn't need to. I came to my senses and realized that you and our family are all I need.' He lifted her hand and kissed her knuckles. '*This* is what's important. Me and you, and our future together.'

Ginny felt her lips quivering and tried to stop them. Maybe the tiredness of almost drowning, and staying up late to talk to Adrian, were catching up with her. 'I can't help thinking what might have happened if I hadn't discovered your profile. Would you have actually met up with anyone? And you've never told me who Miss Peach is.'

'I honestly don't know that woman. It sounds like you got a crank call and you should just forget about it. The dating site was like flicking through a catalogue and looking at new clothes you don't need.'

Ginny winced at the idea of him browsing, dismissing or being attracted to photos of other women. She tried to welcome his assurance and be glad that he'd found *her* on the site. She didn't want to test him, but there was something else she needed to know. 'Did you connect with anyone in particular?' she asked.

Adrian's forehead grew shiny. 'I'll answer your question, then let's drop it and enjoy our day.' He looked deeply into her eyes. 'I chatted to a couple of women online, and that's all.'

Ginny's stomach knotted. A *couple* of women, she thought. Not just Jenny.

'It really was nothing,' he added. 'I've always been faithful to you, Ginny, never even kissed anyone else, in all the years we've been together.'

Ginny felt her cheeks mottle with guilt. The conversations she'd enjoyed with Adrian, while being Jenny, replayed in her head, about rum and cola, and flying and being invisible. All the daft things they'd talked about when they were young lovers, which he was now dismissing as inconsequential. 'I have another question to ask,' she said quietly.

Adrian's face dimmed. 'You said there was only one. What is it?'

'Did you form a friendship with someone named Jenny?' she asked.

The world slipped into slow motion while she waited for his reply. Her heartbeat sounded loud in her ears, as if everyone in the hotel could hear it.

Adrian shook his head slightly as if about to deny it, until Ginny gave him a firm stare.

'How do you know about that?' he asked, eventually.

She wetted her lips. 'I set up a profile on the site . . . under a different name.'

Her confession took time to assemble in Adrian's head. 'It was *you*? *You* were Jenny?'

'It was the only way to reach out to you.'

Adrian straightened himself to his full height, his body language becoming defensive. 'So, you set up a fake profile to check up on me? That's pretty sneaky.'

Ginny's gaze hardened even more. 'It meant I got to chat with my husband, in a way we used to talk, so we could get to know each other again. It proves there was no way to keep us apart.'

Adrian's face set so hard she couldn't tell what he was thinking. Seconds crept by until he forced a laugh. He shook his head in an exaggerated fashion. 'Ginny, *Ginny*. It looks like we're just as bad as each other.' He leaned forwards and kissed the top of her head. 'I enjoyed those conversations with Jenny. They were fun while feeling familiar, and now I can see how it was you all along. It was how we used to talk to each other, a long time ago. Like you say, it just shows we're made for each other.'

His last sentences mirrored the thoughts Ginny had been having, yet she found her body turning rigid. 'It's *not* the same thing at all. You wanted a divorce and joined a dating site,' she challenged.

'You did, too . . .'

'Only because you did it first,' she said.

They sounded like children in a playground.

Gianfranco burst into the room again, rubbing his hands together. 'We are now ready for the happy couple,' he said. '*Both* happy couples.'

Adrian stroked Ginny's arm. 'Come on, let's do this,' he said. 'Afterwards, let's drink rum and cola and discuss who is the best James Bond.'

'It's Daniel Craig,' she said, as she followed him towards the door.

Adrian picked up a bouquet of flowers that she hadn't spotted before. 'Really? I thought you liked Sean Connery,' he said, handing them to her.

Ginny smelled the gorgeous blooms. 'Sometimes, people change their minds.'

Gianfranco held the door open and Ginny and Adrian walked along the corridor together. The doors to the celebration room were open and Ginny heard chatter inside.

'After you,' Adrian offered for her to enter first.

Ginny smoothed a hand down her dress and nervously took a step towards the threshold. She took a moment to fix a smile.

Suddenly a voice rang out from along the corridor. 'Stop,' it cried. 'Ginny, *wait!*'

She stepped back and trod on Adrian's foot. He *ouched*, jumped back and they both turned around to see who was calling her name.

'Who's *that*?' Adrian asked with a frown.

Ginny stood with her eyes fixed firmly on Loretta, who was running towards her. 'She's the landlord's daughter from the hotel,' she said quietly, wondering what the teenager wanted.

'Ginny,' Loretta arrived breathlessly in front of her. She gave Adrian a cursory glance. 'Dad said you were getting married again.'

'Well, yes, it's a vow renewal.' Ginny glanced along the corridor to see if Nico had changed his mind and decided to join them. Hope flickered inside her, but Loretta appeared to be alone. 'I thought you were lunching with friends.'

'I am meeting them soon.' Loretta toyed with her pendant necklace, a gold bird in flight. When she saw Ginny looking at it, she raised it up. 'Isn't it beautiful? Papà gave it to me for my birthday.'

'It's gorgeous.' Ginny turned around to face Adrian. 'It's Loretta's eighteenth today.'

Adrian twitched his lips. 'Happy birthday,' he said, taking hold of Ginny's elbow. 'Come on, we don't want to be late.'

'Can we speak?' Loretta asked, her eyes pleading to Ginny.

Ginny glanced at Adrian.

'I'll see you inside,' he said drily. 'Please don't be long.'

Ginny waited until he was out of earshot. 'What is it?' she asked Loretta.

The teenager gnawed her lip. 'I know you're busy and that your friends are waiting for you . . .'

'It's okay. Please say what you need to say.'

'It's just that, well, I think my dad likes you. I mean, *really* likes you.'

Ginny was thrown off balance. This wasn't the right time and place. It would *never* be the right time and place. She looked over her shoulder and was glad no one else was around to overhear. 'And I like him, too,' she said lightly. 'He's been very . . . um, welcoming and helpful.'

Loretta parted her lips to speak again, but Ginny smiled and shook her head. She had made up her mind and didn't want to think about what might have been with Nico. She had over thirty years of history with Adrian. He was her family and her future. She was going to go through with the renewal, whether Loretta and Nico liked it or not.

'Come and join us, be happy for me,' she told Loretta. 'We're ready to start and I don't want to be late. Happy birthday.'

Loretta gave her a sorrowful smile. 'Happy wedding day, Ginny.'

CHAPTER 32

Bird

Ginny and Adrian held hands tightly as they walked along the red carpet to the front of the room where a celebrant waited to greet them. Phoebe and Pete stood at the side of the floral arch, ready to witness the ceremony and then to take their own turn. A photographer stepped forwards and took snaps as Ginny and Adrian positioned themselves under the floral arch.

Loretta, Edna, Eric, Heather, Curtis and Biscotti sat in the front row and Gianfranco hovered around at the back of the room.

As soon as Phoebe smiled at her, any doubts Ginny harboured flew away. She felt the greatest rush of love for her daughter and could picture herself and Adrian holding their grandchild for the first time. This was the place she'd always wanted to be.

Whatever had happened over the last few weeks, whatever she'd endured, she and Adrian were here and they were strong. He'd made a mistake and she could choose to dissect and examine every particle of his actions, or she could try to move on. Punishing him would only make them both feel bad.

She smiled back at her daughter, noticing that her face appeared strained. Phoebe's lips were tight and her cheeks were a bit pale. Ginny hoped she wasn't feeling too anxious, or queasy after travelling to Italy.

Adrian slipped a hand into his pocket and produced a small black box. He flipped open the lid to reveal a beautiful diamond ring inside.

Ginny blinked hard. 'For me?' she asked.

'Of course.'

'It's beautiful.'

'So are you.' He smiled.

The celebrant motioned for them to move closer together. She was impeccably dressed in a slim-fitting blue dress, her brunette hair up in a tight bun. She was Italian and spoke fluent English.

Ginny tried to calm herself, focusing on the rise and fall of her chest. She was aware of Adrian running his thumb across the top of her fingers and Phoebe caressing her own stomach.

'Ladies and gentlemen, we are ready to begin,' the celebrant said.

A hush fell across the room.

'You were first joined together in matrimony twenty-five years ago, not yet knowing what life had in store for you both. Yet you promised to love, honour and cherish each other, throughout life's highs and lows. You have no doubt persevered through many blessings and challenges over the years, and today you are both here to reaffirm your vows of love and respect for each other.

'As you celebrate your life together and reflect on your shared journey, do you now wish to reaffirm the marriage vows that you committed to twenty-five years ago?'

As the celebrant spoke, random thoughts began to flourish in Ginny's mind, about how she'd been around Loretta's age when she'd first met Adrian. Was it feasible to commit to loving someone for a lifetime at that age? It was romantic, but was it sensible? Had she missed out on beach bars and splashing in the sea with friends? Perhaps she should have dated around more or gone travelling before settling down.

'*Ginny*,' Adrian prompted softly. 'I've said *I do*.'

He and the celebrant were looking at her, waiting for her answer, too. Ginny glanced at Phoebe's stomach again and thoughts kept skittering around in her brain.

'Are you okay?' Adrian asked.

Ginny nodded, but didn't speak. She side-eyed her husband and noticed the tiny hole in his ear again. Adrian had said Phoebe's pregnancy brought him to his senses, but he'd pursued meeting up with Jenny *after* he'd seen the scan.

Memories suddenly rushed back to her of standing under the white rose arch, swaying and falling. A wave of nausea came over her and the room began to spin.

When Ginny looked at her husband, all she could focus on was his piercing and she recalled him hoisting his suitcase out of their home. Walking away from their life together.

She screwed her eyes shut and tried to summon up good advice for herself. If she could reframe her situation it might allow her to feel more in control. Instead of dwelling on Adrian's mistake, she should focus on their long and happy marriage instead. Ginny couldn't change the fact that he'd left her, but she could address her own attitude towards it, to look forwards and not back.

Except, she found her own advice didn't work. Her usual practicality was overtaken by a strong gut feeling instead. It was a sensation in her stomach rather than words in her mind. And it was telling her not to go ahead with the ceremony.

She tried to fight the feeling, not to pay attention to it. In her job, she'd become used to listening to her head rather than her heart. Her windpipe muscles contracted and hurt, as if she'd swallowed a plum. But she knew how she really felt inside.

She *couldn't* renew her vows to Adrian.

Even though the room was turning and everyone was staring at her, Ginny's voice was loud and clear when she spoke. 'I'm sorry, I can't do this,' she said. 'This isn't the right solution.'

The couple of minutes that followed went by at a snail's pace. Ginny was aware of Adrian's face contorting, and her own bouquet falling to the floor with petals scattering everywhere. She saw Pete consoling Phoebe.

Ginny turned around and saw how Loretta's eyes were wide with surprise and that Edna wore a slight smile.

She spun back to face Adrian. 'I'm really sorry,' she repeated. 'You're right that I can't solve everyone else's problems, while denying my own. I can't cover things up any longer. We haven't resolved our issues yet, and promising to stay with you for the rest of my life, in front of others, isn't the right way to do it.'

Adrian took a few moments before moving closer, his eyes full of shock. 'Ginny,' he said, circling his arms around her. He rested his chin on top of her head. 'I thought this was what you wanted. I don't want to force you to do anything.'

'It *was* what I wanted,' she said. 'And now I don't know. Things are still muddy between us and we need time to become friends again.'

Adrian held her more tightly. 'But, I love you,' he said.

'And I love you, too. Sometimes that isn't enough.' Ginny's eyes sought out Phoebe's. 'I'm sorry, darling,' she mouthed.

Her daughter chewed the inside of her cheek. Her eyes flicked between Pete and her mum as she deliberated what to say.

'I'm sorry, please don't let me spoil—' Ginny started.

Phoebe's nostrils flared and she swallowed hard before speaking. 'I don't want to do it either,' she said.

'*Darling* . . .' Ginny reached out for her hand.

Phoebe edged away and caressed her stomach. 'I've got doubts, too. This is so quick and intense . . . and I'm not sure.' She turned to Pete. 'I love you, but this all feels rushed . . .'

Pete's face initially appeared stricken, but then his eyes flooded with relief and he let out a nervous laugh. 'I'm *so* pleased you've said that. I'm not certain either. There's no rush for us to get married, and we'll only have to make things official when we get home. I only want to do this once in my life.'

'If we wait, our child could be part of our big day,' Phoebe said.

The celebrant peered down at her feet and blew out her cheeks.

Adrian looked winded. 'I was trying to do the right thing,' he said.

Phoebe gathered him and Pete to one side, talking to them both to clear the air.

Ginny still felt dizzy and spoke to their backs. 'I really need to go outside.' She felt wobbly as she rushed back along the aisle, refusing to catch anyone's eye. After jogging down the stairs, she headed out into the daylight, letting the sunlight sweep over her cool skin. She meandered around the gardens with her hands clenched at her sides, not noticing the beautiful flowers or the birds singing. She'd done the right thing, but it still hurt. Sitting down on a bench, she lowered her head and wrung her hands.

After a while she heard Phoebe calling out to her. 'Mum. Where've you been?' Her daughter appeared by her side, the gerbera sliding out of her hair.

Ginny stood up and tucked the flower back into place. 'Sorry, I had to get away. It must have been embarrassing for everyone.'

'Your friends took a taxi back. The blonde-haired lady with the suitcase had to leave.'

'Heather?' Ginny's shoulders slumped. 'Oh, no, I've missed saying goodbye to her.'

'She asked me to tell you something.' Phoebe frowned, trying to remember the message accurately. 'She hopes to see you again very soon. You're *the* Ginny Splinter and you've got this. Mistakes are proof that we're trying.'

Ginny solemnly nodded, the Italian sun suddenly feeling too hot.

'Let's sit in the shade,' Phoebe said. She led her mum to a fountain where the sprinkling water cast a light mist on their faces and arms. She placed her mum's hand against her own chest and breathed in and out so Ginny could follow her pace.

'I've made a mess of things,' Ginny said, shaking her head.

'Nothing that can't be fixed.' Phoebe squeezed her hand. 'To be honest, Pete's relieved, and so am I. Dad is . . .' She paused for a second. 'He'll be okay, too. Please be honest with me from now on, Mum. Don't try to hide things.'

It was what Ginny had done with her mum and dad, and that had failed miserably. 'We want to set a good example for you and Pete . . .'

'No one's perfect. You're role models because you love and support me, not because you dress up and marry each other again.'

Ginny marvelled at her daughter. She'd always been the one giving out good advice and now Phoebe was surpassing her. 'So, what do we do now?' she asked, *not* hating the alien feeling of asking someone else for guidance.

'Well, we can have a very awkward family meal together,' Phoebe said. '*Or* you can spend the rest of your holiday with your friends. I've already persuaded Dad it's the best thing for you. You both need time to really think things through.'

'What about you and Pete . . .?'

'You're doing it again, Mum,' Phoebe warned. 'Think of yourself for once. I'm a big girl now and can look after myself.'

Ginny nodded and rested her head on her daughter's shoulder. 'Thanks, sweetheart.'

They both stood up together. 'I'll see you back in rainy England, next week,' Phoebe said.

'Is the weather really miserable back there?'

Phoebe looked up at the blue sky. 'It's much brighter over here,' she said.

CHAPTER 33

Movie

Ginny needed to be on her own. She wasn't ready to see Adrian, or her friends again, so she got into a taxi that had pulled up to the entrance of the hotel. She asked the driver to take her to the one place she might find some peace of mind.

He drove her away from Grand Hotel Castello Bella Vista, along the bumpy road towards Vigornuovo and then up the hill that she'd climbed with Eric and the others. The rocky terrain meant the road petered out halfway, so Ginny paid the fare, got out and trekked the rest of the way.

She walked until she reached the little white chapel with the turquoise door. Wrapping the scarf Heather had given her around her shoulders, she made sure her dress covered her knees. The door creaked as she opened it and she stepped onto the mosaicked floor.

It felt strange to be back inside, especially alone and all dressed up. She lit a candle and watched the flickering flame until her heart rate slowed a little and goose bumps rose on her arms in the cool air.

Her emotions were still chaotic. She'd made a real hash of things and it'd take a long time to pick apart and reassemble them. She presumed all the conversation taking place that afternoon would be about her and there was nothing she could do about it. She was starting not to worry what other people thought about her.

Ginny considered all the people who'd previously married in the chapel, and she could almost sense the joy soaked into the stone walls. Of course, there'd have been many funerals, too, all manner of life events played out in this tiny space. Promises and vows would have been made, with every intention of keeping them, but also with a chance of breaking them.

The longer she stood there, the more her mind calmed and cleared like the morning mist evaporating above the mountains. Sunlight sliced through the windows and she lifted her fingers and swept them through the golden rays, trying to touch the sparkles of dust.

Ginny didn't know what might happen next with her and Adrian, but they would always be parents, grandparents and, hopefully, friends. She had to get to know herself more again, thinking about what *she* wanted, before she could consider the future shape of their relationship.

She now understood that no one else was responsible for her happiness, only her. And there had to be more to it than continually trying to solve other people's problems.

After dropping a few coins into the wooden box, she made her way back outside. Closing her eyes, Ginny lifted her face towards the sun and stood there letting it wash over her entire body, until she heard footsteps approaching.

Eric and Biscotti were heading up the hill towards her and she raised her hand and waved to them. Eric nodded hello and sat down on the grass with Biscotti curled up at his side.

Ginny joined them. If she were Eric, she'd have lots of questions, like what Ginny was doing on top of a hill on her own, why she'd run away from her vow renewal ceremony and how she'd arrived at the chapel. She appreciated it when he didn't say a thing.

She wrapped her arms around her knees and looked down at the village, watching the river sparkle in the sun. People scurried around, as small as ants. Around her, daisies swayed in the breeze and she took off her shoes to wriggle her toes in the grass. She stroked Biscotti's head and thought how simply dogs lived their lives, wagging their tails when they were happy and lowering them when they were sad.

A feeling of acceptance eventually spread through her body, from her feet to the top of her head, and she finally recognized it as the passion she'd been looking for. It was excitement and intrigue for what might come next in her life, whatever form that might take, without looking to others to satisfy her. It was hers for the choosing and taking, and it felt right.

After a while, Ginny felt her scalp tingling from the sun and she slipped Curtis's cap onto her head. She handed Eric's penknife back to him.

He smiled and picked up a small broken branch, whittling the blade against the wood. Time slipped away until he handed something to her, a tiny carved heart with a hole through the top.

Ginny loosened Heather's scarf. She took off the necklace

Edna had given her and slid the heart onto the chain, so it hung alongside the daisy pendant. She twisted off her wedding ring and added it, too.

Eric reached out and helped her refasten the clasp.

He opened his rucksack and took out a napkin embroidered with the Grand Hotel Castello Bella Vista logo. Inside were slices of bread and he cut up an apple to make a sandwich, handing half to Ginny.

She found she was ravenously hungry and relished each mouthful.

Eric took his yellow tin out of his pocket and paused before he opened it. He took out Bess's collar and removed the silver name disk, slipping it into his pocket. He unfastened Biscotti's bow tie and placed the collar around the dog's neck in its place.

'Pink suits him,' Ginny said.

Eric nodded proudly.

The three of them sat together until the tip of Eric's nose shone red from the sun. He stood up and batted grass off his trousers, holding out a hand to assist Ginny to her feet. 'Thank you,' he said, as if their time together had helped him too somehow.

'You're welcome,' she said. Ginny slipped her shoes back on and they climbed back down the hill together without talking.

When they arrived back at Splendido, Nico was draping bunting around the courtyard. He waved when he saw Ginny and Eric. 'Edna has made these pretty flags for Loretta's birthday,' he said. 'You are both in time for cake.'

Eric smiled and went inside with Biscotti.

Nico stood in front of Ginny. 'Loretta has returned from

meeting her friends. She has told me about your celebration. I am sorry it did not take place . . .'

'It is okay,' Ginny said. 'It was my decision and my family supports me.'

'This is what the family is for,' he said.

They both smiled at each other and something unspoken flitted between them.

'Heather has left something behind,' Nico said. He took a packet of tarot cards out of his pocket. 'Would you like to keep them?'

She shook her head. 'They won't help to predict my future. I need to sort that out for myself.'

'I am also giving away the pink vase.'

'Maria's vase?' Ginny asked gently.

'Loretta and I have spoken and I accept my wife is never coming back to me. It is something I knew deep down and tried to deny.' He held a hand to his heart. 'It is the right time for me to move on, too.'

'Perhaps one of your next guests might like the tarot cards, or the vase,' Ginny said.

'Maybe. I will think about this.' He looked back towards the hotel. 'But, right now, Loretta wants to blow out her candles.'

In the dining room, Ginny, Edna, Eric, Curtis, Nico and Loretta stood around the dining table. Nico lit the candles on the cake and the tiny flames reflected in Loretta's eyes. 'It looks so pretty,' she said. 'I told Papà we couldn't light them until you returned.'

'Thank you,' Ginny said, feeling touched.

Nico started to sing, '*Tanti auguri a te,*' to the tune of the

'Happy Birthday' song. His voice was rousing and the others joined in, singing in a strange mix of English and Italian.

Loretta leaned forwards and blew out her candles. '*Grazie, Papà,*' she said softly.

'I hope you are all hungry,' Nico said. 'I have also made pizza.'

'Starving,' Curtis said.

'It's a little too early for my digestive system,' Edna said. 'I can probably force down a small slice of cake.'

Loretta widened her eyes as if a great idea had just landed. 'If we all change into our pyjamas it will be like a slumber party,' she said. 'I have always wanted another one.'

'What . . . with *us*?' Curtis asked.

Loretta cocked her head. 'Sure, if you promise not to dance.' She turned to Nico. 'Please, Papà, can we?'

'Of course. Why not?' Nico rolled his eyes light-heartedly. 'I will get the blankets and pillows. I expect you will want to watch a movie, too?'

Loretta let out a delighted squeal, sounding more like a child than a young woman. 'We won't all fit into my bedroom so we can use the dining room.' She whizzed around throwing cushions onto the floor. 'Everyone, change clothes,' she said.

Her enthusiasm was infectious and they all retreated to their rooms to change into their nightwear.

Ginny took off her cream dress and put on her nightie and dressing gown. She wiped off her make-up as the theme tune to *A Glorious Escape* started up downstairs.

When she left her room, she almost crashed into Loretta on the landing.

The girl had a handful of embroidery thread. 'Edna told me to get this from her room,' she said. 'I want to make friendship bracelets and I'm not sure how to do it.'

'I can show you. I used to make them for my daughter.'

Loretta flashed her a smile. 'Thank you, Ginny.'

Downstairs, they located Nico in the kitchen. His cooking was like choreography as he reached for a copper saucepan with his right arm while opening the oven door with his left. He'd left the back door open, allowing a light breeze to weave inside.

Ginny watched everyone file back into the dining room. Edna sat on the sofa, and Eric curled up with Biscotti. Curtis spread out on the floor. Could there be a stranger sight than five people aged eighteen to eighty, wearing their pyjamas together to watch a film? Yet, somehow it all felt natural, as if it was a ceremony to mark the end of their holiday.

The mozzarella was still bubbling as Nico handed out slices of pizza. He switched off the light and, when he sat down beside Ginny, she noticed how noble his nose looked in the shadows.

He resumed the film and the camera swept across Vigornuovo, giving a bird's-eye view of the river and village square before settling on Sharon Sterling running her fingers through water in the fountain.

Ginny hadn't seen the film before and was quickly hooked by all the costumes and romance. She watched Edna's lips moving as she recited words from the movie. Nico draped his arm across the top of the sofa, so Loretta could nestle under it.

For the next couple of hours, Ginny let her mind escape into the fiction of the film, away from Adrian and her life back at home. Her heart soared when Tim Vincenzo and Sharon Sterling first locked eyes across the village square. She swooned at their first kiss and tears rolled down her face when they said goodbye beneath the medieval archway. Soon, Ginny would have to say goodbye to everyone, too.

As the credits rolled, Edna turned to Nico. 'You have made me see the film through different eyes. In some scenes, Vincenzo towered over Sharon. He must have been standing on a box.'

'I don't know why he lies about his height. It is better to be truthful.'

'He is still magnificent,' Edna sighed.

Nico shook his head. 'I saw him in the village once. He smoked and stared at Loretta for too long.'

Loretta turned to face him, wearing a frown. 'You never told me *this* . . .'

'You were young and I was trying to protect you,' he said.

'I don't need protecting.'

'You may be eighteen, but you'll always be my little girl and—'

His words were interrupted by a snore. Eric and Biscotti had fallen asleep together.

Edna pulled the blanket up to Eric's chin and flipped a corner to cover up the dog.

Ginny showed Loretta how to make friendship bracelets until the village clock struck two in the distance. The three women fastened them around each other's wrists and held up their hands to admire them.

'It is no longer your birthday,' Nico said to Loretta. 'I think it's time for bed.'

She stretched out her arms and yawned. 'It has been perfect, thank you.'

Edna gently shook Eric to wake him and they both went to their rooms, leaving Biscotti asleep on the floor.

'G' night,' Curtis said to Ginny and Nico. He was about to say something else, then smiled and left them standing alone in the dining room.

Ginny felt a little weepy. It was hard to believe they'd all be leaving the day after tomorrow. She turned to Nico, wanting to say so much to him and unable to find the words.

'I should also go to bed,' he said. 'I may not see you tomorrow. I will be spending the day with Gianfranco at his hotel, so he can teach me some things. Loretta will stay here to look after you all. It will be good experience for her.'

Ginny bit her lip to help cancel out her disappointment. 'Will you be around to say goodbye when we leave?' she asked hopefully.

'Yes. I will be there,' Nico said, as he switched off the light. 'I would not miss that for anything.'

CHAPTER 34

Sandwiches

Everyone was too tired to move the next day. After helping Loretta tidy up and make breakfast, Ginny, Edna and Curtis lounged around the hotel and courtyard. Curtis worked on his blog, Edna sewed and Eric threw sticks for Biscotti in the field. Loretta sang as she washed the bedsheets in the sink and hung them on the line to dry.

Ginny felt restless, knowing that Adrian, Phoebe and Pete were in the castle on top of the hill. She had to stop herself from taking a taxi to go and see them, to make sure they were okay. Through a brief exchange of text messages with her daughter, she learned that she, Pete and Adrian were travelling back home the day after Ginny.

She returned to her bedroom intermittently throughout the morning and afternoon, to pack up her things. She opened *The Power of Two* and scanned through the book until she reached the final chapter.

Stage Seven. Acceptance and hope.

Congratulations, you've broken through to the other side. The grass is greener, the stars look brighter and you feel like a butterfly emerging from a chrysalis. You're ready to spread your wings and dazzle the world with your beauty. You're feeling optimistic for the future and ready to fly.

Ginny sighed and closed the book. Had it always been so flowery and condescending? When she looked at the photo of Ben and Ally Prince on the back, she noticed that Ben was a bit cross-eyed, and Ally's smile looked fake.

Trying to mend her relationship with Adrian didn't feel as glorious as the authors claimed it would be. Ginny felt like she'd slugged out ten rounds in a boxing ring and was lying flat on the floor looking up at the ceiling. Still, the book might help out someone else who stayed at the hotel, and she was happy to leave it behind.

Ginny tossed it onto her bedside table and went back outside to sunbathe.

The hallway was stuffed with suitcases and bags, and the air was thick with sadness when Eric, Edna and Ginny gathered to say goodbye.

'Please do not forget anything,' Nico said. 'Gianfranco is waiting outside to take you to the airport.'

Ginny had brought *The Power of Two* downstairs and handed it to Nico. 'You can put this with Heather's tarot cards.'

He held it in his hands. 'My hotel will soon be like

a museum, with all these things people no longer need. Eric has also given me his tin.'

Edna looked all around her. 'Where's Curtis?'

'He left earlier this morning,' Nico said. 'He took a taxi to the airport.'

'Oh.' Edna's mouth puckered. 'Didn't he want to say good-bye to us?'

'Everyone was still asleep and he gave me something to show you all.' Nico took a heartache form from his pocket and unfolded it, showing them what Curtis had written.

Dear friends,

I left a richer man. Thanks for everything.
Have fun!

Curtis

He'd also circled his heartache score for the first time, showing it had fallen from a nine to a five.

Edna blinked hard at it. 'Is that it?'

'I think Curtis's way of dealing with things is to have a good time and then leave,' Ginny said.

As they stood thinking about him for a while, Loretta peered at the form. 'He is still the worst dancer ever,' she said.

Nico stared at her. '*Lolo!*'

'It is true.'

'He was no match for my prowess,' Edna added.

'You can add Curtis's form to the tarot cards, my book and

your vase. It's like people have left pieces of their heartache behind,' Ginny told Nico.

She watched as something flashed across his face.

'I have an idea,' he said to himself.

Ginny loitered in the hallway, experiencing a whirl of emotions about going home. Things could never be the same again, not in her job, at home, or in her marriage. She wanted the opportunity to say goodbye to Nico without the others around her. There were so many conversations they hadn't yet had, and she felt like she was leaving part of herself in Italy.

She glanced longingly at the back of Nico's head as he bent down to pick up Edna's suitcase, and found herself caught between Eric and Edna as they headed out into the courtyard.

Biscotti sat waiting outside, wagging his tail as soon as he saw Eric. Eric crouched down and looked into the dog's eyes. He swept a hand over Biscotti's head and hugged him with tears welling. 'Sorry to say goodbye. You've helped me feel better,' he said. 'Bess would have loved you, too.'

The dog pressed the top of his head under Eric's chin.

'Thanks for everything, boy,' Eric whispered.

'I will make sure he gets the food and water,' Nico said. 'Please do not worry.'

'My vehicle awaits you all,' Gianfranco called out. 'The air-conditioning is as cold as ice.'

Ginny, Edna and Eric moved reluctantly towards his mini-bus.

Nico made a show of shaking their hands, reaching Ginny last. 'Goodbye, Ginny Splinter,' he said, smiling so the sides of his eyes crinkled.

She really didn't want to say it back to him and her voice came out strangled. 'Bye, Nico.'

'Have a safe journey home. *Torna presto!* Come back soon!' he said too cheerfully.

'Yes,' was all Ginny could manage.

Her legs felt weak as she walked to the minibus and got inside. Eric and Edna were already seated and the vehicle shook as Gianfranco shut the door.

Nico and Gianfranco loaded all their luggage and Ginny leaned her temple against the window. She gazed at Splendido longingly. It was too sad to think she might never see the hotel again. Loretta appeared on the doorstep, waving and blowing kisses.

Something deep inside Ginny told her to leap out, to run back to Nico and hug him with all her might. She could hear him behind the minibus, talking to Gianfranco in Italian. They were laughing and Ginny watched Nico walk back towards the hotel. When he reached the doorstep, he turned around and raised his hand. He looked so much smaller, as if the guests were taking a piece of him with them when they left.

Gianfranco got into the driver's seat and started the engine. Ginny gripped her handbag and looked at Nico again. *This can't be it. There has to be more*, she thought. Her chest tightened and she knew she couldn't leave without saying goodbye to him properly.

When Gianfranco released the handbrake, Ginny unfastened her seat belt. 'Wait,' she called out.

Edna stared at her in alarm. 'What's wrong? Have you forgotten something?'

Ginny glanced out of the window again and could no longer see Nico. Had he already gone back inside? She thought he'd stay to wave them off and she grabbed hold of the door handle, willing him to reappear.

Gianfranco muttered something about being late.

Eric was flying home first and he glanced at his watch.

Gianfranco set off slowly and the minibus wheels crunched on the path leading to the gates. Ginny looked back at the hotel with watery eyes.

A banging noise suddenly sounded on the back window, making them all jump.

'*Che diamine*?!' Gianfranco exclaimed.

Nico ran forwards and dashed in front of the vehicle, waving both hands. He darted around and tugged on the door handle. 'Stop. I have forgotten something.'

Gianfranco wound down his window. 'Are you trying to give me a heart attack?' he asked, patting his chest. 'What is it?'

'Lunches. I have made sandwiches for the journey.'

Gianfranco rolled his eyes and tutted. 'Hurry up,' he said.

Edna spoke into Ginny's ear. 'If you have something to say to Nico,' she said. 'Do it now. Don't have any regrets.'

Ginny turned to meet Edna's gaze and nodded. She promptly opened the minibus door and got out. 'I'll help you,' she told Nico, walking side by side with him back to the hotel.

The dining room was cool and quiet and they both eyed the shopping bag full of sandwiches sitting on the table. Then they locked eyes with each other. Nico cupped a hand to Ginny's face and held it there. He pressed his lips against her cheek, so lightly his kiss felt like the touch of a feather.

Ginny's toes tingled and she closed her eyes, willing the kiss not to go any further, while also wanting it so badly. She was going home, to her husband, trying to find a new shape for their lives to take. In a different time, in a different place, who knew what might have happened between her and Nico. But for now, she had to let him go.

'I wanted to say *arrivederci*,' Nico said. 'It means, to when we see each other again.'

'*Arrivederci*,' Ginny whispered.

They stood together, neither of them wanting to pull apart, until Gianfranco blasted his horn.

'I am sure it is the loudest in Italy,' Nico said.

'It certainly sounds like it.' Ginny laughed. 'I have to go.'

'Sadly, yes.'

She carried the bag of sandwiches to the car and handed them out to Edna and Eric.

Nico returned to his doorstep and waved as the minibus swept through the iron gates and onto the road. Ginny looked over her shoulder and watched until he became a speck in the distance and then disappeared. Ordering herself not to cry, she fixed her eyes on the trees along the side of the road. She said a silent goodbye to the not-really-a-castle on the hill.

Inside, the vehicle was quiet apart from the rustle of lunch bags on laps.

The closer Gianfranco got to the airport, the more Ginny felt she was leaving a different life behind. Something she wasn't yet ready to let go.

CHAPTER 35

Coffee

It was soon time for Eric to go to the boarding gates. He waited with Edna and Ginny under the screen displaying his flight details, with his rucksack hoisted high on his back. 'This is it,' he said. 'Back to reality.' He patted his hands to his sides.

Edna stepped over and gave him a tight squeeze with her cheek pressed against his chest. 'Take care of yourself, young man.'

'Will do, Edna.' Eric looked over her shoulder. 'Thanks Ginny.'

She nodded and was the next to hug him.

'Thanks for accepting me as I am,' Eric whispered into her ear, which made Ginny hold him even tighter.

He pulled away and with a brisk wave was gone.

Edna dabbed a handkerchief to her eye. 'I'll miss him. I'm going to miss everyone.'

Ginny took her by the crook of her arm. 'Come on, let's get a coffee,' she said. 'It won't be as good as Nico's, but it'll be hot and wet.'

'I don't want to go home,' Edna grumbled in a café, a few

minutes later. 'Bloody Shady Pines. I suppose they aren't allowed to call it Shady Prison. I'm feeling all pernickety just thinking about it.'

'You might like it,' Ginny said. 'People might want to contribute to your quilt. There might be bingo.'

'Everywhere has bingo except for Splendido,' Edna said, laughing and breaking her mood. 'Nico will be pleased to learn I've left my game behind in my room, for his next guests to play. I've also left my quilt.'

Ginny frowned at her in astonishment. 'Really? Why?'

'It was irreparable, really. Leaving all our blocks behind was a little like casting off our heartbreak stories and moving on from them. Daisy will always be a part of me and I don't need scraps of fabric to feel that way. I have many happy memories of her to enjoy.'

'I promise to look after her necklace,' Ginny said, touching the chain around her neck where the daisy charm, wooden heart and her wedding ring hung. 'I bet you never imagined that calling my show would lead to all this.'

Edna looked into her coffee as if it was a bottomless well. She patted her eye with her handkerchief again.

Ginny touched her arm. 'Please don't look so sad about it.'

'I have something to tell you.' Edna's voice was low and quiet. 'It's about my phone call . . .'

Ginny sipped her drink. 'What about it?'

'I actually made two calls to your show, one about the holiday and one *before* that,' Edna said. 'We spoke to each other.'

'We did?' Ginny frowned. She tried to recall what problem Edna might have called her with. 'Did you use your real name?' she asked, sure that she'd remember a Mrs Edgerton-Woods.

311

'I used an alias.' Edna worked her jaw for a few moments. 'It was . . . Miss Peach.'

Cogs cranked in Ginny's head. 'Miss Peach?' She frowned. 'The lady who asked me how well I knew my husband, live on air?'

Edna nodded meekly.

Ginny squinted as she tried to recall *that* conversation and her temples started to throb. The caller had been unhappy in her marriage and stayed for the sake of her child. She'd felt stuck and said she'd wasted precious time. Edna hadn't admit- ted to any of this in Italy, only to her sense of loneliness and grief for the loss of her daughter. 'I thought that you missed Desmond . . .' she started.

'I do, but we separated emotionally a long time before he died. We lived together but had separate lives and I wished I'd been brave enough to leave him. Daisy was the only mortar holding us together, and it totally crumbled when she died. It's why I've been trying to encourage you to make the right choices.'

Ginny rubbed between her eyes, trying to take in this information. Her nostrils flared at the thought of Edna keeping this from her, for three whole weeks. Adrian had betrayed her and now *this*. Something she'd forgotten arrived in her head. 'You asked if I knew what Adrian got up to after work . . . How *do* you know him?'

'I feel ashamed for not telling you everything sooner. I didn't know how to admit to what I'd done.' Edna pushed her cup away. 'After Desmond died, I didn't get around to selling his car for some time. I took it to The Vehicle Emporium and dealt with Adrian Splinter. I recognized him from photos I'd seen of you both in a magazine. He has very blue eyes. I sat in his office while he went off to print some paperwork. Maybe he'd just finished his lunch break because a laptop was on his desk with the screen still lit up.' She paused and pointed at her eyes. 'I told you, twenty-twenty vision.'

'I saw a dating site was open and there was a photograph of him on display. When he returned to the office, we locked eyes and I think he knew I'd seen it. He hurriedly switched it off and acted like nothing had happened.'

Ginny's mouth hung open. 'Before the vow renewal, Adrian said you looked familiar . . .'

'He probably couldn't place who I was, here with you in Italy. When I sold Desmond's car, I was miserable and wearing dark clothes. Not like now,' Edna stroked her patchwork waistcoat. 'When I called your show and said my name was Miss Peach, I was feeling lonely and bitter. I heard you on the radio sometimes, sounding chirpy, as if you didn't have a care in the world. Your life looked so perfect in the magazine photos and something snapped inside me. I'd not talked to anyone for days and my words spewed out.' A tear fell from Edna's eye onto the table.

Ginny ran her fingers down her neck. 'You were Miss Peach?' she repeated numbly.

'I really am sorry.'

'Why *that* name?'

'It was Daisy's favourite fruit.'

At the time of the call, Ginny remembered jumping to defend her marriage. If Edna hadn't called her show, Ginny might not have become aware of Adrian's misdemeanours. She wouldn't have travelled to Italy, to meet the four strangers who'd become friends.

She couldn't help feeling a touch of her customary empathy towards the older woman sat hunched in front of her, especially when she spotted they were both wearing the friendship bracelets Loretta had made for them.

In many ways, Edna had changed Ginny's life for the better. 'You were right, my life wasn't perfect,' she told Edna. 'No one's is. Everyone has problems that can shape or break us. It's weird, but I'm glad you made that call. Otherwise, I wouldn't be here, and you wouldn't be here either.' She ducked to seek out Edna's eyes. 'Or does that make me sound like an advice expert?'

'It makes you sound like a perceptive young woman, and I hope you'll be happy, whichever path you choose in life.' Edna reached out and patted the back of Ginny's hand. 'And I'm going to aim for the same thing, too.'

When the screens showed that Edna's plane was ready for boarding, Ginny walked with her towards the departure gate.

'Sadly, this is where we say goodbye,' Edna said.

Ginny could swear she saw the old woman's chin trembling and it made her own bottom lip wobble, too. 'I prefer the Italian word *arrivederci*,' she said.

Edna nodded and wiped a tear from her eye. '*Arrivederci* and *grazie,* Ginny. I'm truly grateful for everything.'

Ginny planted a kiss on her cheek. 'Have a safe journey home and keep in touch. Using your own name this time,' she added with a smile, and the two women waved until they were out of sight.

CHAPTER 36

Cymbal

Ginny
Ten months later

Ginny found that wearing jeans and a sweater to work was more comfortable than her skirt suit. She'd retired her leopard-print heels, thinking that callers wouldn't mind what she was wearing, so long as she could help them out. Things were much quieter and less fraught without Tam around trying to shake things up.

She wrapped Heather's new scarf around her neck and tied it in a loose knot. The early morning April sky was still grey, though sunshine was trying to break through the clouds.

A couple of emails had arrived for her over the weekend and Ginny read them while making herself a coffee. One was from a lady who needed time to herself after caring for an injured relative for months. The other was from a young woman who'd been devastated to discover her fiancé had been cheating on her with his ex-girlfriend.

Ginny replied to both women, suggesting a solution that might help with their heartache.

When the first phone call of the day came through, she sat down at the dining table to answer it. 'Hello, this is Ginny Splinter speaking. *Sì, questo è Splendido, l'hotel per cuori infranti.*' She hoped her attempt at Italian was correct. 'Yes, this is Splendido, the hotel for broken hearts.'

She listened sympathetically to the caller's story, about how the man had lost his aunt and grandmother in the same month. Ginny made caring noises until he'd finished talking.

'I think I need help,' the man said with a sigh.

'That's what we're here for. Thanks for reaching out to us.' Ginny picked up a pen. 'At Splendido we understand there's no set way to deal with heartbreak. We're here to listen, to look after you and give you the space to feel better. You can spend time alone or be with others who are looking for support, too. There's some beautiful walking trails and we offer access to luxury spa facilities and workshops at a local castle. If you prefer to get out and about, we can take you to Venice and Florence.'

She now knew that heartache could be loud or quiet. Sometimes it needed to make itself known to the world, and other varieties needed space and time to settle down on their own. Heartbreak took many shapes and Ginny would never be an expert, but she could try to listen and help out if she could.

Following her holiday with strangers in Vigornuovo, Ginny returned to the UK with the intention of working on her relationship with Adrian, starting with becoming friends again. The shift in their marriage had been seismic, like how a small earth tremor can damage the sturdiest structure. Any rebuilding would take much care and time.

Things between them were stilted and rocky at first, but they were both determined to devote time to each other. Adrian cut back on his hours at The Vehicle Emporium. He made dinner, sparked conversation and paid Ginny lots of compliments. He moved into their spare bedroom to give her space and time to trust him again.

Ginny listened to Kizzi Matthews on Talk Heart FM and heard how the young woman brought a fresh perspective to problem-solving. She was blunt and funny, urging callers to think of their own solutions rather than doling out advice to them.

Ginny decided it was time to graciously move on and had handed in her notice. She took up a part-time job writing an advice column for a local magazine and even tried out some of Kizzi's methods. She tried not to solve Adrian's life any longer.

Sitting at home, around their dinner table in the evening, Ginny and Adrian pored over old photographs, reminiscing on shared memories. In one shot, there was a smudge of icing sugar on her nose as Adrian fed wedding cake to her, and in another, they grinned proudly as they held baby Phoebe.

Despite these warm moments captured in time, Ginny had to remind herself that no one ever took and kept photos of the bad times.

As the months progressed, Ginny found some of her old feelings for Adrian filtering back. Her hurt and anger subsided so things began to feel more normal again.

Except *normal* didn't make Ginny's heart sing or fill the hole in her life that she felt was still there.

The old Ginny would usually get on with things and put

others first, perhaps buying a new dress or shoes for herself. But the different life she'd tasted for herself had left her wanting more. Old layers were still peeling away to reveal a fresh new woman underneath, one she was still getting to know. How could she tell that person to be quiet and shut her away, to become the former Ginny again? She'd spent half a century being a daughter, a wife and a mother. Entering into the second half of her life, Ginny wanted to explore being *herself*.

She explained to Adrian how she felt and through many conversations together, about both of their worries and hopes, they grew closer to each other than they had in years, but not yet in a romantic sense.

Their love and respect for each other had been further enhanced by the arrival of Phoebe's daughter, Erin.

As soon as Ginny saw her tiny fingers and pink face, her heart melted. Her granddaughter was utterly perfect though, as she held her in her arms, a doubt niggled in the back of her mind.

Should I rely on the arrival of this tiny new person to fulfil me?

It was a question that wouldn't go away and she shared this thought with her husband. After his own episode of uncharacteristic behaviour, Adrian claimed that he understood.

So, when Ginny received an email from Nico, inviting her back to Vigornuovo one day, she felt comfortable telling her husband about it. Apparently, the little Italian hotel was going through a transformative phase. Nico was enjoying welcoming guests again, though he was struggling with his workload, now that Loretta had returned to school. She was currently revising for her final exams and would head off to university, in Milan, in the late summer.

Upon receiving Nico's email, Ginny revisited the hotel website. Nico had rewritten Romeo's copy.

> The Hotel Splendido offers you simple delights in a picturesque location not too far away from Venice and Florence. What makes it different are the special ingredients to help heal a broken heart – time, love, relaxation and the good food. You're not alone. Welcome, friend.

The descriptions and photographs brought back memories for Ginny, like the scent of bougainvillea and freshly cooked tomatoes. She remembered dancing like no one else was watching, admiring art, sailing the canals of Venice, padding quietly into a tiny chapel on a hill, releasing her emotions to the sound of gongs, the ache of her calves as she climbed a hill, and laughter around Nico's dining table. She was reminded of how she'd rediscovered a part of herself that made her feel oh-so-alive.

A thought lodged in Ginny's mind that she couldn't shake. What if she returned to Vigornuovo to assist Nico at the hotel?

The idea sprouted and soon grew into a burning desire. Thinking about it excited her and, during the long nights she spent helping Phoebe to settle Erin to sleep, it grew, taking shape until she eventually felt compelled to share it with Adrian.

'I feel torn,' Ginny told him. 'I know my place should be here with you and our family, but I feel the strongest pull back to Italy. I'm thinking about going back there, to work at Splendido for a while . . .'

Adrian's mouth slackened. 'So, you want to give up your new job and work as a receptionist or a housekeeper in Italy, at a hotel you stayed at for three weeks last summer, leaving your husband, daughter and baby granddaughter behind?'

Ginny paused and took only a moment to think. 'Yes,' she said.

That one word had an impact like the crash of a cymbal. Adrian looked like he'd taken a surprise stumble and was trying to right himself. 'I thought we were working on things between us,' he spluttered. 'They're going well.'

'We are . . . and they are. But I'm not sure if I'm *really* happy, or if you are either.'

He frowned, as if happiness was a far-off destination he didn't have a ticket for. 'We're getting along fine, just like we used to. We've got a grandchild and we still love each other. You hated it when your dad used to leave you and your mum behind.'

'That was different, I was only a child,' Ginny said. 'He didn't listen to Mum's needs and their partnership wasn't equal. I've spent my entire life listening to others and trying to help them, and now I'm asking *you* to listen and to help *me*.'

She reached out and stroked the face she'd loved for more than three decades, wanting to be truthful, even if it hurt him. Hurt them both. Her throat constricted as she spoke. 'I'm not sure what's missing from my life, but I think going to Italy might help me find it.'

'But—' Adrian started.

'We're still working on rebuilding our relationship and I'm not sure what shape it will take. Does being married mean living together all day, every day?' She shrugged. 'Shouldn't we support and encourage each other to spread our wings? We both love Phoebe, but she's left home and has her own life, has created her own family. Italy is only two and a half hours away, the same as if you or I took up a job in London. It's easy to keep in touch. It's not like my father who constantly flitted in and out of my life. It'd be nice to travel and to see new things on my own terms, for once.'

Her words hung in the air like dust particles during spring cleaning.

Adrian dipped his chin and thought for some time. 'I know what *I* want and it's you. I'm willing to try anything to keep us together, but I want you to be certain, too. If you're not sure about us, and you want to return to Italy, then of course you should go. I'll be waiting for you when you get home. I never want to walk away from you again.'

'Adrian—' Ginny started, unsure where her sentence was going. This was what she'd always wanted to hear, what she'd wanted to feel. 'I need time to find myself again . . . I don't know how long it will take.'

'You're not *asking* me to do this, I'm *offering*,' he said, taking her hands in his. 'I'll wait for you.'

Relief washed over her. This wasn't about wanting to be with another man, or meeting other people, or escaping her life. It was a *need* to learn more about herself again, what she was good at, what she liked, and what she wanted to do for the next part of her life. Could she be happy on her own, or did she need the security and stability of family around her? The only way to find out was to throw off her comfort blanket and embrace the unknown. If she didn't, she'd always wonder what might have been. 'Thank you,' she said, kissing Adrian on the cheek.

Ginny sat down with Phoebe to explain her decision. She promised to come home on a regular basis.

'I kind of get it,' Phoebe said, stroking Erin's wispy hair and holding her close. 'I'm a mum now and will never be *just me* again. If you go, we'll come to visit you. I just hope you and Dad work things out.' She held up her crossed fingers.

Adrian drove Ginny to the airport where they held each other tightly and said their goodbyes. She leaned her head against his shoulder and he circled his arms around her back. 'Love you,' he said.

She breathed in the scent of his skin and relished the prickle of his cheek against hers. She knew she'd miss him a great deal. 'Love you, too,' she said, and this time the words felt right.

CHAPTER 37

Hearts

Ginny and Nico

Ginny had spent her first week in Italy on her own, staying in a remote Tuscan farmhouse. She'd walked all day and tried to make soup that was as good as Nico's in the evening, never quite managing it.

She'd moved on to the beach resort of Lido di Jesolo, where she'd mingled with holidaymakers in the boutiques, bars and on the miles of golden beach. As she'd watched all the couples and families, the singles and the children, Ginny sometimes worried if she was doing the right thing. Yet, surely it was better to lay herself open to the world, to feel the discomfort of the new, rather than the numbness of the known. In Loretta's words, she would not know what was right or wrong for her until she tried it.

She'd next travelled to Vigornuovo, where she'd now been working at Splendido for one month, staying in a tiny room that was once used for storage because all the guest rooms were fully booked.

Ginny was trying to learn Italian by listening to the radio, especially any advice shows. Nico talked patiently to her in the language while they made pasta together for his hotel guests. She appreciated his kindness and friendship.

The renewed interest from holidaymakers in Splendido had come courtesy of Curtis. After leaving Italy, he'd updated his blog with details about his health struggles. His last piece said:

CURTIS'S BRAIN BLOG

Man Alive.

I'm not a sophisticated man, never been particularly talented at anything except making my own luck in the world. I've spent the last few months enduring hospital visits, scans and treatment and my luck's finally running out.

If you get sad reading this – don't. Because I'm not. And I've got four strangers to thank for it.

This summer, I spent three weeks at the Hotel Splendido, in Vigornuovo, Bologna. It wasn't that long, and everyone feels better after a holiday, right? Except it helped me put things into perspective. I learned life isn't just about me and it came as a big surprise. Playing bingo, eating olives at midnight, picnics, sightseeing, drinking nonalcoholic cocktails (yes, really), the sea lapping my ankles and even listening to weird gong music – the little things meant a lot. Splendido was a haven for broken hearts and I had a great time.

Now I'm keeping busy, decorating my apartment and staying grateful. (Copper and dark wood look great together

– try it!) I wish I could go back to Italy but the demon in my head is calling the shots.

You only get one life. So, my advice is laugh often, try something new, talk to people. Why not?

That's all for now.

Cheers,
Curtis x

The piece was illustrated with photos of him with Edna, Eric, Heather, Ginny, Nico and Loretta, playing bingo, nightclubbing, listening to gongs and touring Venice, accompanied by a video of him throwing rocks into the sea.

A passage had been added, posthumously.

We're heartbroken to share that Curtis Dunne passed away in November. He was comfortable and listening to music. He lived his final weeks with his usual humour and zest for life, and he'll be sorely missed. As per his request, any proceeds from the sale of his business will be donated to cancer charities.

A few weeks after his death, Curtis's story and generous donation had featured in a local newspaper, and had been adopted by the national press.

His description of Splendido as *a haven for broken hearts* had sparked interest and Nico started to receive calls and emails from people who wanted to stay at his hotel. His business began to flourish and his dining table became filled with tears and laughter again.

Splendido no longer had a fusty air and was brimming with positivity and life. Nico had consigned the photographs of his relatives to a small area in the dining room, freeing up space in the hallway. He'd framed Edna's fabric blocks, the lid of Eric's tin, *The Power of Two* book and Heather's tarot cards, adding small handwritten notes to tell their stories. He'd added a Polaroid, taken on Heather's camera, of them all together in Venice.

The 'strangers' had all remained in touch with Nico and each other, sending items to Splendido that Nico also added to his display.

A photograph of Eric showed him with Biscotti at his feet, proudly displaying wooden board games he'd started to make inspired by Italian marquetry. Nico had helped with Biscotti's adoption in the UK, and man and dog looked happy together.

Edna had sent a flyer for a fashion show she was hosting at Shady Pines. She'd introduced a sewing class for the residents and an accompanying photo showed her wearing a garment as spectacular as Joseph's Amazing Technicolor Dreamcoat. Ginny managed to spot a few patches of pale grey fabric among the silk and cotton.

A card from Heather featured a rainbow drawn by one of her pupils and a long note inside it. She was still learning to embrace and love the new version of her mum instead of mourning the old one. She and Renee had enjoyed looking at the photos of Venice together.

Taking pride of place in the centre of the wall, Nico dedicated a large picture frame to Curtis, featuring his final heartache form, a printout of his last blog entry and a flattened baseball cap.

If Ginny ever felt pinpricked by life, she polished the glass and thought about Curtis. She'd only known him for a short while, but he'd made her rethink her life and be grateful for it, whatever shape it took from now on.

It was becoming a tradition for other guests at Splendido to also leave behind a token of their heartbreak, including a badly drawn Valentine's Day card, a plastic tiger from a Christmas cracker, rosary beads and the cork from a champagne bottle. Nico had asked each guest to write a small story on a form to accompany their item, and he planned to add them to his display.

After Ginny had entered the latest hotel booking into the system, she dusted the dining room and made two cappuccinos. A rhythmic banging noise sounded from the courtyard and she carried the cups of coffee outside. Nico was making a new sign for his hotel.

Welcome to Hotel Splendido
Give your heart a holiday

Instead of featuring stars, as per the sign for Grand Hotel Castello Bella Vista, he'd added the outline of six hearts.

'If Tim Vincenzo's trousers can attract tourists to Vigornuovo, my hotel has a good chance, too,' he said, standing up to survey his handiwork. 'I think my mamma would be proud of this new direction.'

'I think Loretta will be, too,' Ginny said.

She and Nico stood side by side, sipping their coffees. They watched the sky lightening through the branches of the trees, promising a bright day ahead. A light breeze made the coral bedsheets on the washing line drift backwards and forwards.

Ginny felt a buzz of excitement in her stomach, passion for what the day might bring, and what might happen beyond it. She might not have all the answers yet, but that was okay. She had a good feeling that everything was going to turn out just fine and any solutions would appear by themselves.

ACKNOWLEDGEMENTS

I couldn't have written *The Little Italian Hotel* without the help and support of some important people in my life and I give thanks and much gratitude to the following.

The entire team at Darley Anderson Literary, Film and TV Agency, who help to nurture me and my stories, finding new homes for them around the world. Special thanks goes to my super-agent Clare Wallace for her continuous encouragement and all she does for me.

My amazing US editor Erika Imranyi, ably assisted by Nicole Luongo, and to all the wonderful team at Park Row/ HarperCollins. Also, to my fantastic UK editor Emily Kitchin and the HQ/HarperCollins crew. I'm proud to be part of your publishing families and truly appreciate everything you do for my books.

A special mention goes to my friend Janine McKown for her medical advice and expertise with regard to Heather's mum's diagnosis and also to Curtis's illness, to make sure I presented them correctly.

I've been fortunate to travel to Italy several times and the country's magnificence and friendliness of its people helped to inspire the idea for this book. I created the village of Vigornuovo from my own imagination and experiences, spending many happy days living there in my head, while writing. However, I am English not Italian, so I'm deeply grateful to Marianna Riccuito and Alberta Torres for their valuable contribution to my use of the Italian language, nuances, and depictions of Italian places and people. Any errors are entirely my own.

My thanks go to booksellers, independent bookshops, librarians, bloggers, reviewers and readers everywhere who read and champion my work. A special shout out goes to Daniella Pintar and the team at the Oldham Waterstones for their brilliant support (and my own dedicated display table in the store), and to Suzanne Hudson and the team at Oldham Library.

A big hello and thank you to Barnes & Noble booksellers across the US for their support and sharing of my last novel, *The Messy Lives of Book People*. You guys were all incredible!

Last but not least, I'm forever grateful to my family – Mark, Oliver, Pat and Dave – for always supporting and celebrating my writing. Much thanks and I love you all.

BOOK CLUB QUESTIONS
THE LITTLE ITALIAN HOTEL

1. If you could choose to go anywhere in the world for a special holiday, where would it be? Who would be your ideal travel companion?
2. Ginny likes to solve other people's problems while glossing over her own. Do you tend to tackle your own issues head on, or try to bury them? Do you turn to others for advice?
3. Does joining a dating website count as being unfaithful in a relationship?
4. Which "stranger" out of Eric, Edna, Heather and Curtis was your favourite and why? Whose story did you relate to the most?
5. What were your first impressions of hotel owner Nico? How does he change throughout the book?
6. There are some funny and uplifting moments in the book, also some sad and reflective ones. How did you feel after reading it?
7. Adrian undergoes "a midlife crisis." Do you believe they actually exist? Is midlife more difficult for men or women?

8. Ginny turns to *The Power of Two* book to help with her heartache. Do you find self-help books useful? Which one would you recommend to others?

9. Out of all the heartache cures – art in Florence, making a quilt, visiting Venice, dancing in a nightclub, hiking and sound healing – which activity appeals to you the most and why?

10. Ginny makes a choice at the end of the book, to listen to her own needs. In your opinion, was her decision the right one? What do you think (or hope) will happen next for Ginny?

Read on for an extract from
The Book Share, the charming and
uplifting novel from bestselling author
Phaedra Patrick.

CHAPTER I

The Flat in the Clouds

Liv Green wore her polishing cloth draped over her arm in the same proud way a maître d' might wear a napkin. She'd already cleaned Essie Starling's two bathrooms, each bigger than her own bedroom, polished the white marble kitchen worktops, and left uniform vacuum cleaner tracks on the dove grey carpets, just how the bestselling author liked them. She wore one earbud while she worked, listening to the audiobook of Essie's nineteenth novel for the second time and leaving her other ear free in case the author called out any commands.

As Liv carried her cleaning box into the third bedroom, she averted her eyes from the floor-to-ceiling windows. After three years of working here, the panoramic view still made her dizzy. If she were Rapunzel, she'd need a plait thirty-two storeys long to reach down to the pavement. Not that many forty-two-year-old mums, wearing bleach-specked jeans and an ancient Rolling Stones T-shirt, ever appeared in fairy tales.

Outside, cars were beeping in the Friday evening traffic. Liv really should be home by now, but there was always something about Essie that made her want to stay.

The flat's white walls were lined with shelves populated with framed photographs and a rainbow of books – contemporary novels, battered tomes, childhood favourites and copies of Essie's own novels in forty languages. Liv loved to gently wipe their covers and admire how various countries depicted Essie's famous heroine, Georgia Rory.

If she ever told anyone she cleaned for the author, the common reaction was wide eyes and a dropped jaw. 'You really work for *the* Essie Starling?' people would ask. 'What is she like? Why is she so reclusive?' Liv couldn't blame their fascination. She could still hardly believe she worked for her favourite writer, and, out of her three cleaning jobs, she relished this one the most. In response to eager questions about Essie, she gave a slight smile and a shrug, adding to the author's enigma.

For the past decade, Essie had refused most interviews and no longer took part in book tours. Invitations to give talks, attend literature festivals or go to parties were ignored. She didn't even take calls from her agent and publisher, contacting them by email or via her latest personal assistant instead. On the rare occasion Essie left the flat, Liv never knew where she disappeared to.

As she straightened up the books on the shelves, Liv spotted a chunk of A4 pages, stained and dog-eared as if handled many times. It looked like a manuscript and was obviously in the wrong place. She picked it up to return it to Essie's writing room and recognized the author's indigo scrawl on the front page.

Book Twenty, it read.

Liv let out a small gasp, her heart dancing in her chest. She was holding Essie's latest story, the new Georgia Rory adventure.

The series of novels originated in the late eighties. Although literary critics were sniffy about Georgia's clean-cut character, positivity and verve, readers across the world adored her. They camped outside bookshops on publication day, and copied Georgia's eclectic outfits of floral tea dresses, school ties, a black blazer and battered biker boots. Young adults and grown-ups alike enjoyed the stories, passing the books on across generations. All the novels became book club favourites, and Liv was happy to label herself as Georgia's biggest fan.

And here, finally in her hands, was a draft of Essie's twentieth book. Other readers would kill for this moment.

Pulling out her earbud, Liv looked over her shoulder towards the closed writing-room door. For a moment she wondered if Essie had intentionally left the manuscript for her to find, as she sometimes did with books by other writers. *No, it's not possible*, she told herself. Mere mortals were never allowed to clap eyes on Essie's work before it was published, except for her agent Marlon and editor Meg.

For the first couple of years that Liv worked here, the author had been strictly out of bounds, and her writing door remained closed. But over the last twelve months, things had begun to change. Essie called out to Liv for reminders of plot points, and her characters' likes and dislikes.

'Nobody knows Georgia Rory like you do,' Essie once said, making Liv feel like a child wrapped in a hot towel fresh off the radiator.

If she had to find one word to describe it, she'd say Essie was *thawing* towards her.

Warmth spread in Liv's chest, the delicious yearning she felt whenever she held a new book. When she fingered the tatty edges of paper, anticipation shimmied down her spine. Was there any harm in peeking at a page or two?

She nervously glanced at a photo on the shelf of the author. Essie wore a blue evening gown with embroidered birds on the shoulder. Her round glasses had lenses as dark as licorice, and her trademark patterned silk scarf was tied around her sharp black bob. Tangerine orange was her preferred lip colour. She once attended all the best parties and award ceremonies, and her fans voted in droves for her to win the global Constellation Writing Prize ten years ago.

And then, on the eve of the Constellation afterparty, Essie vanished.

Post-award interviews were cancelled, and journalists were left hanging. Speculation raged – was she ill, what had happened, where was she? As the months ticked by, her fans clung to the hope she might emerge from hiding to grace a local bookshop or appear on TV. But Essie hadn't been seen in public for a decade.

Liv always wondered how and why things changed so dramatically for the author. Why would someone with the world at their feet cut themselves off from society? Now *that* would make a great story.

Unable to resist the lure of the manuscript, Liv sat down cross-legged on the carpet and began to read the first chapter. She'd always had a vivid imagination, allowing her to slip into books and become one with the characters. The room and the photographs faded away.

Aware of nothing else but the story, Liv kept on turning the pages.

Georgia swallowed her worries away as she strode into the airport. Old-fashioned fans rattled on the ceiling and did little to circulate the stifling heat. It was a tiny place with a dusty track for a runway and

two propeller planes on standby. She gripped the handle of her battered
leather suitcase, full of trepidation. She'd travelled the world, and been
on many adventures, but this time her throat was scratchy and her
anxiety was rising. 'I'm not sure where I'm going, or what I need to
do,' she said aloud. 'Is there anyone who can help me?'

'*Olivia*. What on *earth* are you doing?' a woman's voice said.

Liv's bookish world snapped away and her cheeks flooded with colour. Essie was the only person who used her full name. How long had she been standing in the doorway?

Liv frantically gathered the pages of the manuscript together before realizing they weren't numbered. Questions rumbled in her head about what she'd just read. Where was the warmth and fun in the story? Where was Georgia's usual quick wit and confidence?

Her eyes crept fearfully towards Essie's beige Tory Burch pumps, up her slim black trousers and silk blouse, before reaching the patterned Hermès scarf in her hair and her narrowed eyes. 'Essie, I'm *so* sorry,' she spluttered. 'I started to read and couldn't stop.'

Essie's glasses slipped down her nose, so Liv could see her steely grey irises. 'My writing room in ten minutes, please,' she snapped. She turned on her heels and left the room with the grace of a prima ballerina.

Liv's palms were clammy as she tried to return the manuscript pages to their correct order. Essie employed a revolving door of personal assistants. As one exited, another one showed up. Liv had overheard her firing her last one, Matilda, and was never sure why *she* was the only employee left standing.

She couldn't afford to lose this job. Her husband, Jake, was fighting to stop his family business from going under, and her son Johnny was joining his older brother Mack at university this summer. He needed enough stuff to fill a small truck. Liv's wages were on the modest side, but every penny counted in the Green household. If she was going to be dismissed, she hoped it would be quick, like ripping a plaster off a hairy knee.

Returning the manuscript to its shelf, Liv's eyes narrowed when she saw something glinting behind a trophy. She carefully reached up and plucked out a small label-less glass bottle. As she lifted it to her nose, the sweet smell of juniper made her stomach churn.

It was the fifth miniature gin bottle she'd found that week, not to mention the full-size vodka beside Essie's bed. Liv sighed and pushed the bottle into the back pocket of her jeans. Really, where did Essie think they disappeared to when she left them around the place? She wondered if the author had been drinking while reading her own manuscript, and why.

Her pulse performed a quickstep as she padded along the hallway towards the writing room. She said a mental goodbye to the designer side table, books and huge display of lilies.

Before she entered the writing room, Liv clenched her fists. *You've been through worse*, she told herself, trying not to think back to her childhood when she was scared and alone in a strange bedroom clutching her Georgia Rory books for comfort.

Think. What would Georgia do?

Essie's writing room looked like it had been transported from a cottagey holiday home, a contrast to the starkness of the rest of her flat. Her desk was made of old oak, and there was a wall of dark wooden bookshelves displaying more editions of her books.

'Be seated,' Essie said, without looking up from her notepad.

Her cut glass English accent had a slight American twang, which made Liv feel very ordinary. Essie was only ten years older than her yet their age difference felt like a generation.

Essie turned and steepled her long, slim fingers. 'So?' she said.

Blood thumped in Liv's ears, but she had a touch of Georgia's bravery running through her veins. 'I only read a few pages of your manuscript.'

Essie's face was still and unreadable. 'You know my work is off-limits.'

'It wasn't in your writing room, and I couldn't help myself.' All of her emotions felt on edge. 'Are you going to sack me, or not?'

Essie's mouth twitched into a brief smile, then settled back just as quickly. As she stroked the handle of her vintage teacup, her stare seemed to laser through Liv's skin. 'No, I'm not going to dismiss you.'

Relief flooded Liv's body. Before she could say anything, Essie continued, 'I'd like your opinion on something.'

Liv's stomach jittered, and she wasn't sure if it was with fear or excitement. 'Oh, okay.'

Essie opened her top drawer and took out a magazine, the *Chicago Globe Literary Review.* She tossed it towards Liv and folded her arms. 'My agent sent this recent review to me, for *Few and Far Between*,' she said. 'It's dated April Fool's Day. I assume it's not a hoax.'

Liv gulped. She wasn't good with dates, always forgetting birthdays and anniversaries, but the author was highly superstitious about them. She read a section of the critique, for the novel she'd just been listening to. It was a fair summary, albeit with a weary tone of voice.

The complexities and delicate emotion of Starling's earlier work are missing in this flat novel. The writing is uncomplicated, and the story unoriginal. Georgia Rory's feistiness has been replaced with a dithering reticence and lack of direction. Once a writer of considerable promise, Ms Starling continues to let her once considerable talent fly south. It is therefore no surprise she avoids the public eye. Nevertheless, her devoted fans will undoubtedly buy the book in their millions, guaranteeing her yet another bestseller.

Liv quickly considered what she should say. Forget about being caught reading during work hours — saying the wrong thing about the review would surely cost her this job. Did she try to flatter Essie? Should she use a conciliatory tone, or a firm, resolute one? Whatever she said would be judged.

'The truth, please, Olivia.' Essie tapped a fingernail on her desk. 'And get straight to the point.'

Liv ran her tongue around her mouth to get rid of a metallic taste. She tapped into Georgia's mindset once more and tried not to falter. 'I think your earlier books had a warm, easy charm, like you really enjoyed writing them. However, if I'm honest, like you're asking me to be—' She hesitated. 'I... sometimes feel you've lost your true passion for Georgia.'

Essie raised a palm, as if stopping traffic. 'And the pages of the manuscript you read?'

Liv lowered her eyes. 'Kind of the same thing.'

'I see,' Essie said through gritted teeth.

8